COLO

ANNE ot GREEN BAGELS

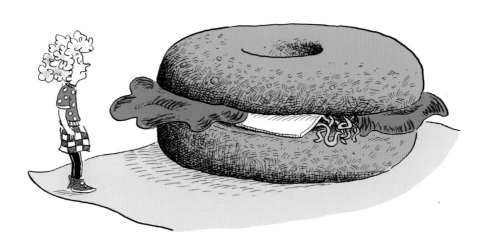

PAPERCUTZ ™

ARiOL Graphic Novels available from PAPERCUTZ

ARIOL graphic novels are also available digitally wherever e-books are sold.

ARiOL
Just a Donkey Like You and Me
PAPERCUTZ

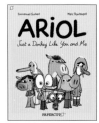

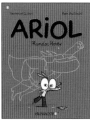

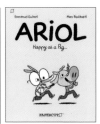

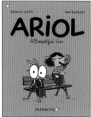

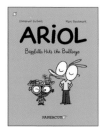

ARiOL #1
"Just a Donkey Like You and Me"

ARiOL
Thunder Horse

ARiOL #2
"Thunder Horse"

ARiOL
Happy as a Pig...
PAPERCUTZ

ARiOL #3
"Happy as a Pig..."

ARiOL
A Beautiful Cow
PAPERCUTZ

ARiOL #4
"A Beautiful Cow"

ARiOL
Bizzbilla Hits the Bullseye
PAPERCUTZ

ARiOL #5
"Bizzbilla Hits the Bullseye"

ARiOL
A Nasty Cat

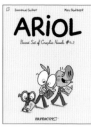

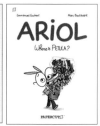

ARiOL #6
"A Nasty Cat"

ARiOL
Top Dog
PAPERCUTZ

ARiOL #7
"Top Dog"

ARiOL
The Three Donkeys

ARiOL #8
"The Three Donkeys"

ARiOL
Boxed Set of Graphic Novels #1-3
PAPERCUTZ

Boxed Set of Graphic Novels #1-3

ARiOL
Where's PETULA?
PAPERCUTZ

"Where's Petula?" Graphic Novel

Coming Soon

Emmanuel Guibert
Marc Boutavant
ARiOL
The Teeth of the Rabbit
PAPERCUTZ

ARiOL #9
"The Teeth of the Rabbit"

ARiOL graphic novels are available for $12.99 only in paperback, except for "Where's Petula?" which is $9.99. The ARIOL Boxed Set is $38.99. Available from booksellers everywhere. You can also order online from papercutz.com. Or call 1-800-886-1223, Monday through Friday, 9 - 5 EST. MC, Visa, and AmEx accepted. To order by mail, please add $4.00 for postage and handling for first book ordered, $1.00 for each additional book and make check payable to NBM Publishing. Send to:

Papercutz, 160 Broadway, Suite 700, East Wing, New York, NY 10038.

ARIOL graphic novels are also available digitally wherever e-books are sold.

papercutz.com

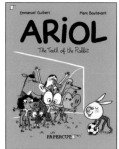

for
LUCY MAUD
MONTGOMERY

... and with special thanks to Sophia Harvey, Geoffrey Conklin, and Judy Hansen!

ANNE OF GREEN BAGELS
Created by Jon Buller and Susan Schade
Dawn Guzzo — Production
Brittanie Black — Production Coordinator
Bethany Bryan — Editor
Jeff Whitman — Assistant Managing Editor
Jim Salicrup
Editor-in-Chief

ISBN: 978-1-62991-465-7

Printed in China
August 2016 by Toppan Leefung Printing Limited
Jin Ju Guan Li Qu,
Da Ling Shan Town,
Dongguan, PRC
China

Papercutz books may be purchased for business or promotional use.
For information on bulk purchases please contact Macmillan Corporate and Premium Sales Department at (800) 221-7945 x5442.

Distributed by Macmillan
First Papercutz Printing

BAGEL SURFING DREAM

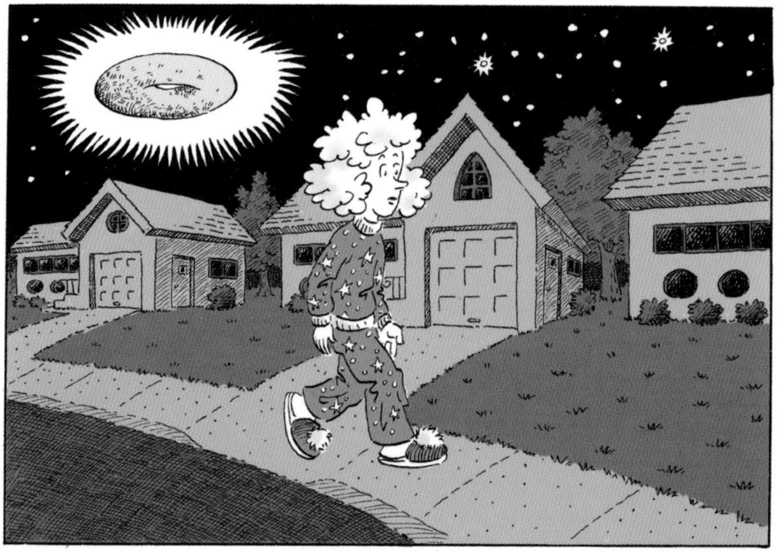

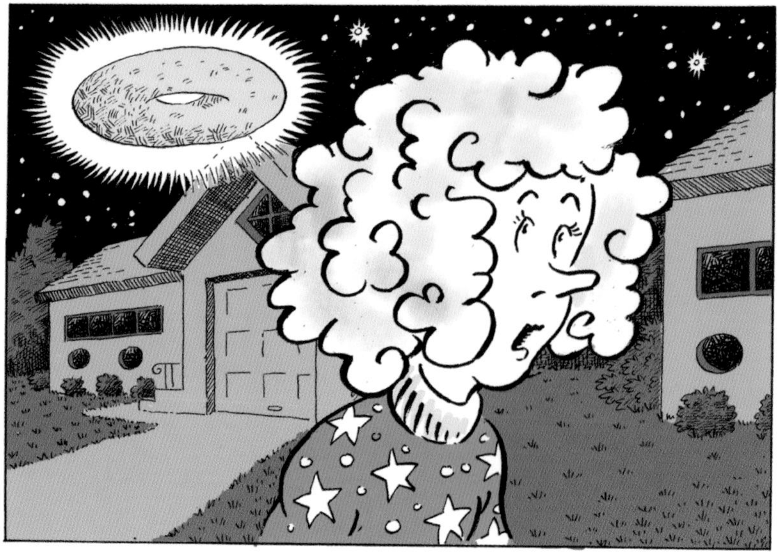

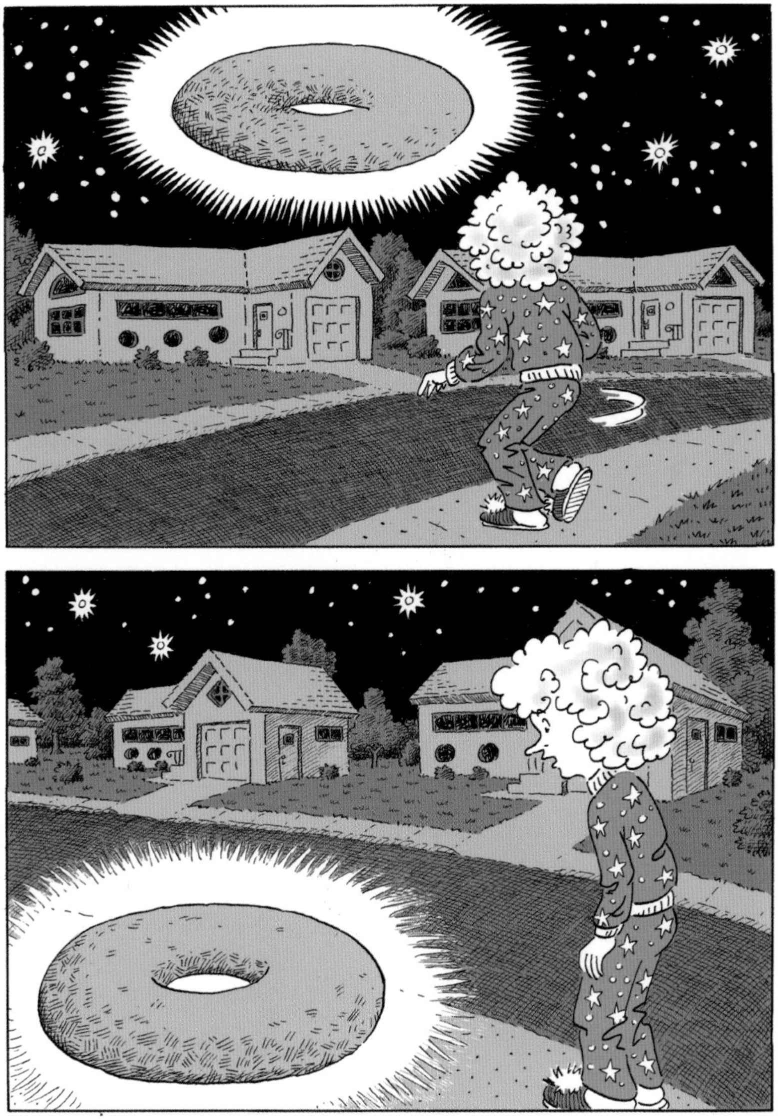

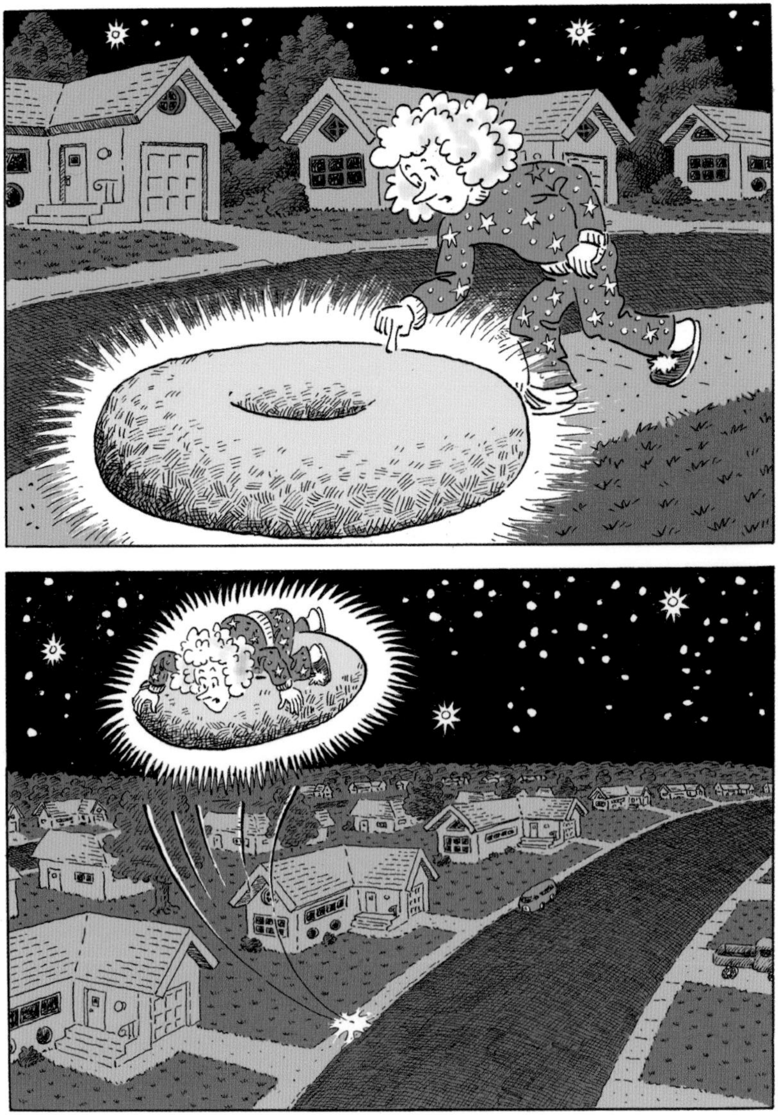

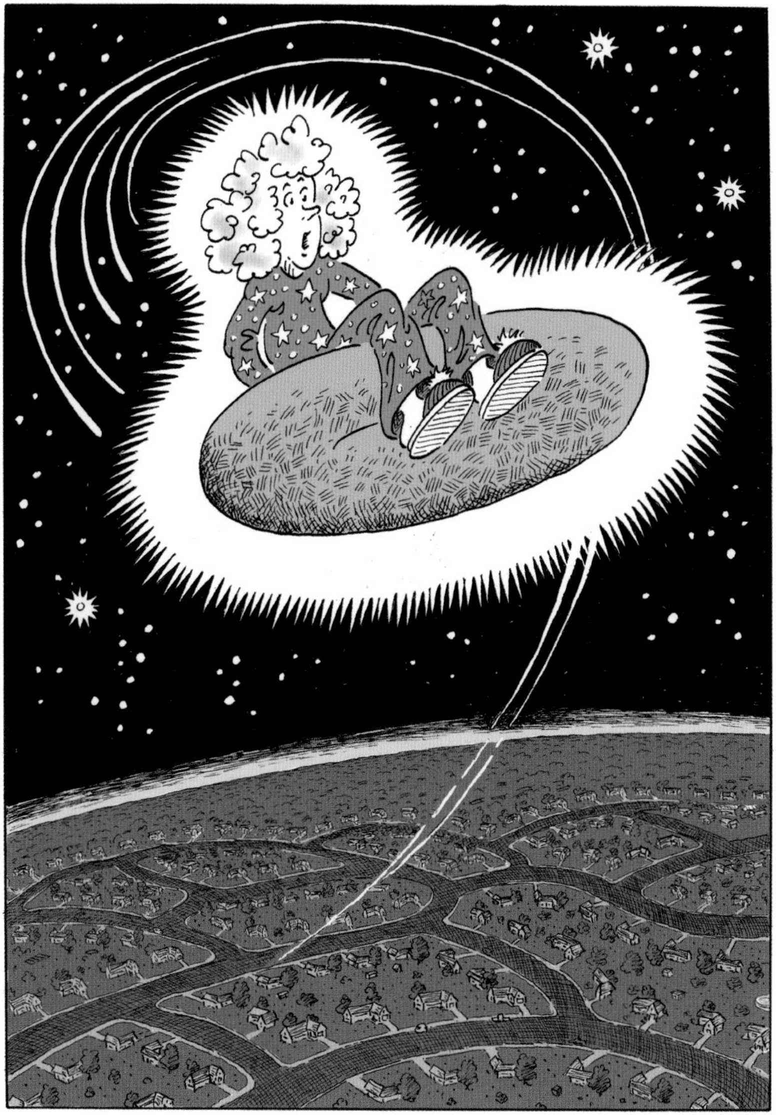

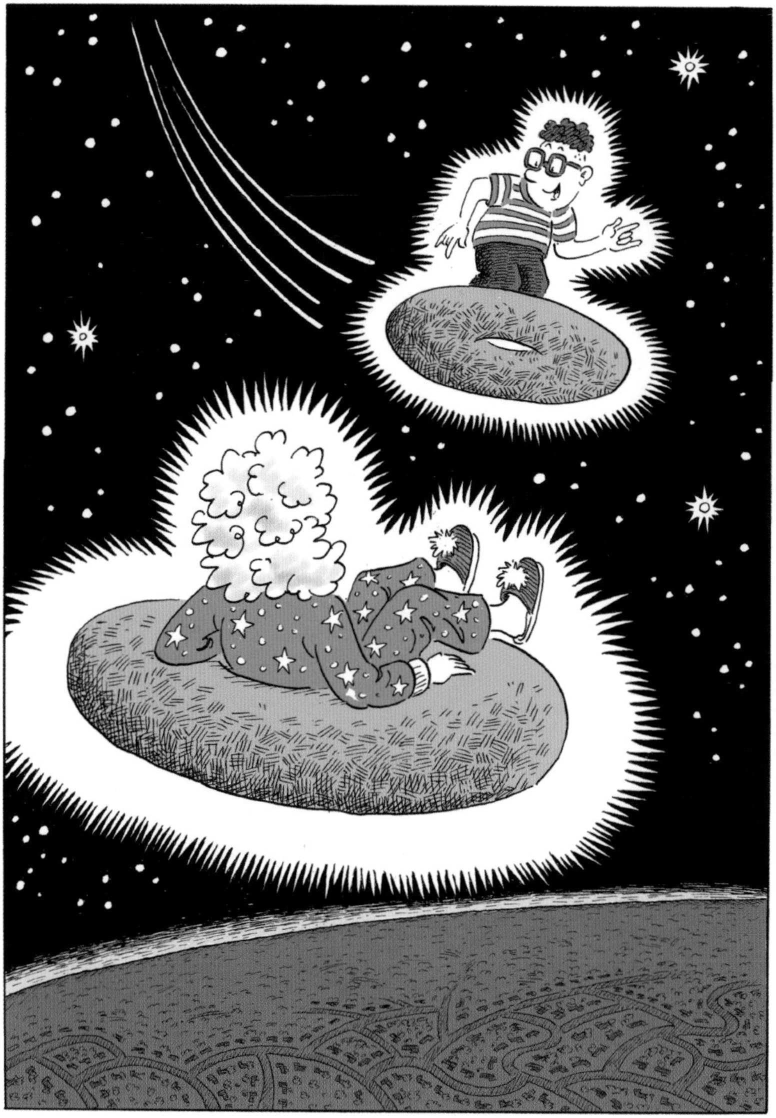

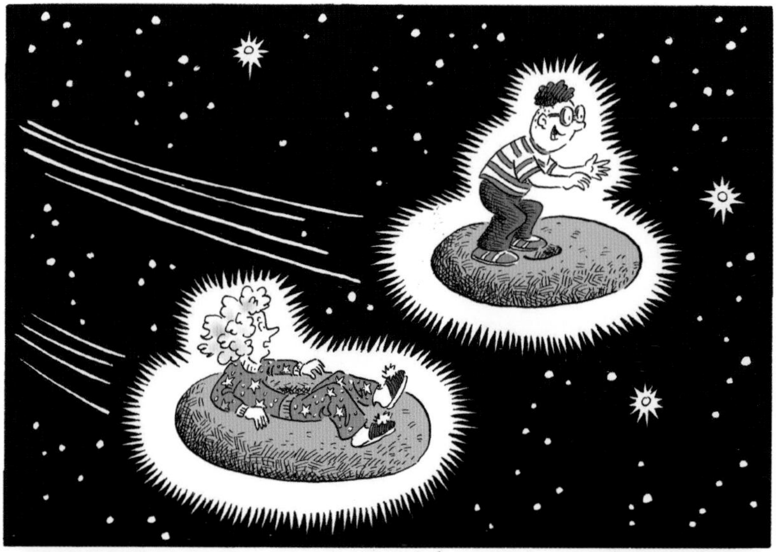

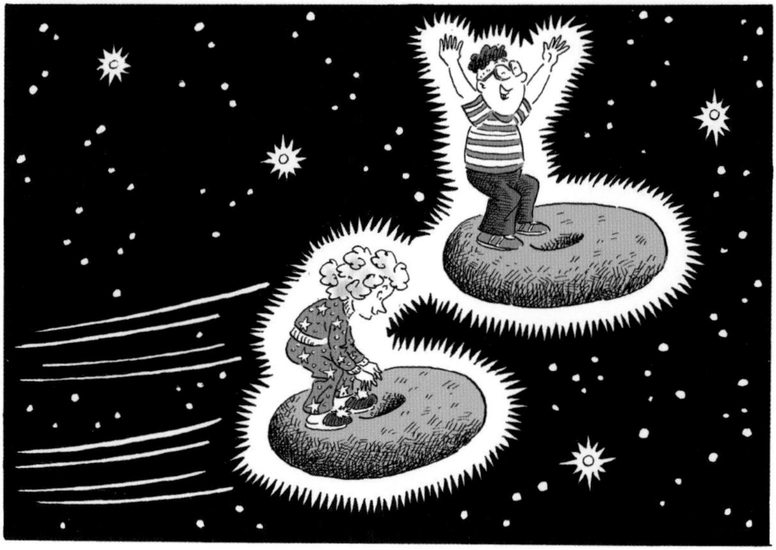

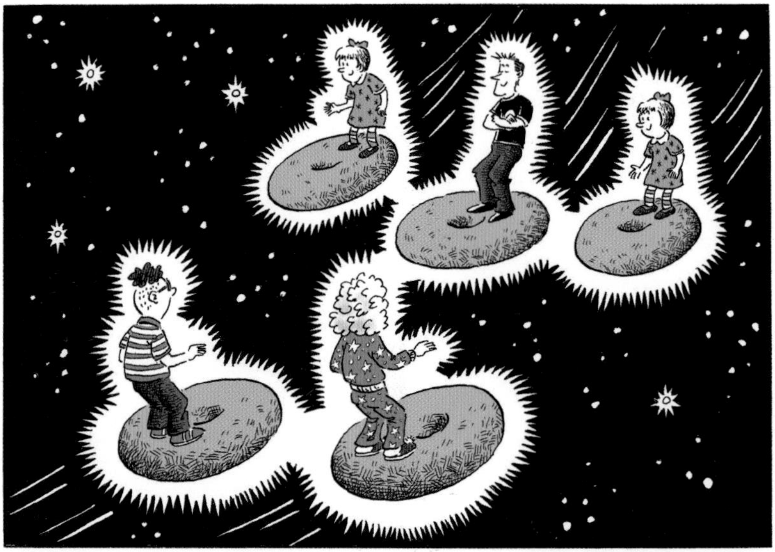

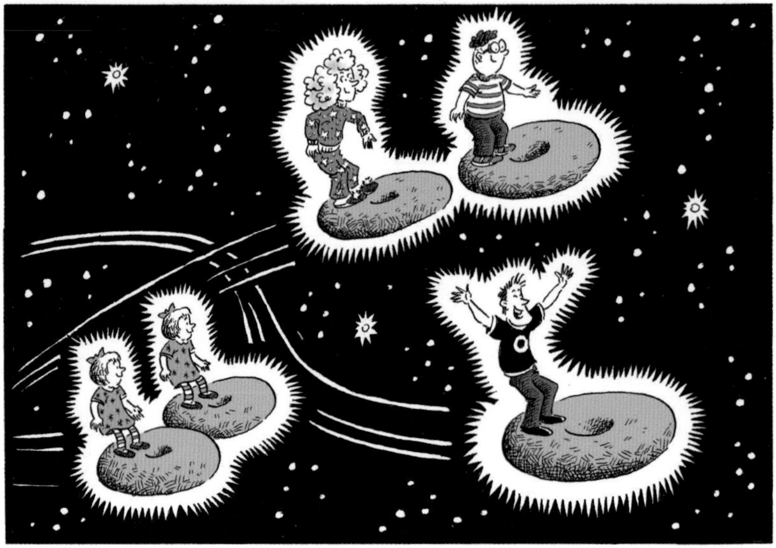

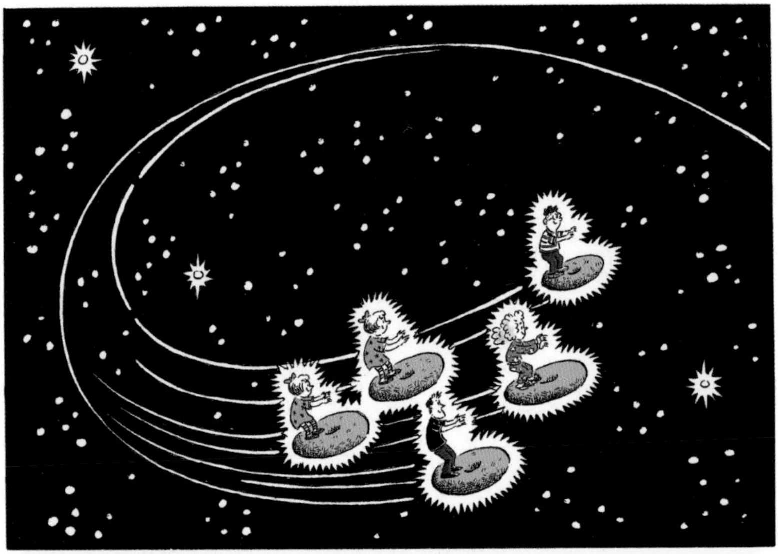

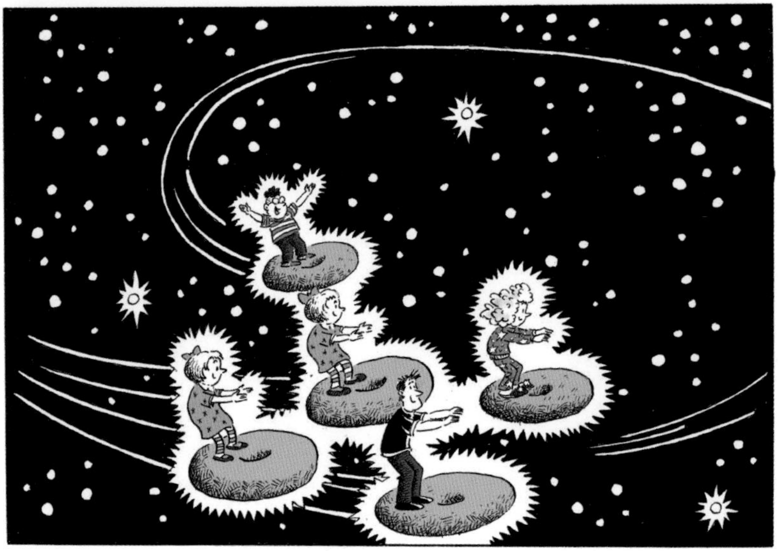

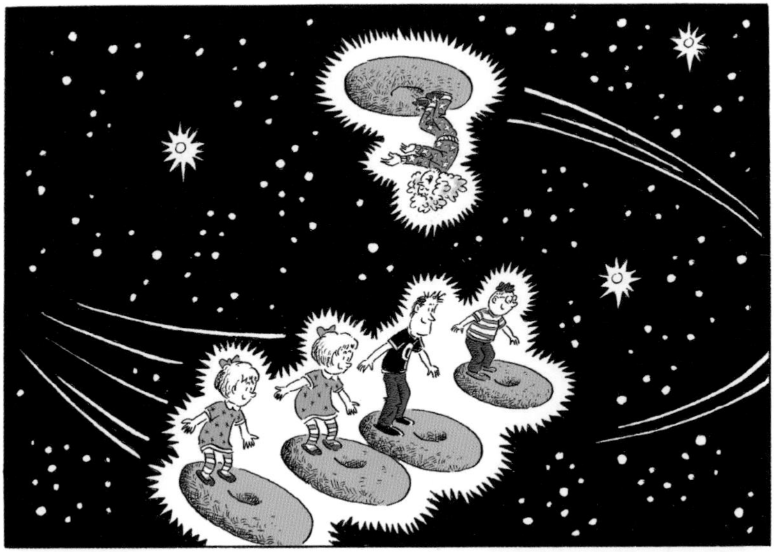

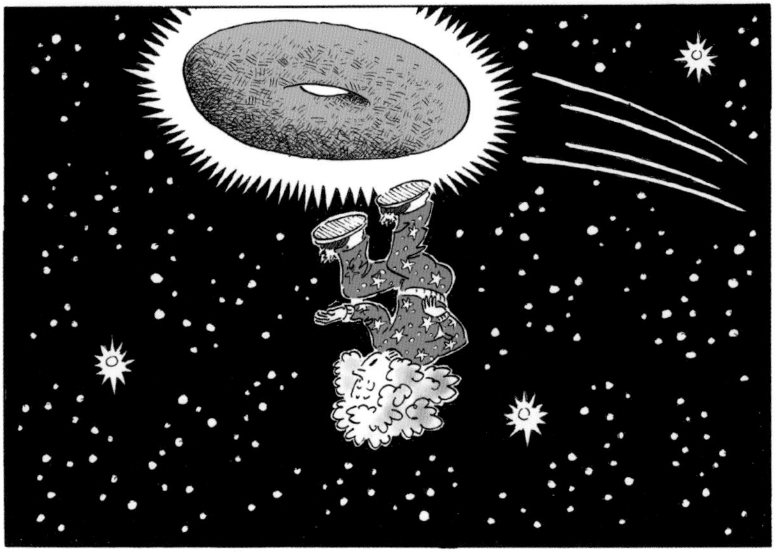

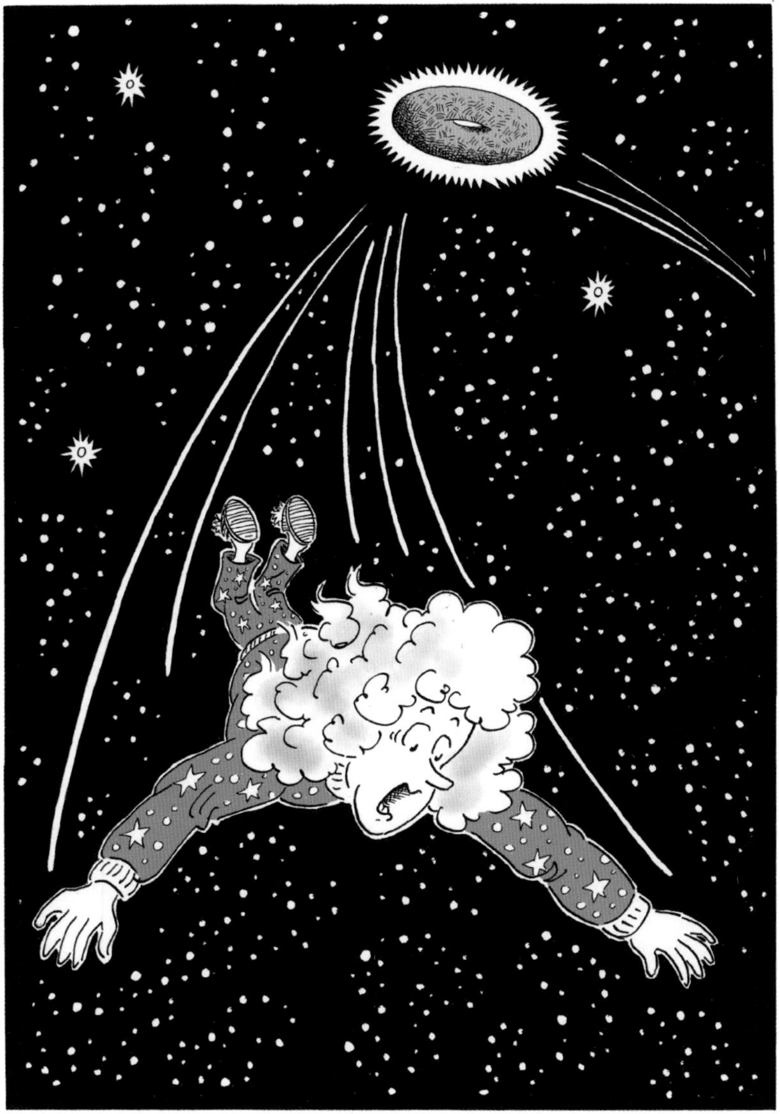

2

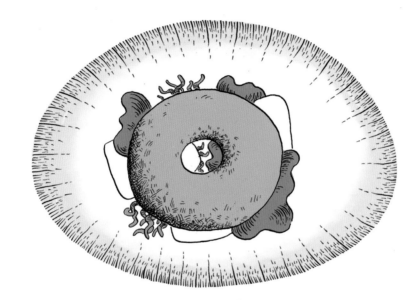

THE FATEFUL BAGEL

I don't remember when I first started having weird dreams.

Was it when my father left home to try out his latest wacky invention and didn't leave a forwarding address? Or when we hadn't heard from him for over a month, and Mom had started seeing a therapist? Or was it when we left the trees and mountains of New Mexico for the weird, suburban sameness of Megatown, New York? Or maybe it was after my first day at my new school — the Norbert E. Megget Middle School, grade 6, when they made fun of my green bagels.

Starting sixth grade at the new school was a lot more scary than starting kindergarten back in New Mexico when I was five.

In Megatown most of the kids can walk to school. Because it was my first day, Mom walked with me and made sure I knew the way.

At first nothing horrible happened. I didn't look anybody in the eye or talk to anybody, and the teachers didn't call on me. But at lunch it was a different story.

You have to sit at long tables with other kids. When I walked in with my lunch bag from home, every table had kids already sitting there. And not only that. They all stopped talking and looked at me to see where I would sit.

So I just slid into the nearest seat and started unwrapping my sandwich. I kept my eyes down, but I could feel the others all looking at me.

I picked up my sandwich to take a bite. The girl next to me said,

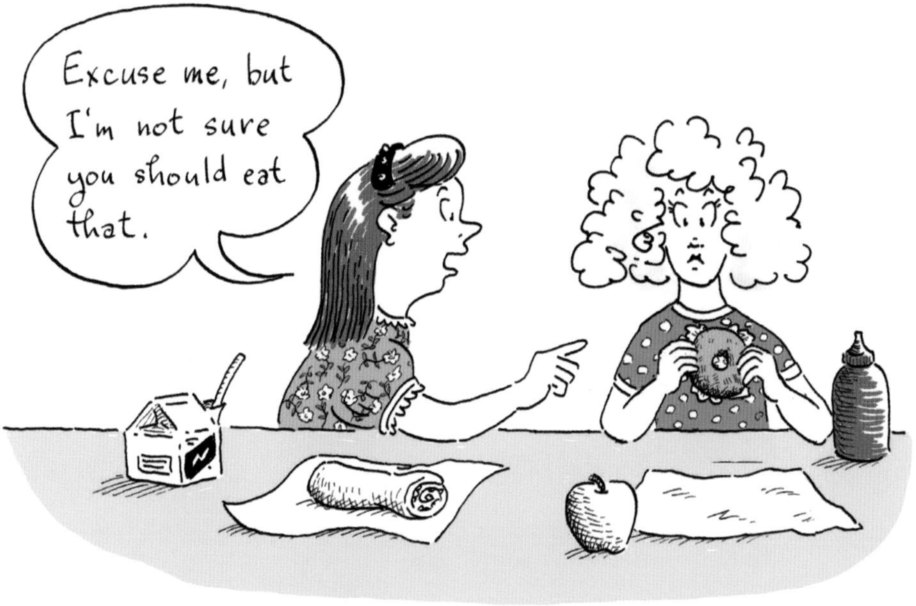
Excuse me, but I'm not sure you should eat that.

I looked at her sideways. "Why not?" I asked.

"Your bagel is all green. It looks moldy."

"It's just spirulina," I kind of whispered.

"What?"

"SPIRULINA!" That came out louder than I meant it to. "It's health food. Made out of seaweed."

"Green bagels! HAHAHA!"

The other kids were all looking at my sandwich now.

Then this tall kid named Brendan said in a loud voice, "Isn't your name Anne?"

"Yes," I mumbled.

"Green bagels! And she even has red hair," he said to the other kids. "Get it? She's Anne of Green Bagels!"

"HAHAHA!"

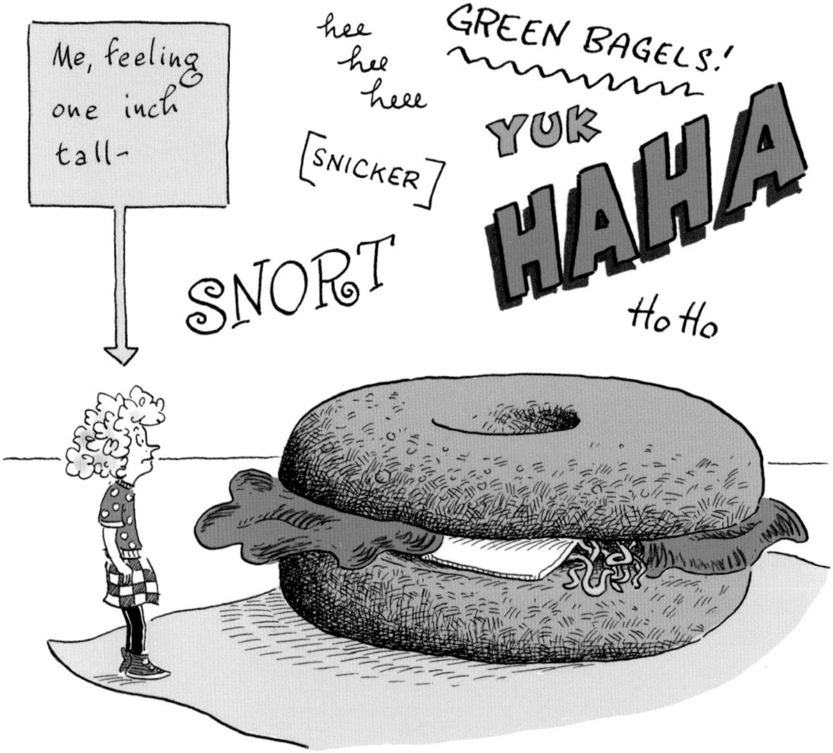

Me, feeling one inch tall-
hee hee heee
GREEN BAGELS!
YUK
[SNICKER]
HAHA
SNORT
Ho Ho

I could have died right there.

I'd heard of that book, *Anne of Green Gables*. Who hasn't? I think I saw a show of it on TV once. I'd heard it was a good book, but so what? Now I had to go to a school, maybe forever, where everybody pointed at me and said, "Look! There goes Anne of Green Bagels. HAHAHA!"

I wished I was dead. And I decided I was never going back to that school again.

At my old school I had lots of friends. I even had a *best* friend. I hadn't heard from her lately and I suspected she had already forgotten me.

I did meet one nice kid though. His name was Otto. He called out to me while we were walking in the hall.

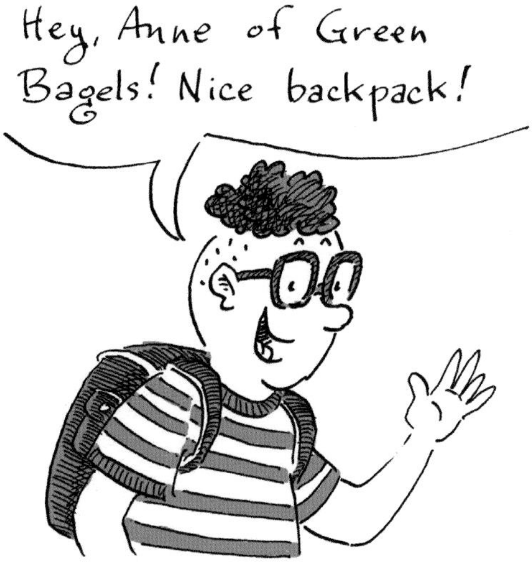
Hey, Anne of Green Bagels! Nice backpack!

I said, "Don't call me that!"

And he said, "No offense. I meant it as a friendly kind of nickname."

He started walking beside me.

"You know, the other kids used to call me Bob Blob. I kind of liked it when I was younger until I figured out what it meant. But Anne of Green Bagels — that's a tag of *respect*. Did you ever read the book?"

I shook my head.

"Well, you should," he said.

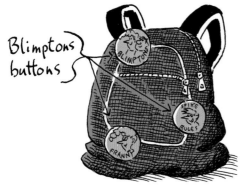

Blimptons buttons
BLIMPTONS
SPIKE RULES
FRANNY

The reason he said I had a nice backpack was because he saw my Blimptons buttons. It turned out that he was a Blimptons collector like me. He said I should come over to his house sometime to see his collection.

When I got home Mom asked me how the first day went.

"It was okay," I said.

3

THE
TOWER

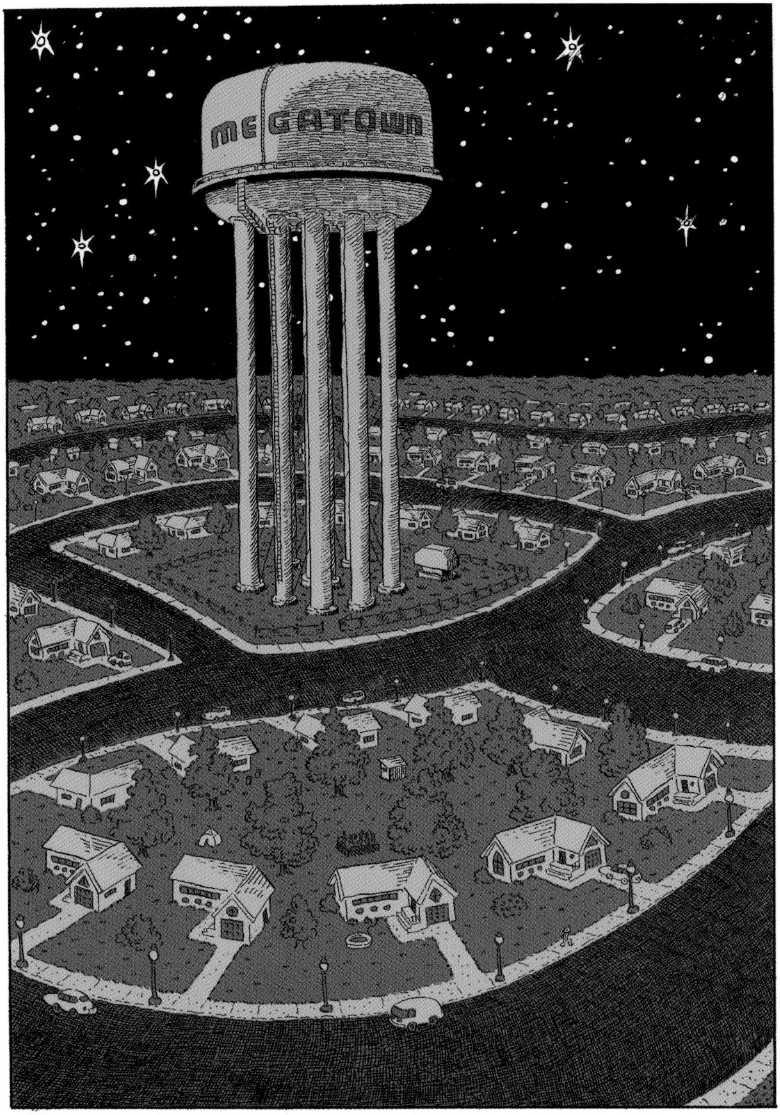
MEGATOWN

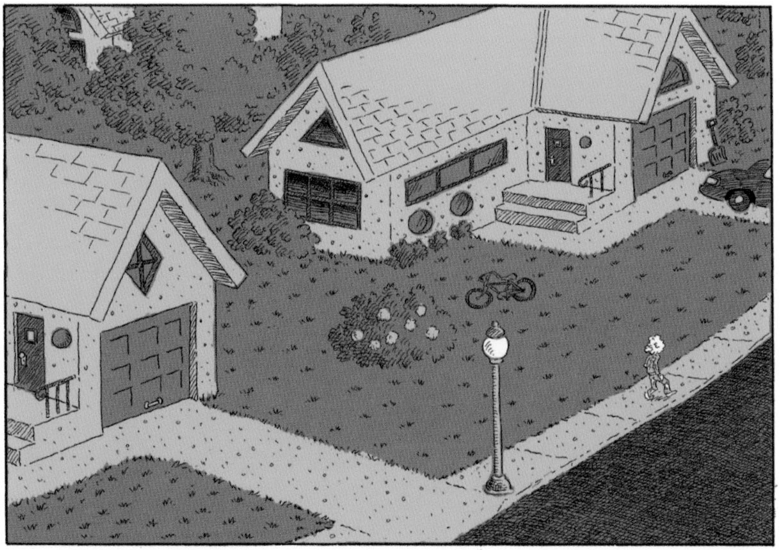

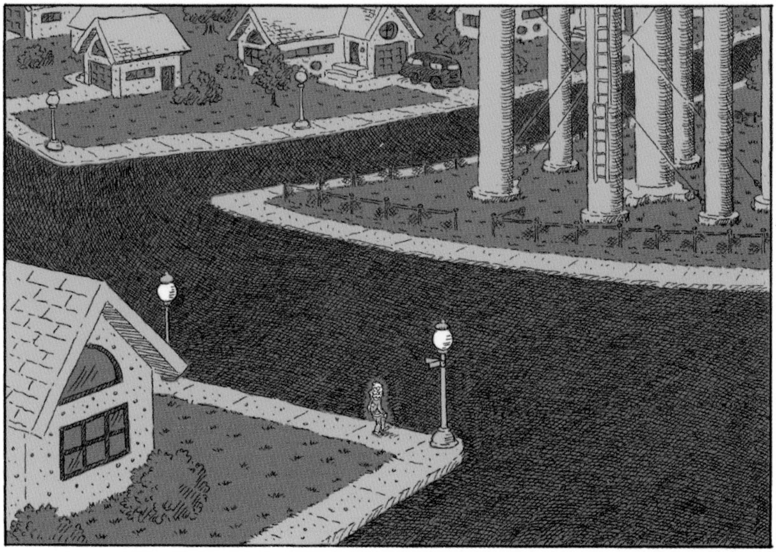

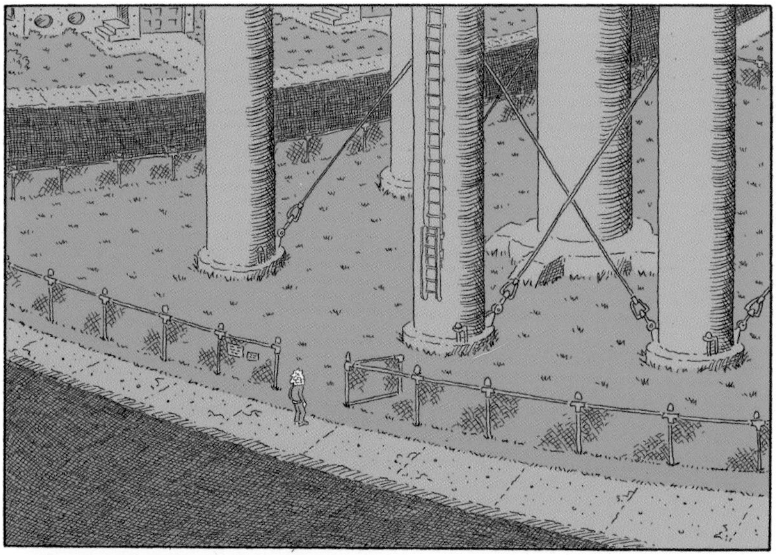

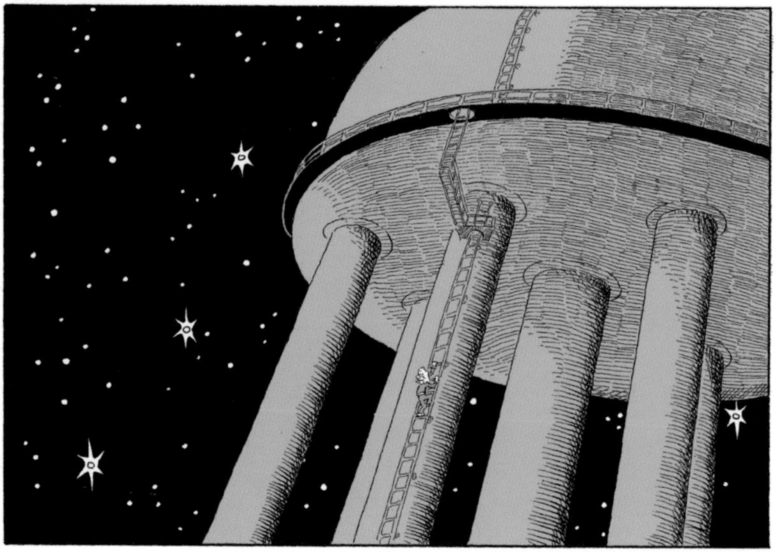

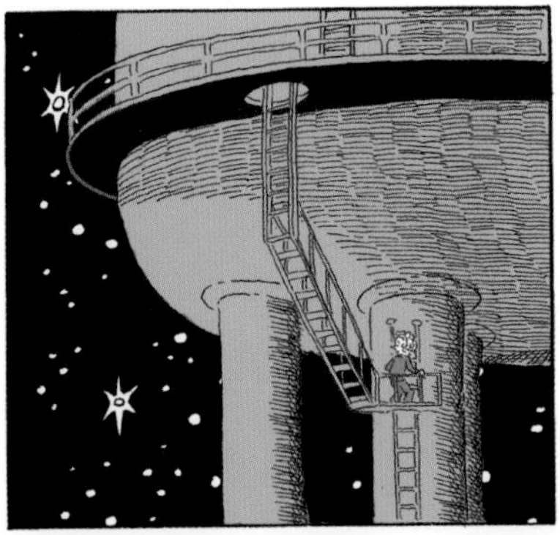

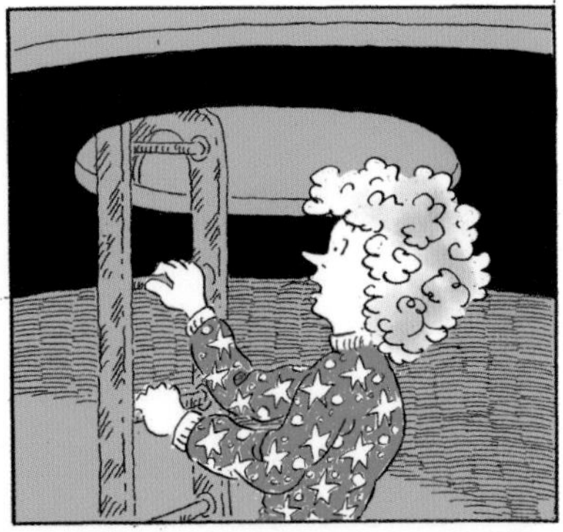

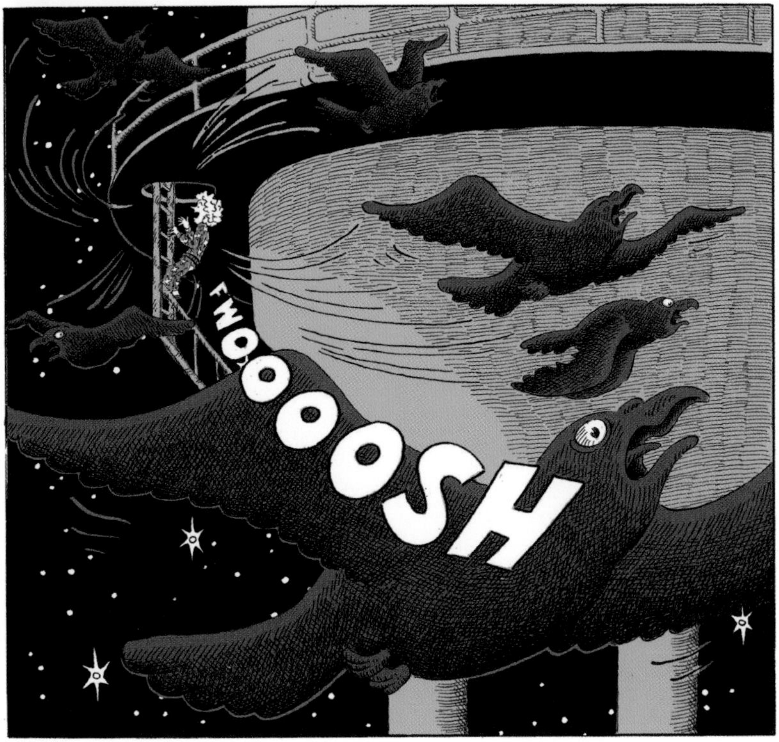
FWOOOOOSH

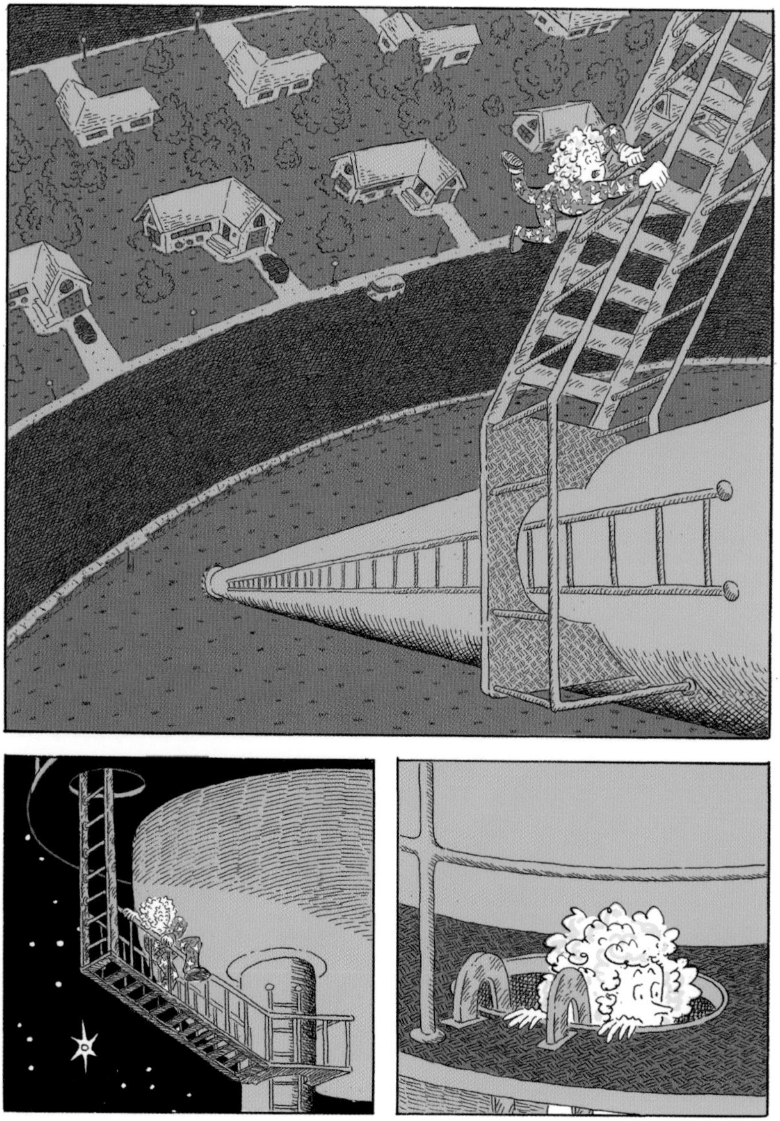

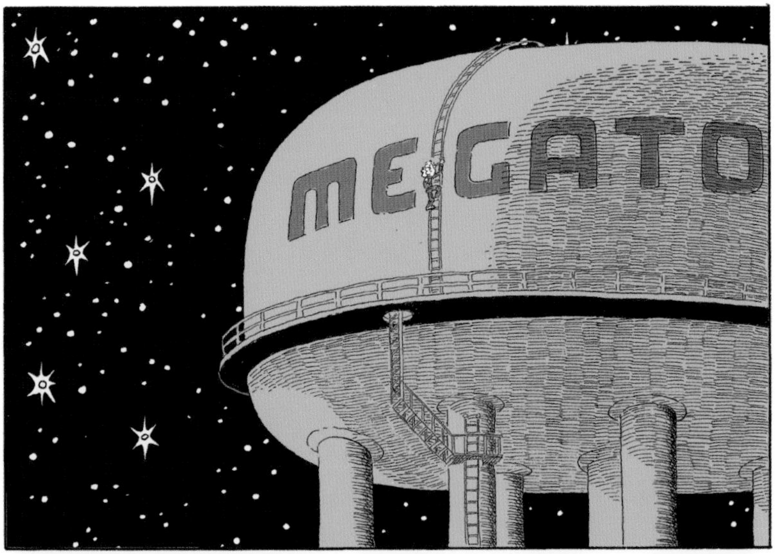
MEGATO

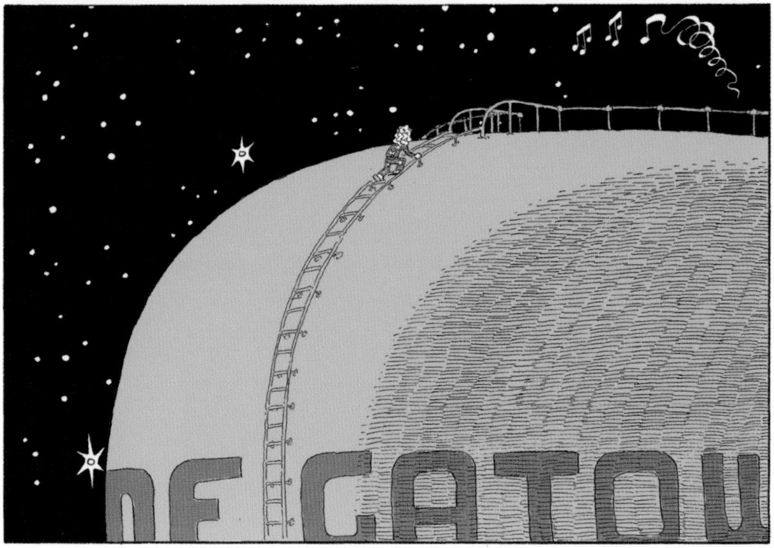

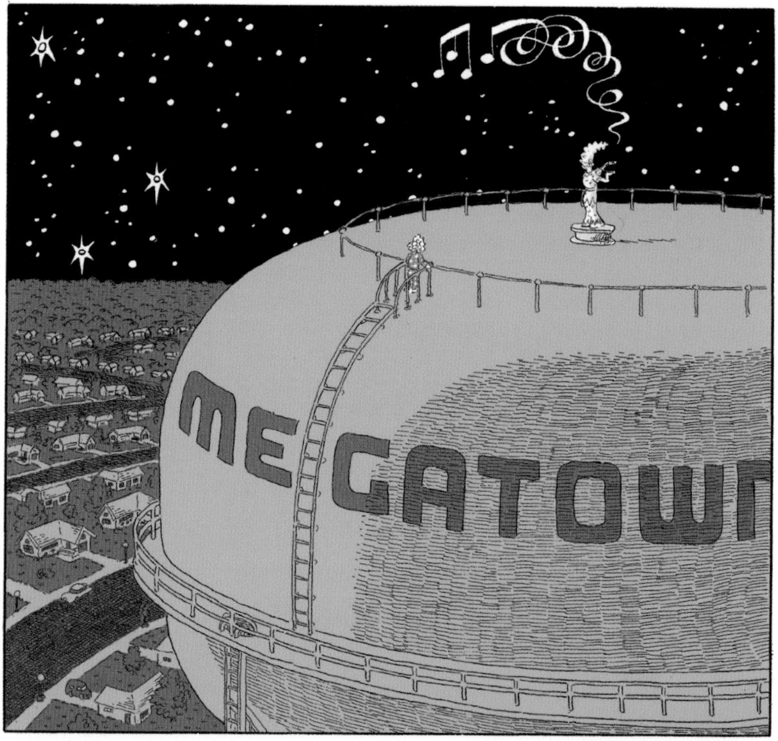
MEGATOWN

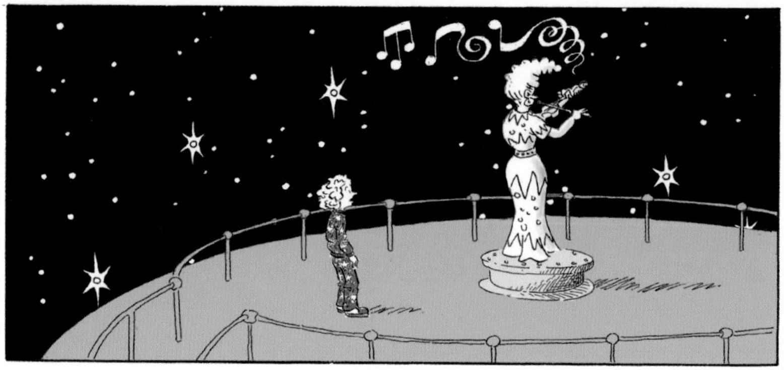

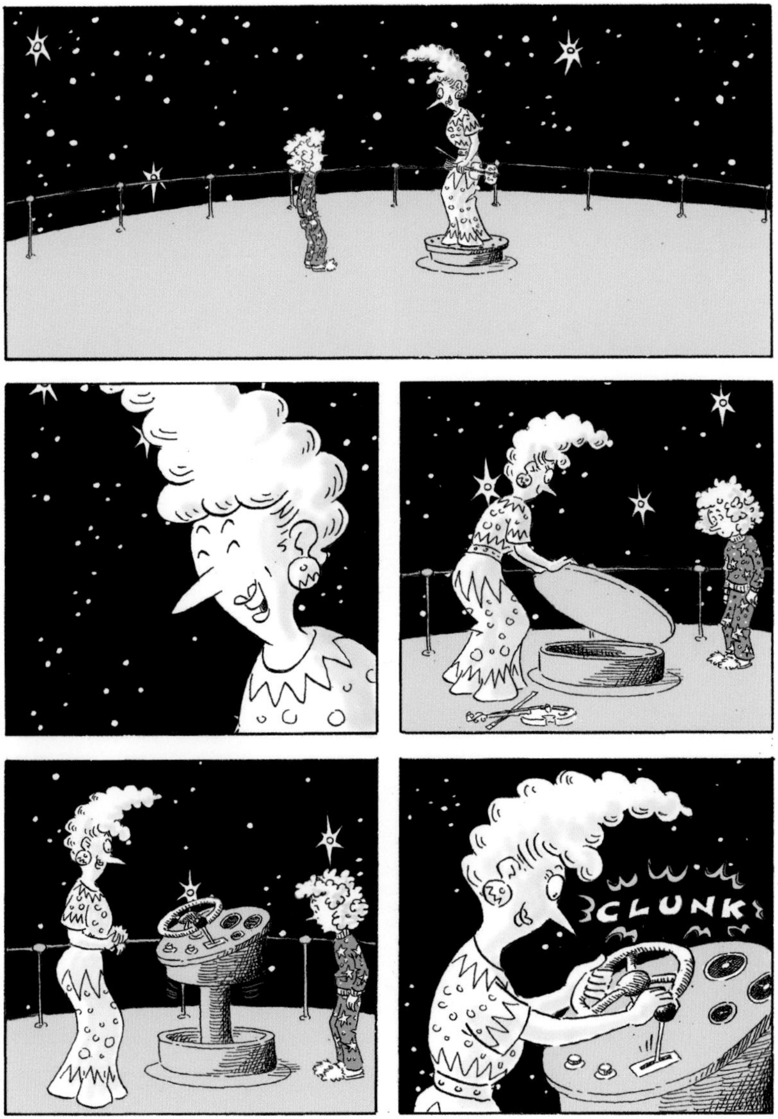
CLUNK

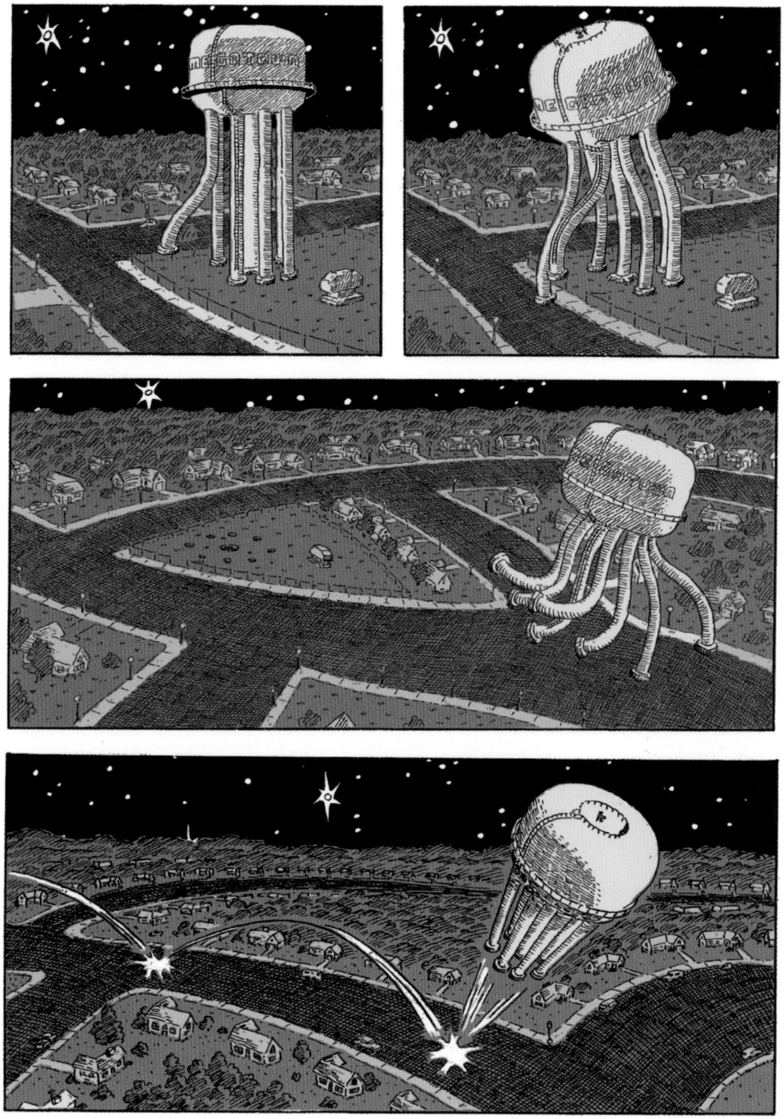
MEGATOWN

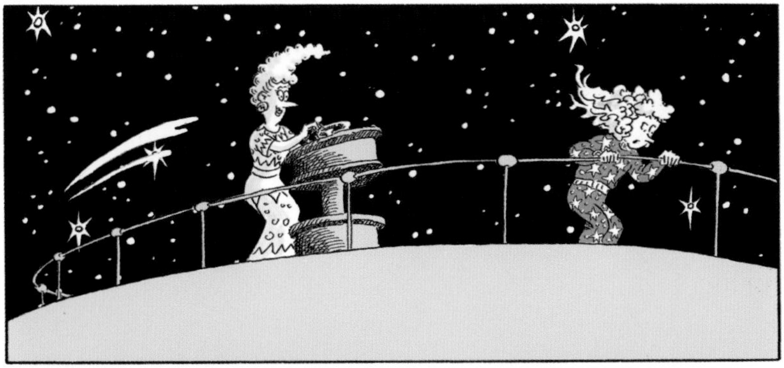

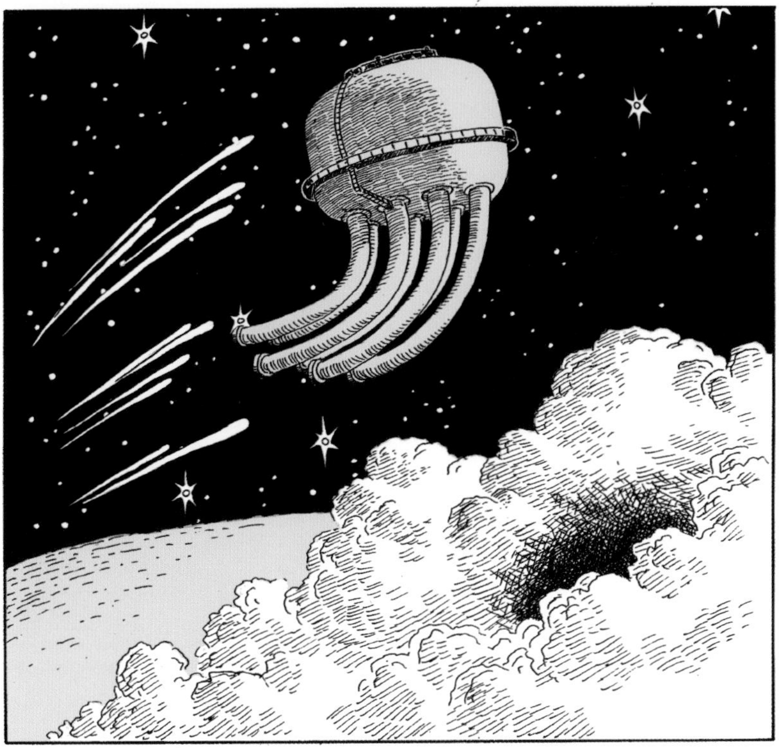

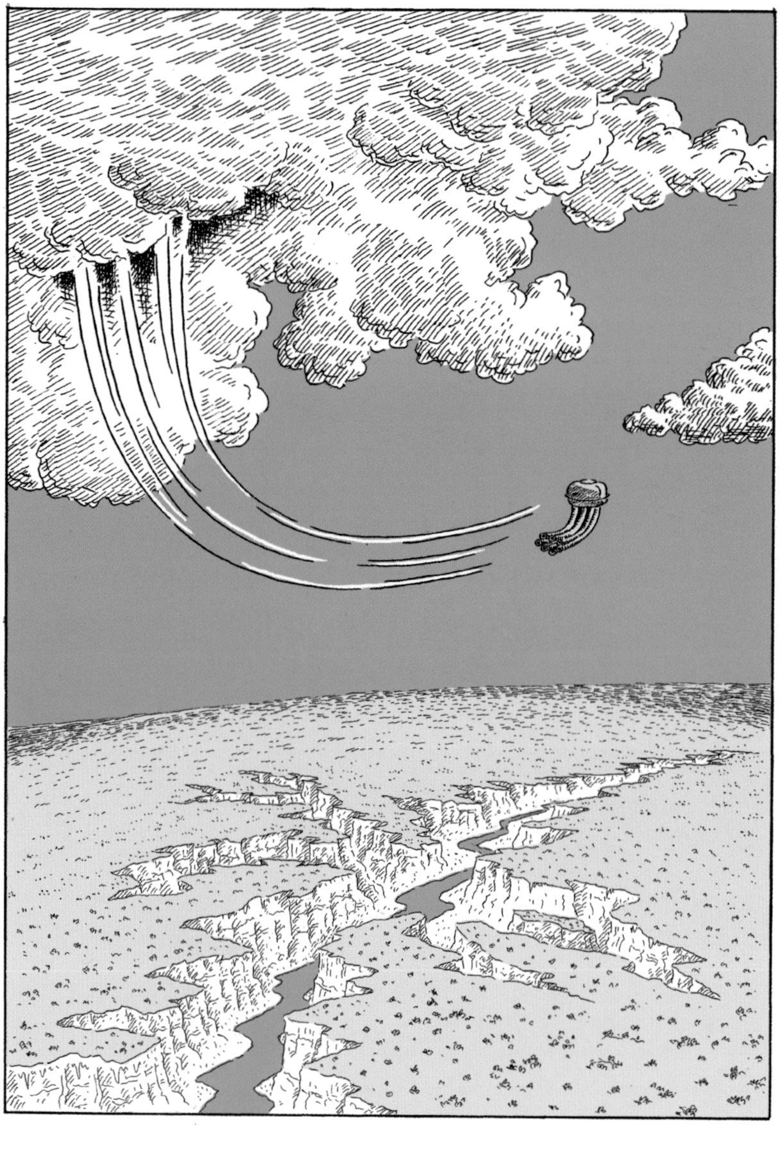

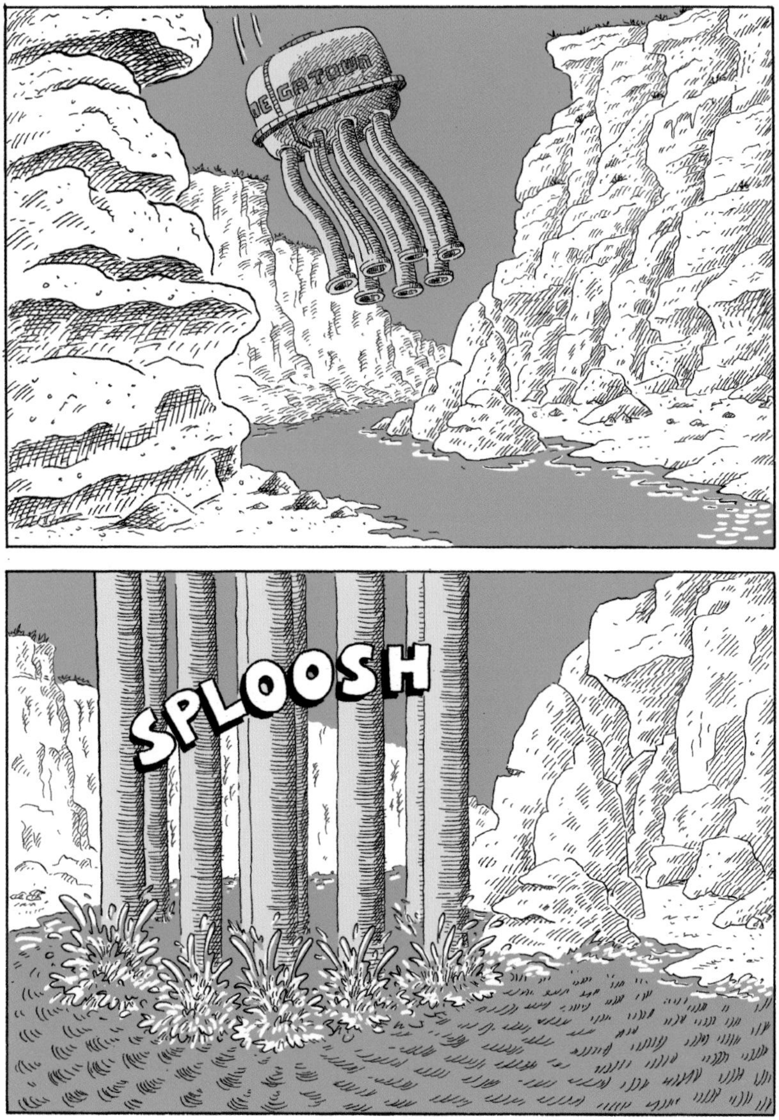
EGATOWN
SPLOOSH

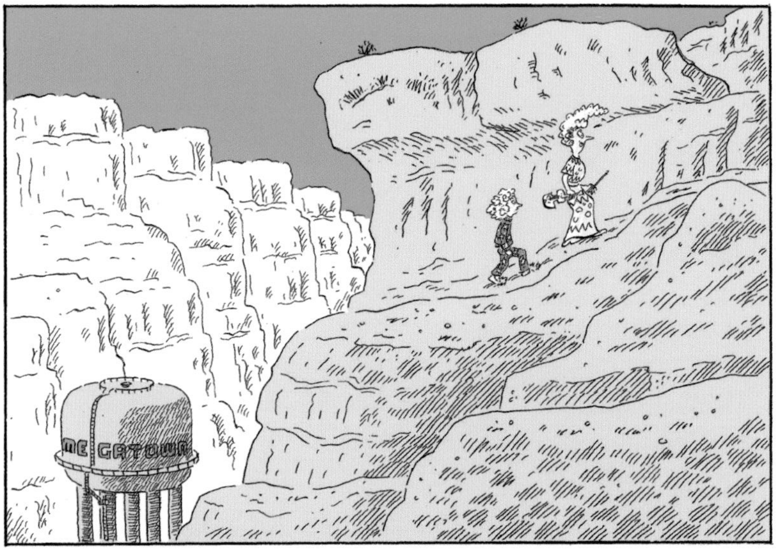
ME GATOWN

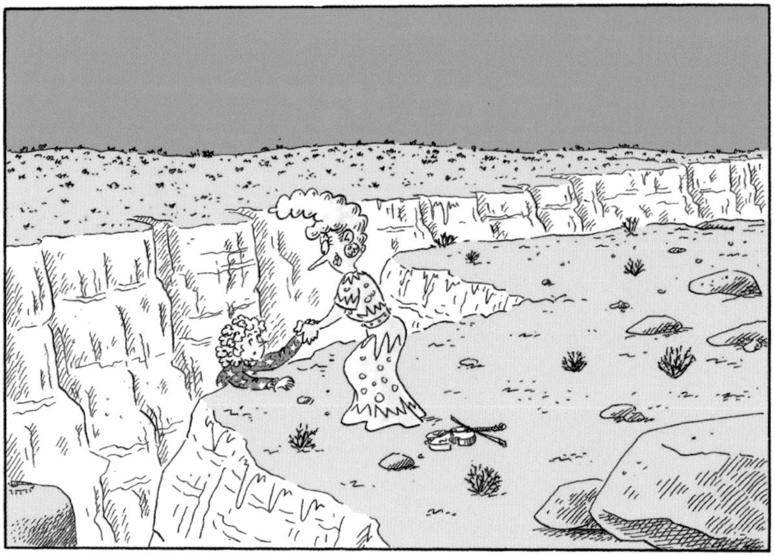

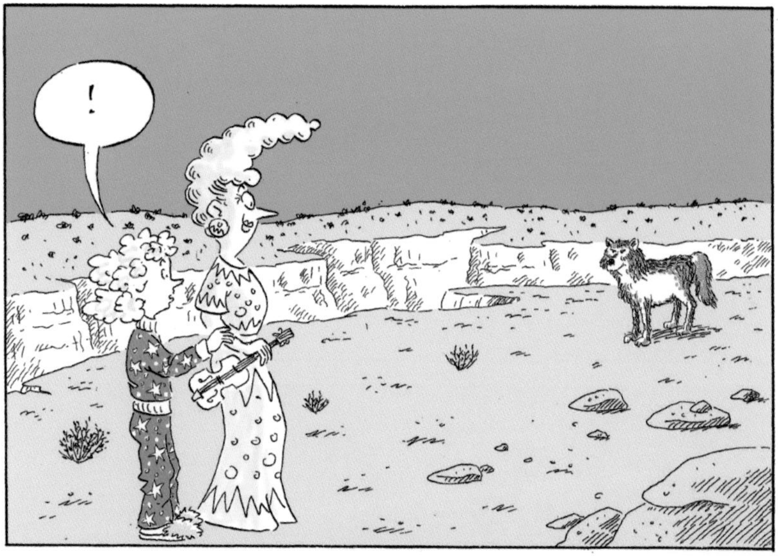
!

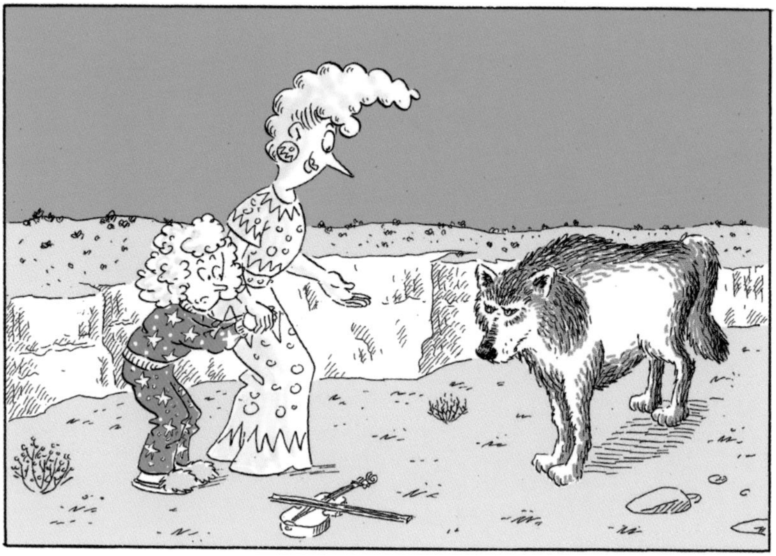

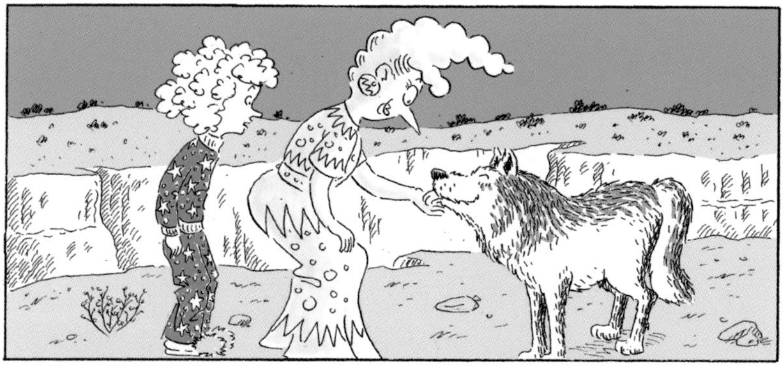

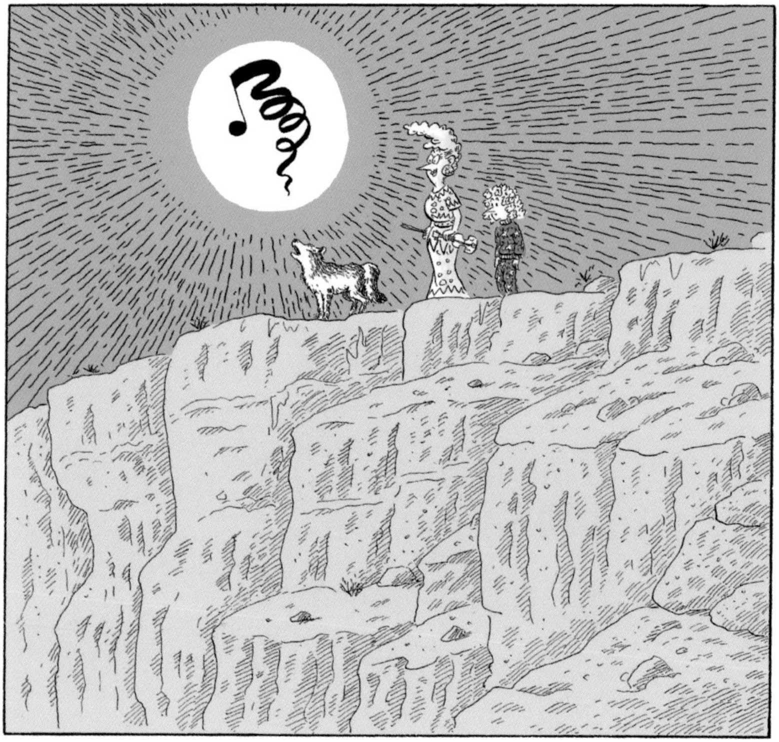

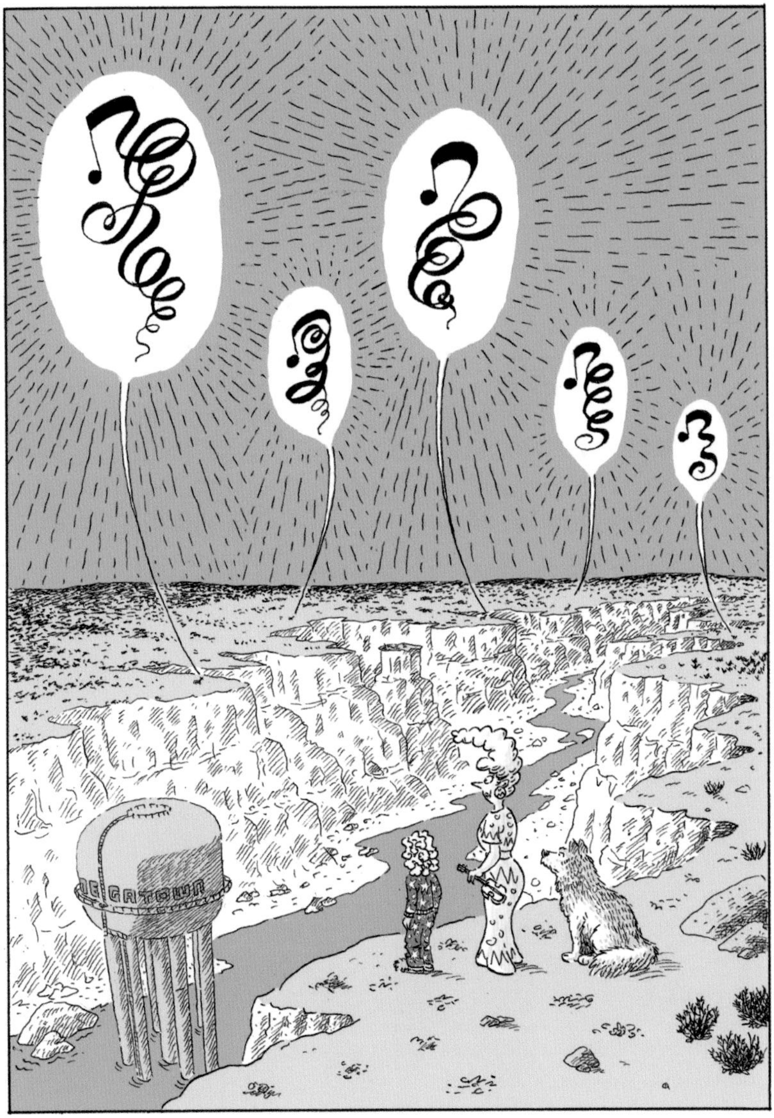
EGATOWN

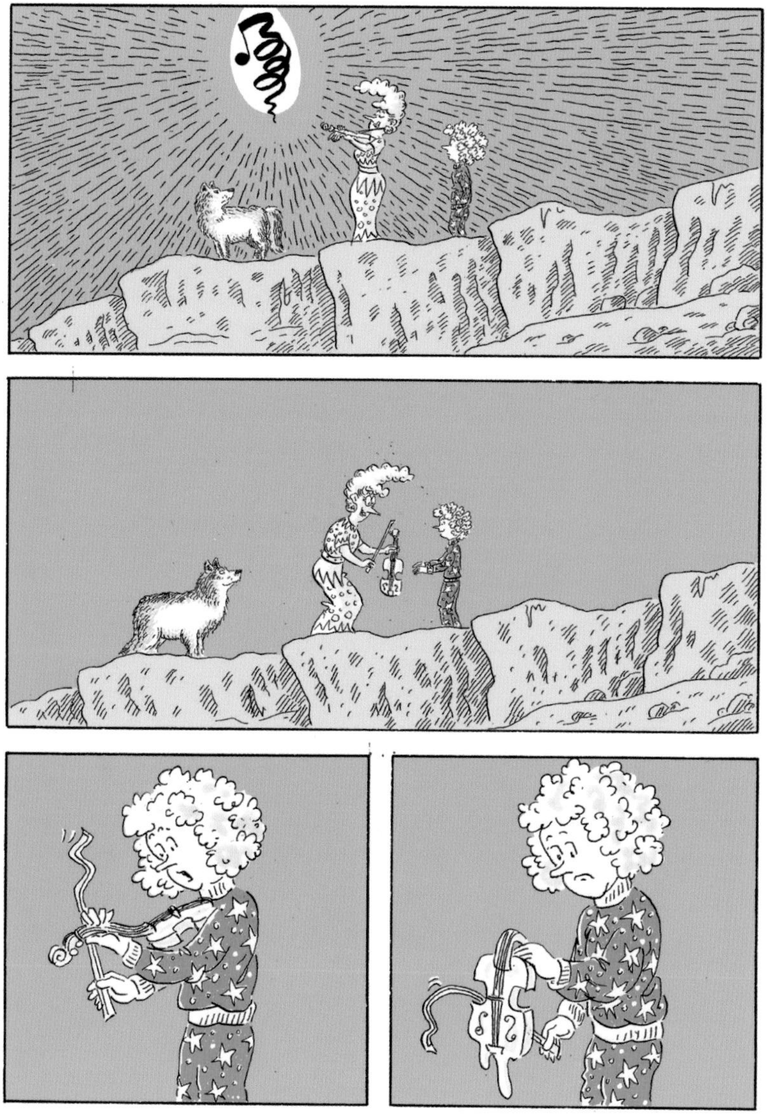

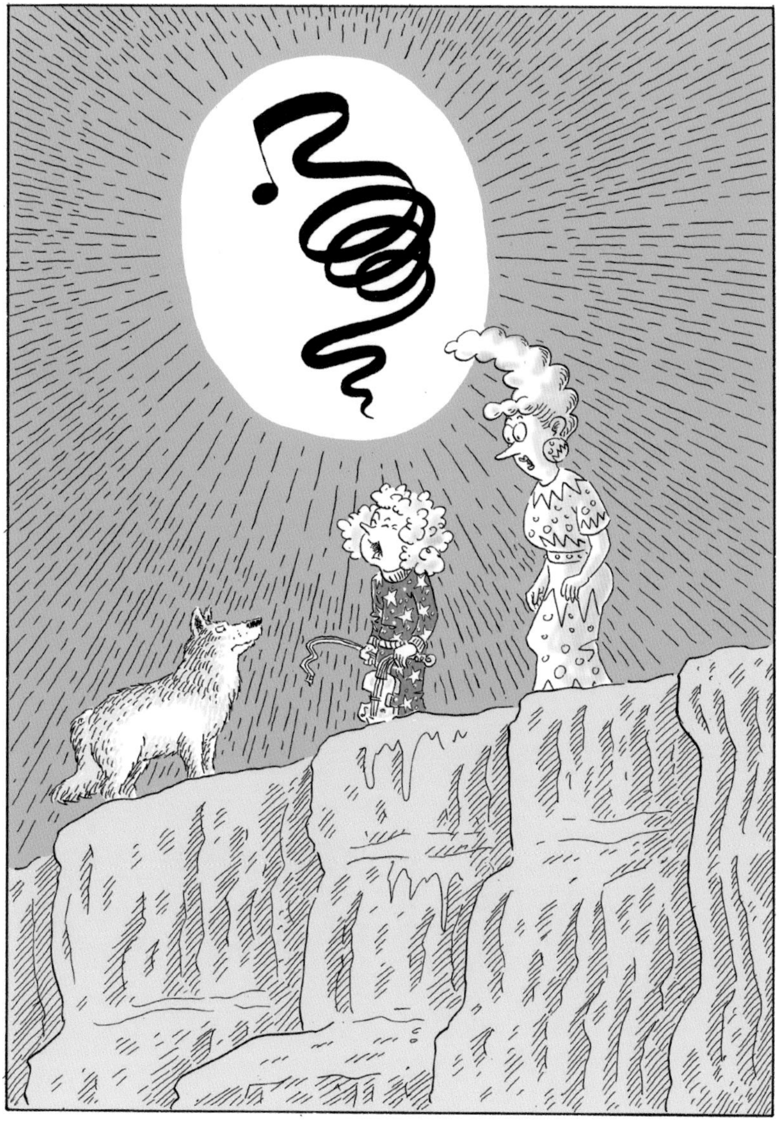

4

WEIRDO

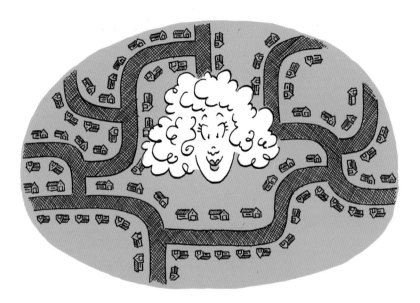

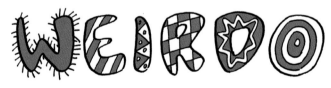

On the morning of my second day at the new school, I woke up feeling sick to my stomach. But Nana said it was just nerves, and she gave me some chamomile tea and sent me off.

Nana and Grandpop are into health food. They have a health food deli on the turnpike and bagels are their specialty.

Which is why I had that green bagel sandwich in the first place.

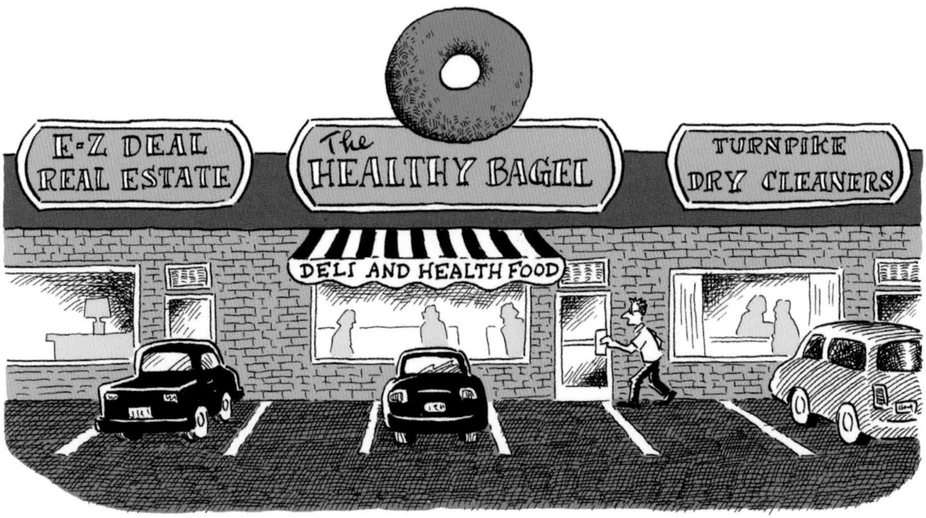

E-Z DEAL
REAL ESTATE
The
HEALTHY BAGEL
TURNPIKE
DRY CLEANERS
DELI AND HEALTH FOOD

For my lunch I had asked Nana if I could have my sandwich on rye bread instead of on a green bagel, but I still felt pretty tense walking to school. The truth was, I knew I would never fit in at the Norbert E. Meggett School. Because, let's face it, I'm a weirdo.

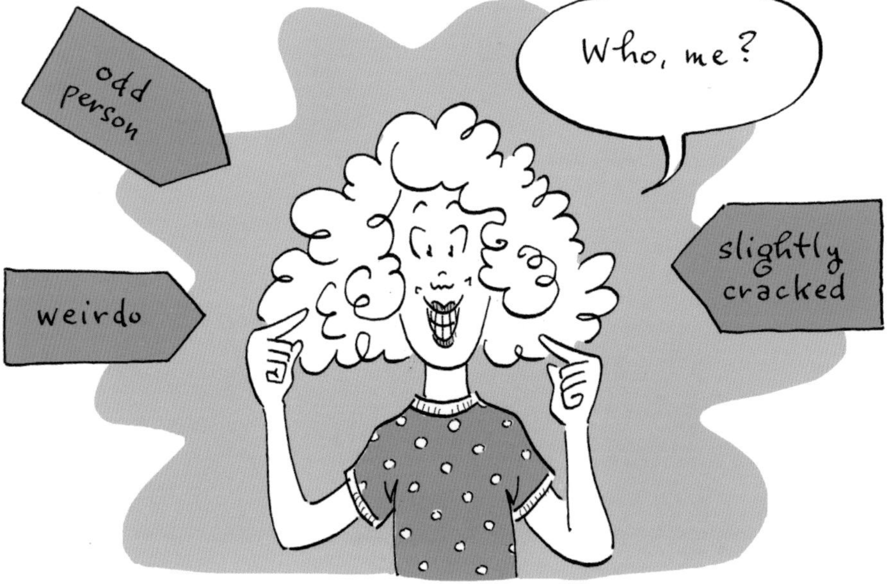
odd person
weirdo
Who, me?
slightly cracked

I get it from my dad. He's a weirdo too. And we're cool with that. We make up crazy music. We make up stories. We draw. Dad has cool ideas. I have cool dreams.

Flying on the Megatown water tower with Frannie Blimpton was one of my coolest dreams ever.

See, there's this show on TV — *The Blimptons* — and Dad and I used to watch it together. (Before he did his disappearing act.) It cracked me up right from the beginning, but Dad wasn't so sure. The first time he saw it he looked dumbstruck. He said, "I don't believe it!" Then he snorted and said, "Oh, no, not that old line."

But pretty soon he was as into it as I was. And he started buying me Blimptons collectibles. I have a pretty good collection.

Anyway, after my second day at the new school I had this dream. I think Frannie Blimpton was trying to tell me to loosen up and play whatever weird kind of music I wanted — just like the music Dad and I used to play together when Mom wasn't around.

So where is my dad now, and why did he disappear? It wasn't because he doesn't love us.

It was because . . . well, here's what happened.

One night, last August, he came home from work and looked at us as if he wasn't seeing us. He said,

I quit my job today.

"Oh, Ross!" Mom said, "Not again!"

Then Dad grinned suddenly and picked her up and swung her around.

"Don't worry, Naomi," he said, and he laughed out loud.

Uh oh, I thought. *He's got another big idea.*

"You know that pedestrian mobile home I've been working on?" he continued. "It just came to me — it's perfect for the HOMELESS!"

Just think of it! They can travel the country in comfort!

"And here's the kicker — FUNDING! I'm going to take this idea to Senator Feebler. I'm sure as soon as he sees it he'll help us get government funding!"

"Put me down right now," Mom said, kicking her feet in the air.

Here it comes, I thought.

"What about *us*?" Mom said. "What about Anne's violin lessons? What about the bills? I hate to bust your bubble, Ross, but we're the ones who are going to end up homeless! And I'm not living in any tiny pedestrian mobile home!"

But when Dad gets going on a new idea, there's no busting his bubble. He kissed Mom on the nose and said,

You're so cute I can't believe it!

SLORCH

Then he rushed out to his workshop to work on his idea. "Want to come, Anne? You can help with the brakes."

"I'll be out in a few minutes, Dad."

Mom and I looked at each other.

I said, "He'll get another job, after he finishes making his pedestrian mobile home. Don't worry so much.

We have some money in the bank, don't we?"

Mom sighed. "I don't like living like this," she said.

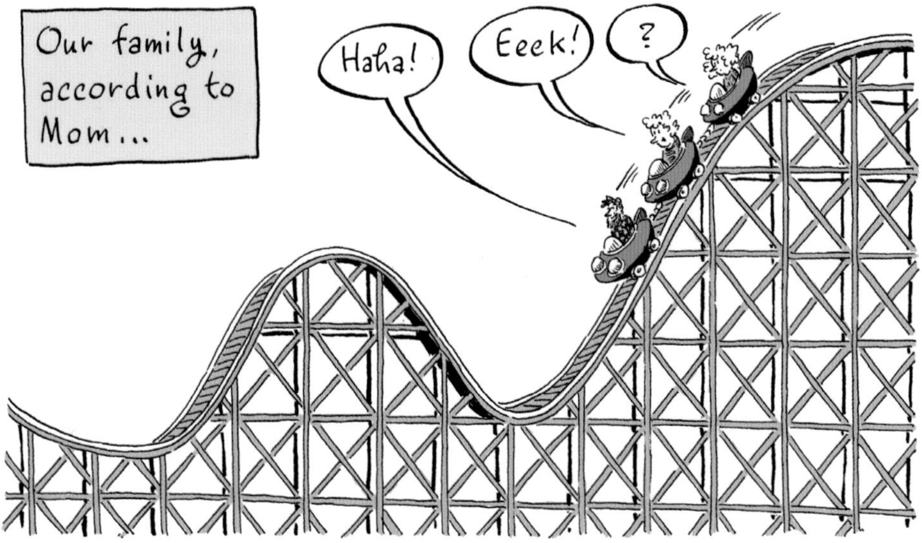
Our family, according to Mom...
Haha!
Eeek!
?

"It's always up or down. Up or down!"

"I know he doesn't like a nine-to-five job," she continued. "A lot of people feel the same way, but they do it anyway. I've done it. Do you think I like waitressing?"

Mom definitely does not like waitressing.

"If any of his projects were *successful* that would be one thing." And she took the vacuum cleaner out of the closet and began vacuuming the rug as if she was trying to teach it a lesson.

I went out to the workshop to help Dad work on his idea.

I thought the pedestrian mobile home was a lot of fun. It was about eight feet long and two feet wide, with wheels, and Dad had an air mattress and a sleeping bag to put inside it, and there was a place to carry a little cook stove.

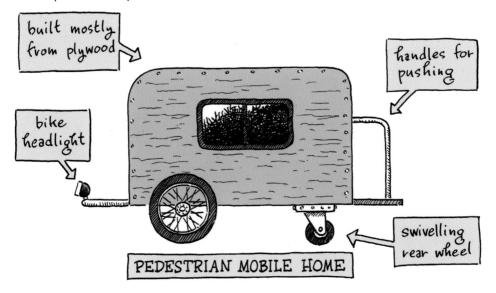

built mostly from plywood

handles for pushing

bike headlight

swivelling rear wheel

PEDESTRIAN MOBILE HOME

About two weeks later, at breakfast, he told us he was taking the pedestrian mobile home for a test run. "Not just around the block, you know," he said, putting down his napkin. "I'm going to be homeless . . ."

"HOMELESS! Is this the thanks I get?"

"Take it easy, Naomi. I just mean to try her out *as if* I was homeless. I want to really get the feel of it."

"Ross, homelessness is NOT A JOKE! I think you should try to show some real compassion for these people."

"That's just what I plan to do," he answered. And he kissed us both and went off with a spring in his step. I don't think he had the slightest idea where he was going.

Mom yelled after him, "What about your cell phone?" And, "What are you going to eat?"

He just waved and went whistling down the road, pushing his pedestrian mobile home in front of him.

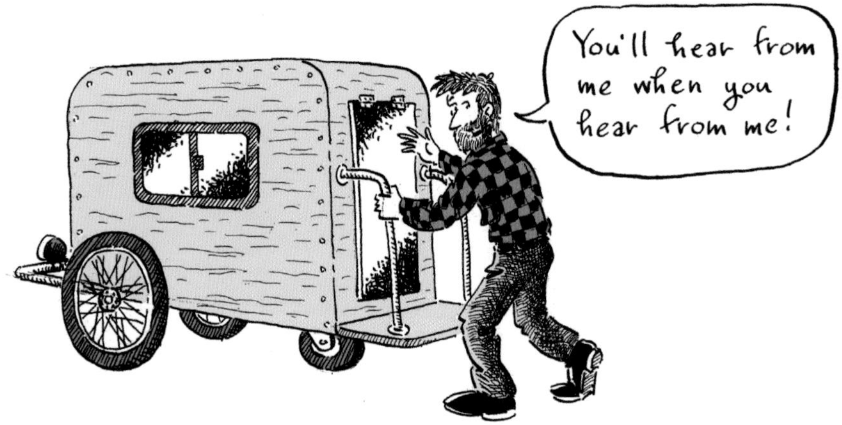
You'll hear from me when you hear from me!

It wasn't the first time Dad had taken off to try out one of his inventions. But after he had been gone a couple of weeks without calling, Mom started to worry.

"What if he's had an accident?" she said. "What if he has amnesia! Well, at least he has his wallet and his driver's license. If anything happens I'm sure we'll hear about it."

But she didn't stop worrying. In fact she started going to a therapist. The therapist told her it wasn't her fault.

And then, a few days later, a package came for me.

It was a plastic collectible of Franny Blimpton driving a little cartoon car.

There was a card inside that said, *From your Father*.

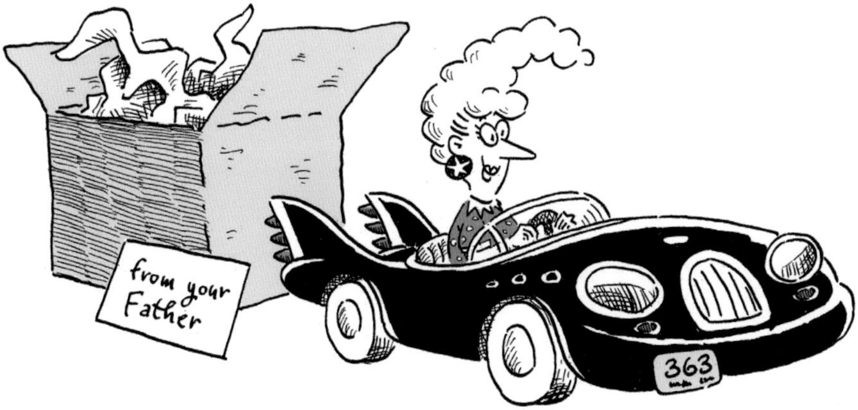
from your Father
363

So at least we knew he was still alive. But there was no return address. It came direct from *The Blimptons* online store. Mom blew her stack.

"He can send you a stupid toy? And he doesn't even let me know he's okay?"

"You can tell he's okay *because* he sent a toy," I said, which I thought was totally sensible.

"Oooooh," growled Mom. "So the homeless can't make a phone call, but they can order expensive toys online? Well, I'm not sitting here fretting any longer. And I'm not getting another waitressing job. We'll rent the house!"

"But . . ." I said.

"We'll go stay with Nana and Grandpop."

"But Dad won't know where we are!" I cried.

"Of course he will. Unlike some people we know, I'm a responsible parent and everyone knows how to reach me. I have *my* phone. And the people we rent the house to will have our address." And she put an ad for the house online.

It took a while to find good tenants. Meanwhile, I got another package from Dad — Mountain Girl, from the Yeti episode.

We moved our personal stuff into Dad's workshop and locked the door. The new tenants said they would look after our cats.

Zorro ⇨   ⇦ Phoebe

And then, around the middle of September, we left to drive 2,000 miles to Megatown.

Boom chick-a
unh unh
oowah wah!

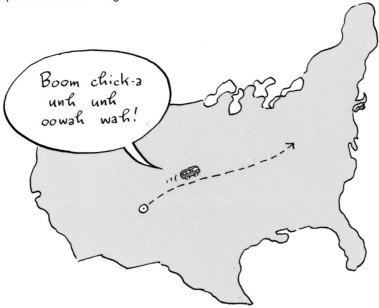

I passed the time in the car by practicing my beat boxing. That's where you make drum noises with your mouth.

Mom said it was very annoying, but by the second day she was beat boxing along with me. (Mom can be a little weird herself.)

By the time we got to Megatown we were both exhausted.

Nana and Grandpop met us with hugs and kisses.

Nana hustled us into the house and told Grandpop to bring the bags. He was standing around looking vague.

"He's losing his memory," Nana whispered.

"But not my hearing," he shouted.

5

DESERT DREAM

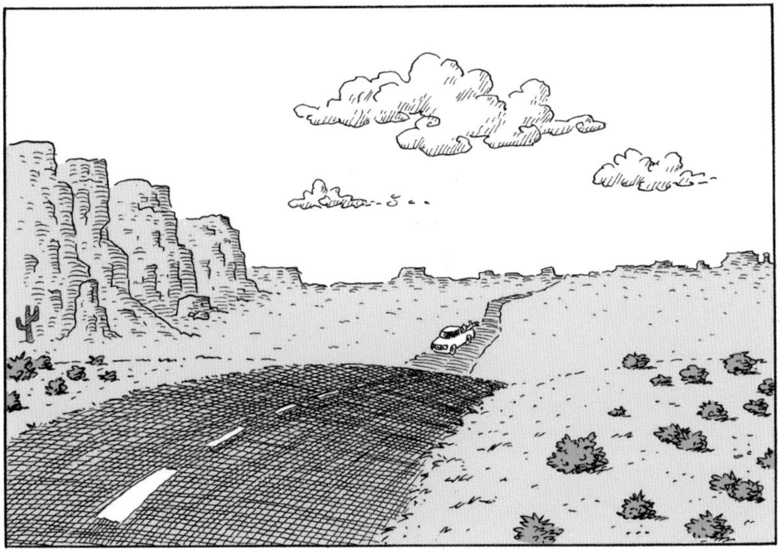

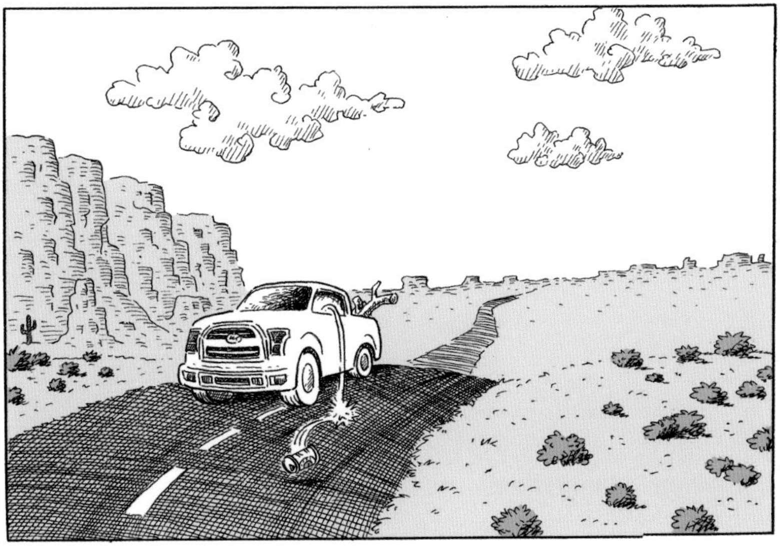

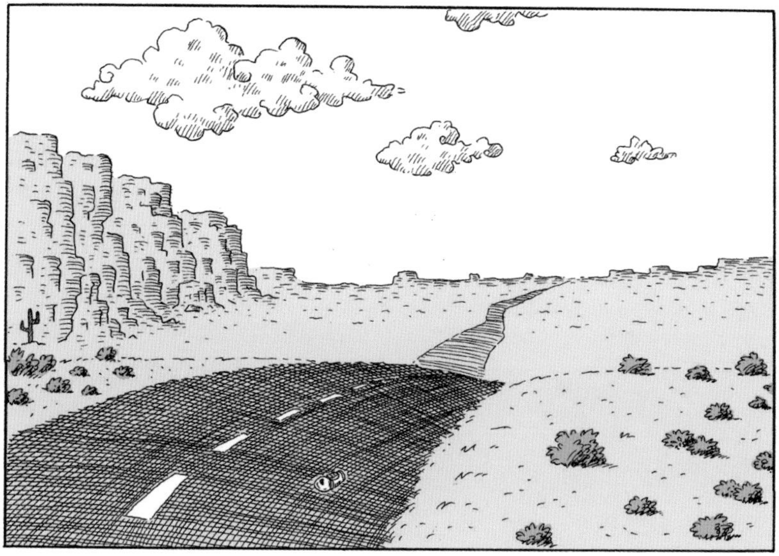

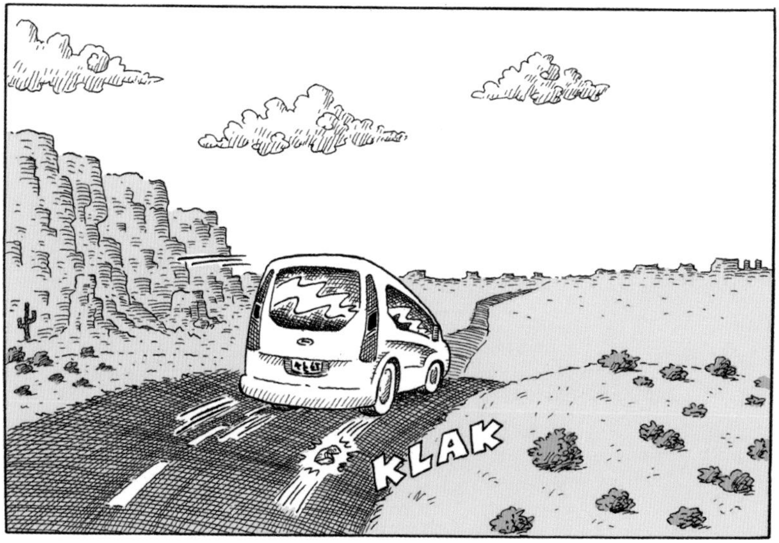
KLAK

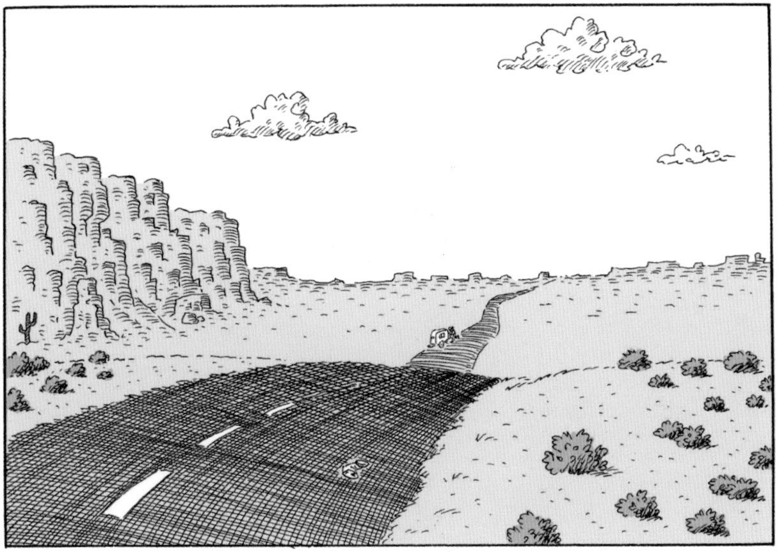

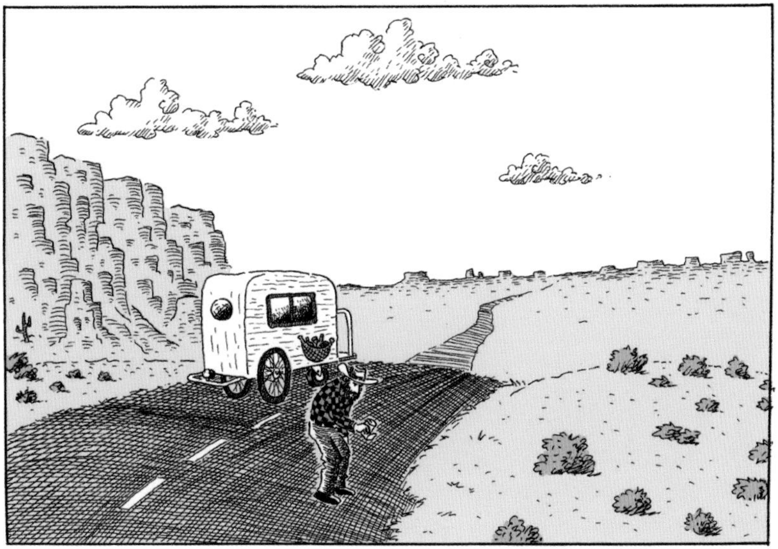

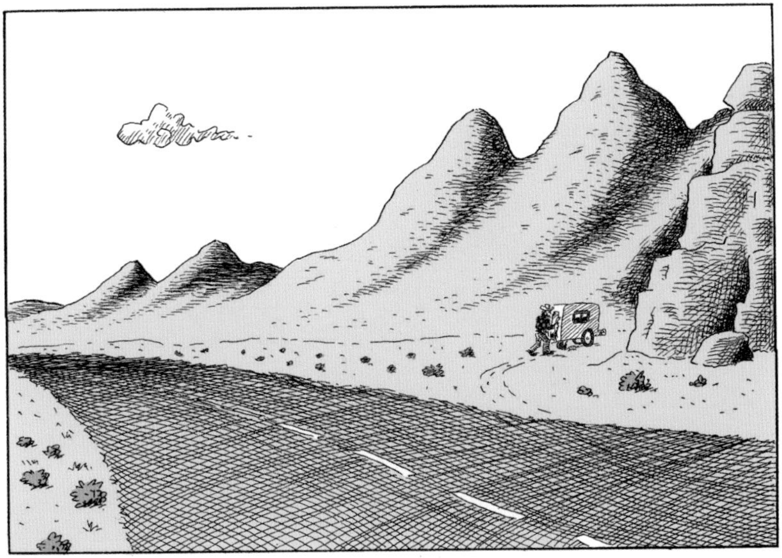

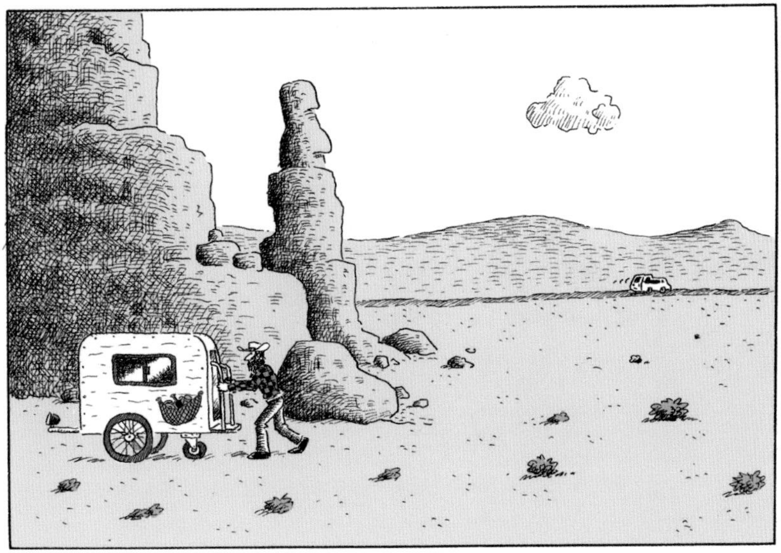

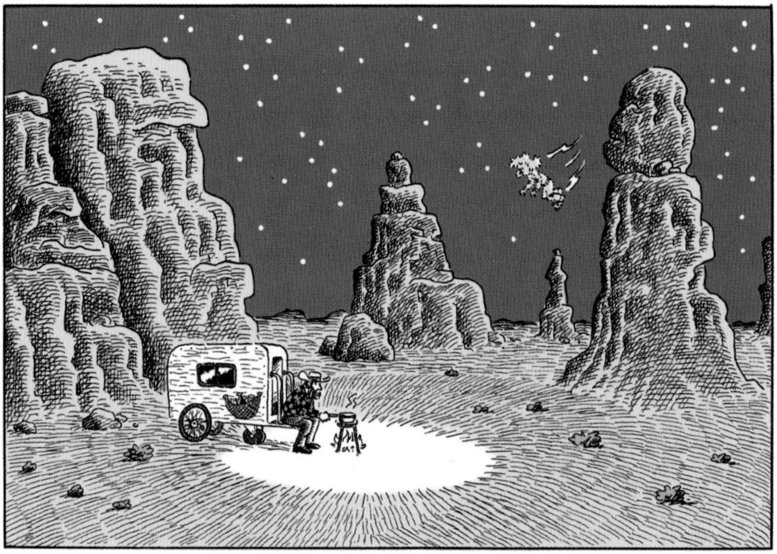

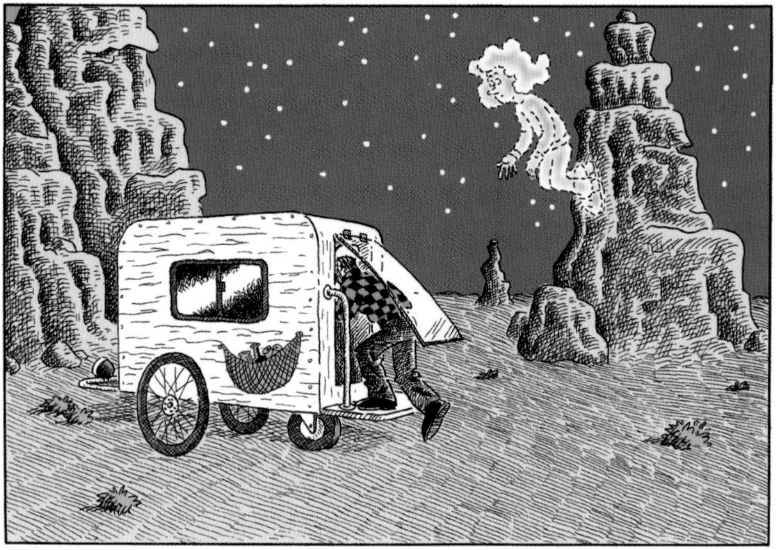

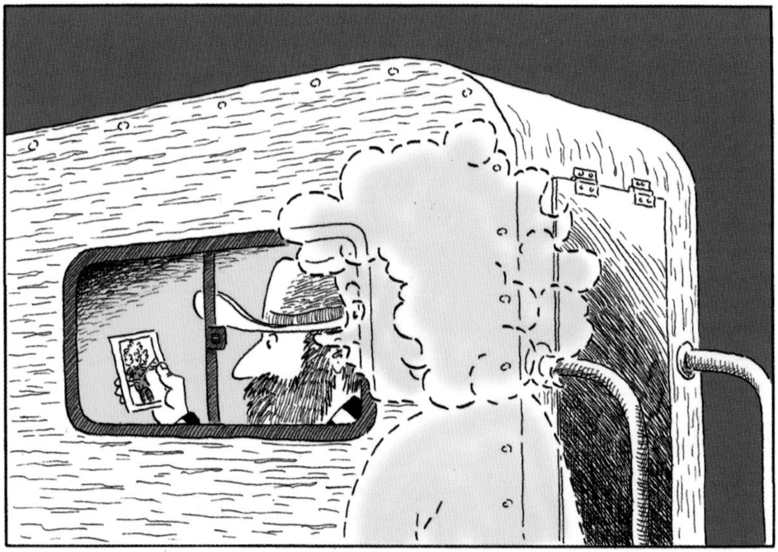

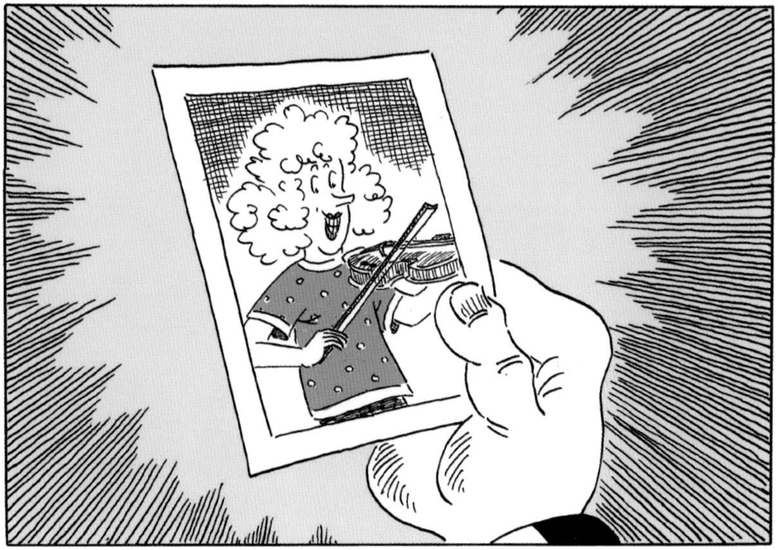

6

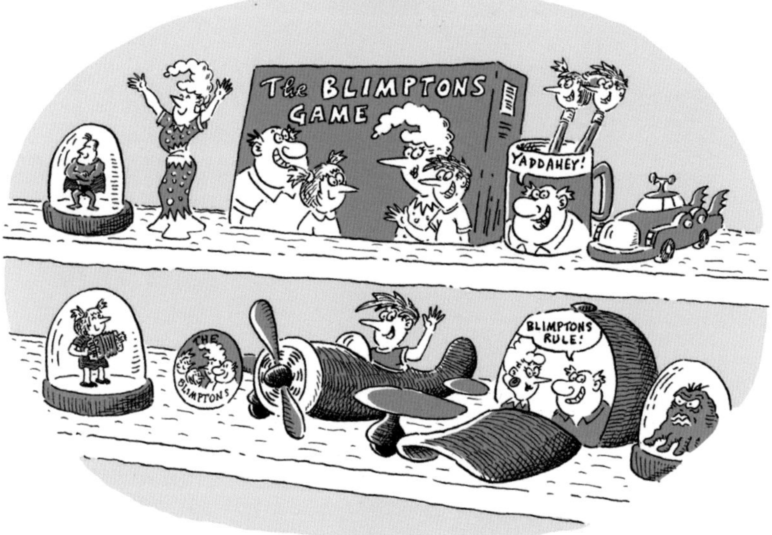

The BLIMPTONS GAME
YADDAHEY!
THE BLIMPTONS
BLIMPTONS RULE!

OTTO'S GARAGE

It turned out that school wasn't so bad. I didn't like the way Brendan Boyle and his friends still teased me, but I had made a good new friend — Otto Immaculata.

On Friday, Otto asked me if I wanted to come over after school and see his collection. I called Mom and she said it would be okay, so Otto and I walked to his house together.

"Megatown is like a *maze*," I said as we walked along. "It's a wonder people don't get lost in it. I know I would if I was by myself."

"You wouldn't if you had lived here all your life like I have," Otto replied.

"I think it's weird the way all the houses are the same. Why don't they add on porches or something?" I asked.

"It's because of crackpot Norbert Meggett."

"The man our school is named after?"

"That's right. He built Megatown," Otto said. "And he thought it was so perfect he didn't want anyone to change it. So when you move in you have to sign a contract saying you won't make any changes, and promising to make whoever buys your house sign the same contract. It's called in perpetuity, or something."

"But the houses aren't all exactly the same," he added. "Can you tell what the difference is?"

"I give up," I said. "They all look the same to me."

"It's the shape of the garage windows! Take a look. You'll see that there are four different shapes."

round   half-round   diamond   arch
(Otto's)   (ours)

"Here we are," he said, and turned up his driveway. We went right into the garage.

Otto yelled, "MA! I'M HOME!"

Otto's garage isn't used for cars. It's Otto's own room.

"There's no bed in here," I said, looking around.
"My bedroom is in the house," Otto said.
"So you've got your own playroom?"
"I prefer to call it my boy cave."
Otto showed me his Blimpton collection.

I've got every snowglobe except the Demented Doctor. That's been retired.

"I've got the Demented Doctor," I said.
Otto looked me in the eye. "What d'you want for it?" he said.
"I don't think I want to sell it," I said.
"Trade?" he asked.

Blimp baby carriage?
Got it.
Blimpbird house?
Got it.
Blimp Go-Round?
Got it.

Otto looked really disappointed.

"Let me think about it," I said.

One corner of Otto's garage was taken up by a huge set of drums. I suspected that was why Otto had his own boy cave.

"Nice drum set," I said.

"I don't play them any more. Now I play accordion. Want to hear?" He strapped on his accordion. "This is an old classic Elvis Presley number," he said. "You may have heard of it. It's called 'Heartbreak Hotel.'"

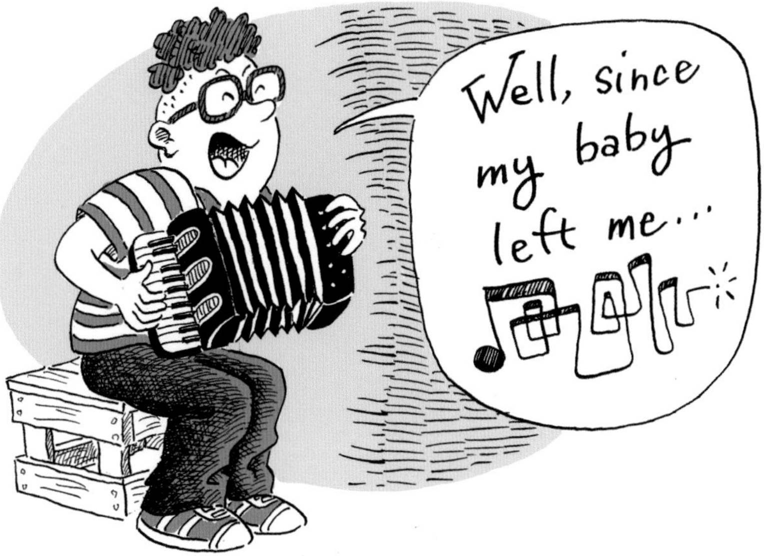
Well, since my baby left me...

So after that I started hanging out in Otto's garage a lot. I would bring over my violin and we would play music together. He liked my violin playing, but he didn't think much of my beat boxing.

"You should stick to the fiddle," he said.

"Violin," I said.

"The way you play it, it sounds more like a fiddle. Same instrument. It's all in the way you play it."

"Whatever," I said.

My mother was happy to know that I had a friend and that I was keeping up with my music. She might have felt differently if she could have heard us play. It wasn't much like the minuets and études I learned with my violin teacher in New Mexico.

Otto said, "I like it when you play two strings together so it sounds like a wolf howling."

"Oh, good," I said. "I wasn't sure if people could tell what it was supposed to be."

"I could tell," Otto said. "It sounds strange and lonely."

"Yeah," I said. "I was sort of thinking about my dad."

"What about your dad?" Otto asked.

"I had a dream about him the other night. He was walking along a road in the desert pushing his pedestrian mobile home and collecting cans. I don't know if he's in the desert in real life, but if he is I'm sure he'll be collecting cans. He has a thing about recycling."

"What's a pedestrian whatsit and how come you don't know if your father is in the desert or not?" Otto asked.

So I told him all about it.

When I was finished Otto said, "Is your father a wack-job?"

"That's not a very polite question! And no, he's not! He's cool and weird. And he's always inventing stuff.

Like he invented a pen the size of a toothpick."

"Did it work?"

"It worked great, but my mom used it to pick her teeth and got ink in her mouth. Then she yelled at him and it hurt his feelings."

"One of the first things I remember from when I was really little is lying on the rug with Dad and drawing funny pictures. He taught me to draw a lady looking over a fence."

"And he got me my first musical instrument — a set of bongo drums. We used to play music together. And after Mom made me start violin lessons Dad and I would jam."

"My dad is a huge Blimptons fan," I told Otto.

"We always used to watch the show together, and he knew every single episode. Like if you lost your shoe or something he would say, 'Hah! That reminds of the episode where Barney loses his rubber pencil!'

"Mom didn't think the show was very funny, and that really cracked us up. Sometimes it made me and Dad laugh so hard we could hardly talk."

"So he just took off? What did your mom say?"

"She worries about him," I said. "When they were first married, they had an RV and they drove around the country staying at trailer camps and doing odd jobs. I think they were really happy then.

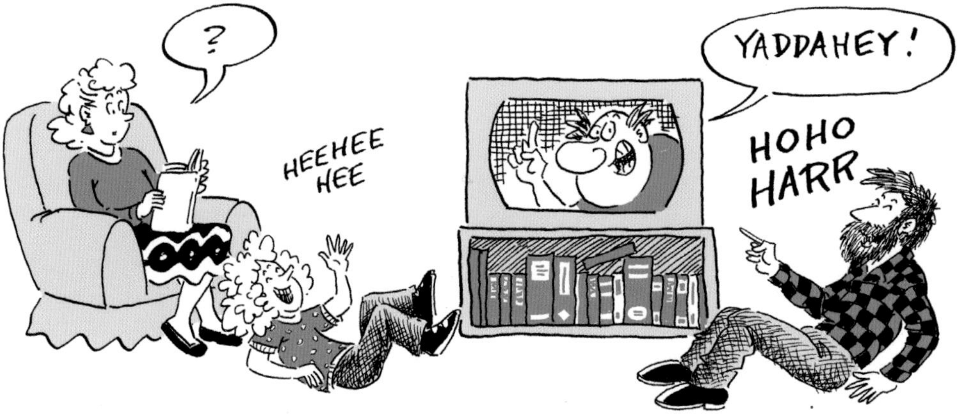
?
HEEHEE
HEE
YADDAHEY!
HOHO
HARR

Now they usually aren't both happy at the same time. Dad is happy when he's inventing new stuff and fooling around in his workshop. But Mom is happy when he has a steady salary and she doesn't have to worry about money. I wish they could both be happy at the same time."

"Well," said Otto, "your father still sounds like a wack-job to me. Maybe he needs to see a therapist."

"Maybe you need to mind your own business!"

"Hey! You brought it up."

I said I was sorry. "People don't understand him. Well, Nana understands him. She says he's an 'independent thinker,' and he'll find us when he's ready."

"Is Nana your father's mother or your mother's mother?"

"My father's mother."

"You know what? I'll bet your father grew up right here in Megatown. He probably went to our school and lived in your house. Your room was probably his room when he was a kid! Maybe he even left some stuff around. Like old comics or something."

"Nah," I said. "It *was* his room, but it got totally cleaned out. They even repainted it. Pink."

"Pink! Eew!"

"Yeah. They thought I was going to be younger."

"What's the matter? Can't they count?"

"Hey," I said, "don't make fun of my grandparents. They're doing their best for me."

"Sorry," Otto said. "I didn't mean anything."

"Besides," I said, "I kind of like pink."

Otto picked up his accordion. "Want to play a duet?" he asked.

"What key?"

Oh, and just for the record, in spite of what some creepy people might be saying around school, Otto does not have a crush on me, which is a good thing. Otherwise I would feel awkward about going over there all the time.

He actually has a crush on Isabel Morton who is cute and has blonde hair. She's okay. Otto asked me once if I thought Isabel liked him at all.

I said, "Sure, but not like she likes that creep Brendan Boyle. Haven't you noticed how she laughs every time he opens his mouth?"

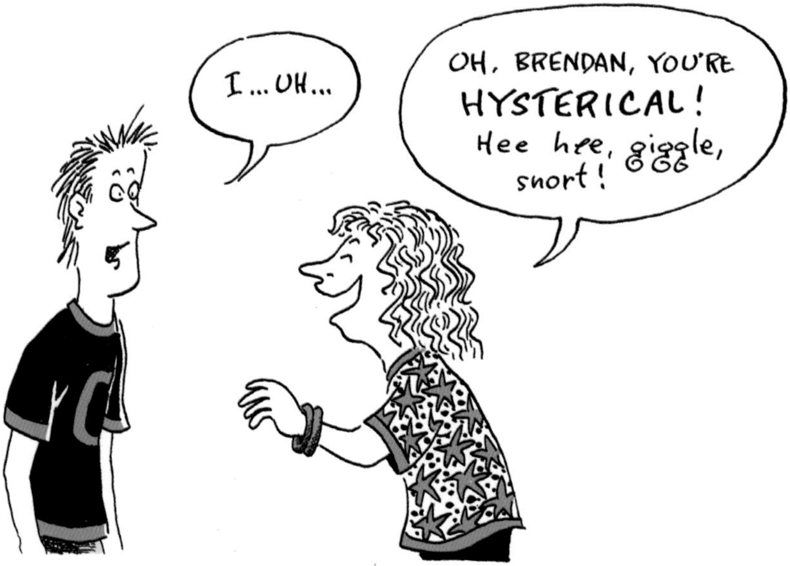
I... UH...
OH, BRENDAN, YOU'RE HYSTERICAL! Hee hee, giggle, snort!

"Yeah," Otto said, "And he's not even that funny. He's not really a creep, though. He's okay. And he's a good singer. Last year he won the school talent show."

That was the first I had heard about the school talent show. And it occurred to me right away, *I wonder if Otto and I could be in it!*

7

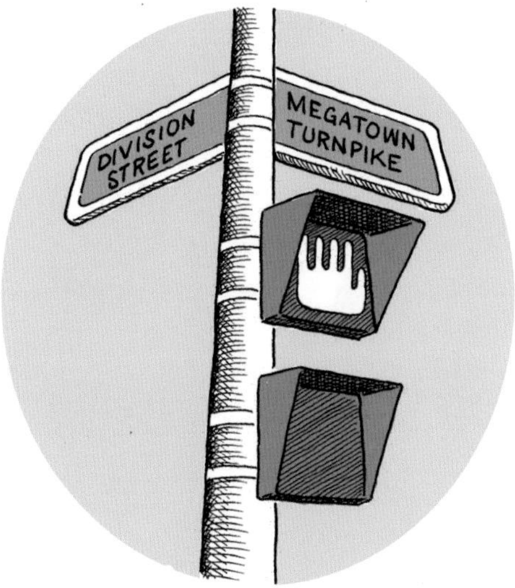
DIVISION STREET
MEGATOWN TURNPIKE

MEGATOWN TURNPIKE

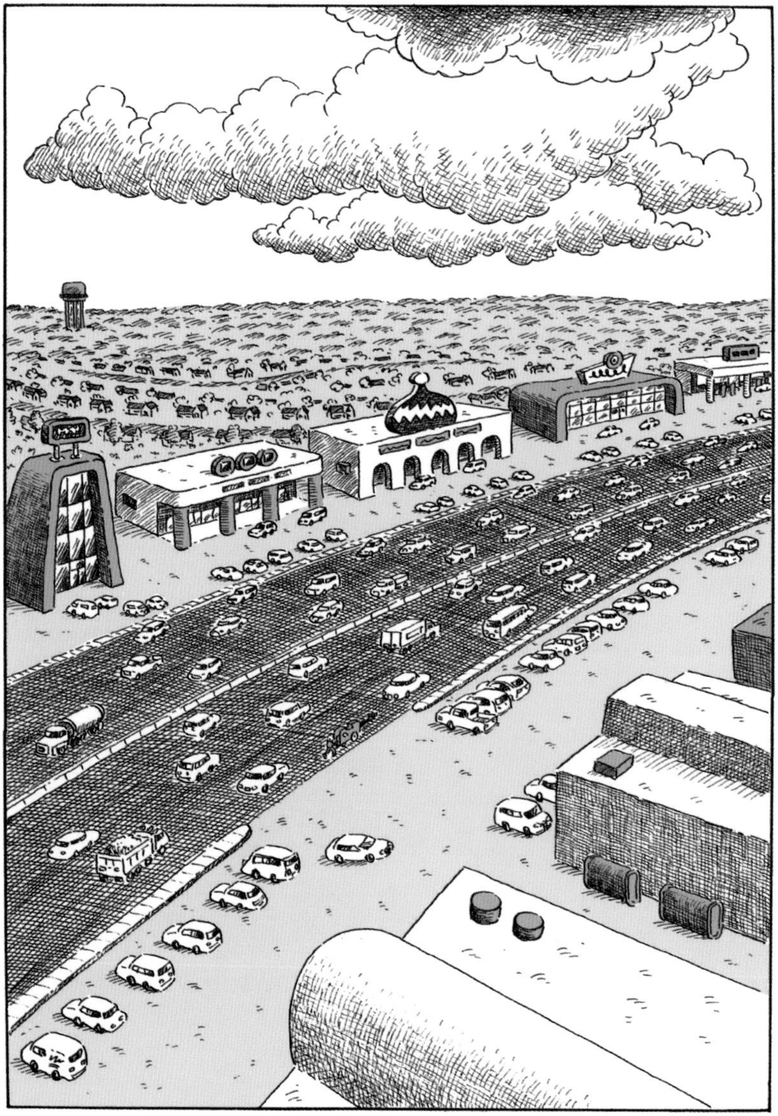

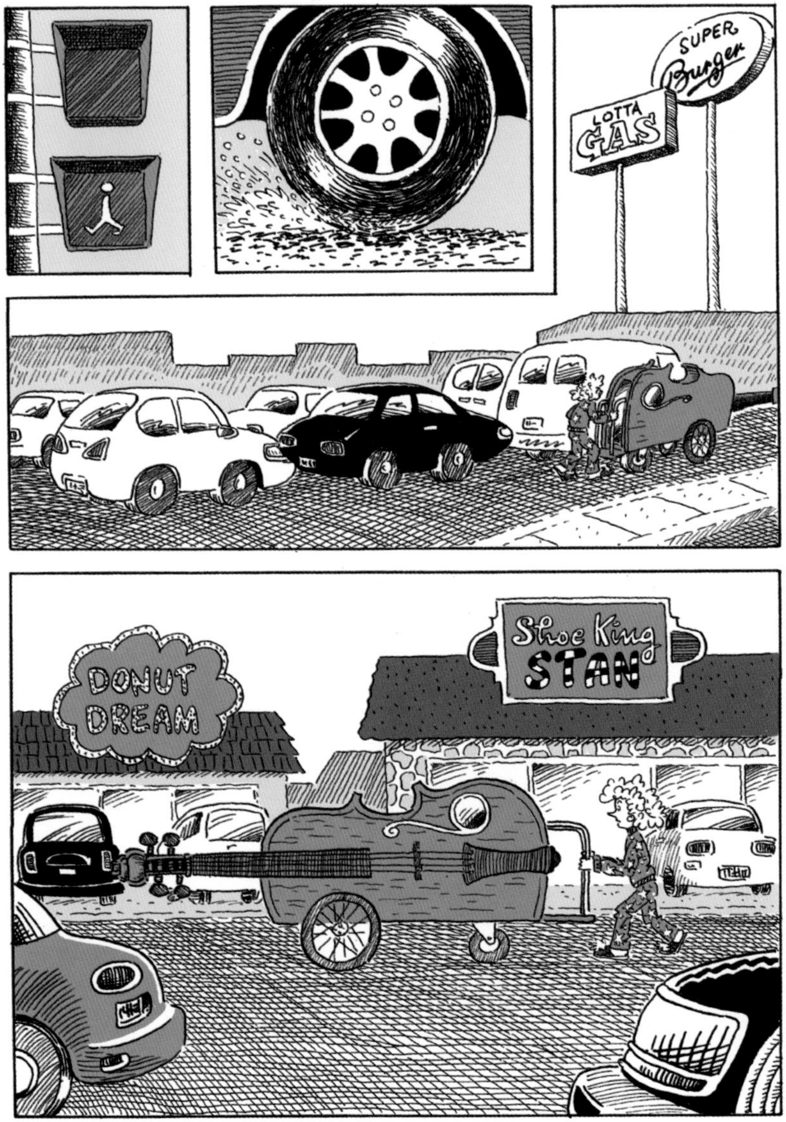
SUPER Burger
LOTTA GAS
DONUT DREAM
Shoe King STAN

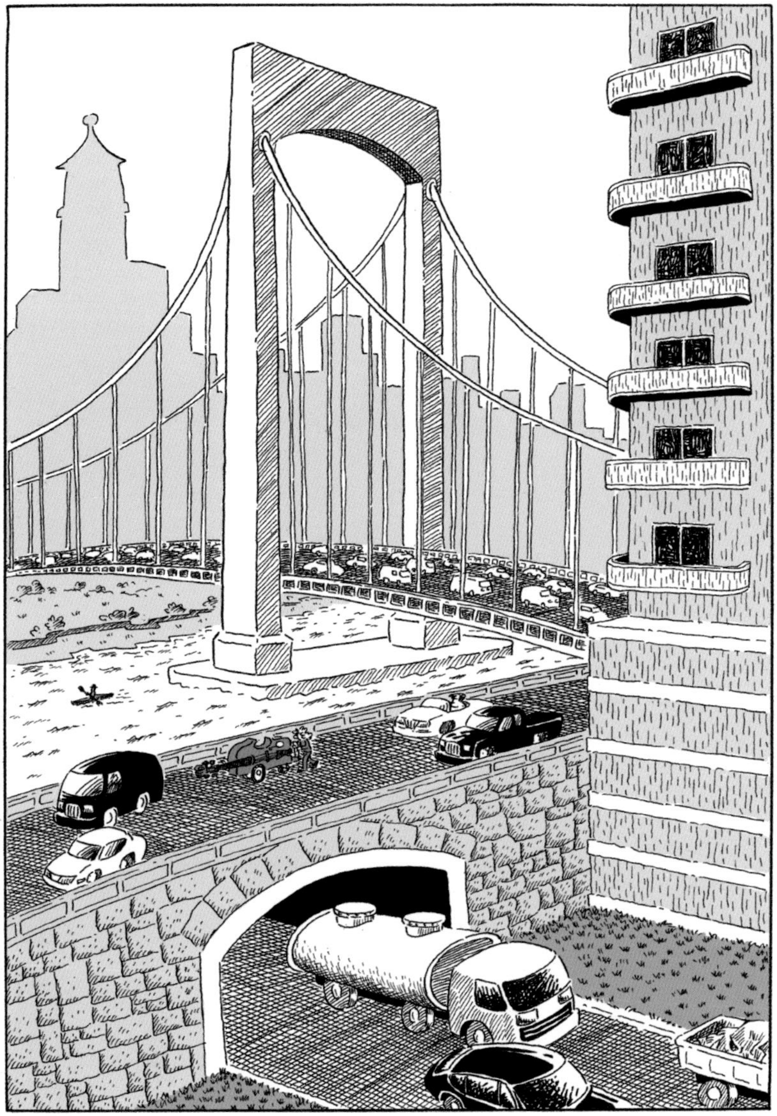

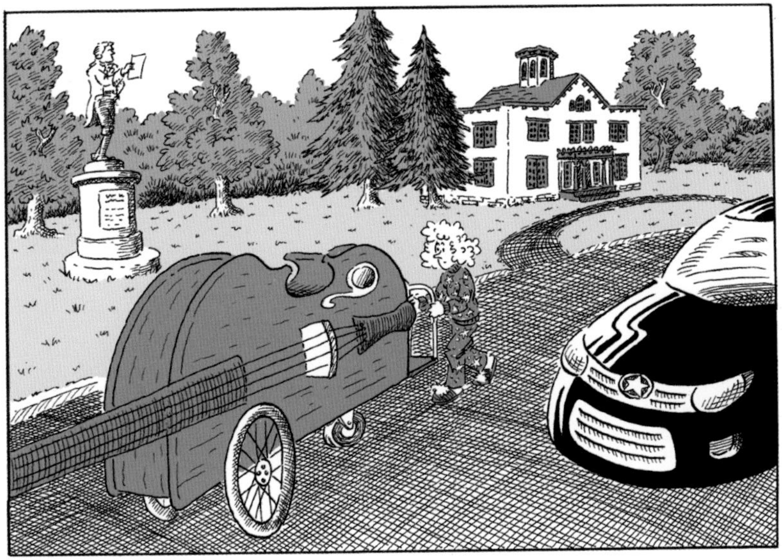

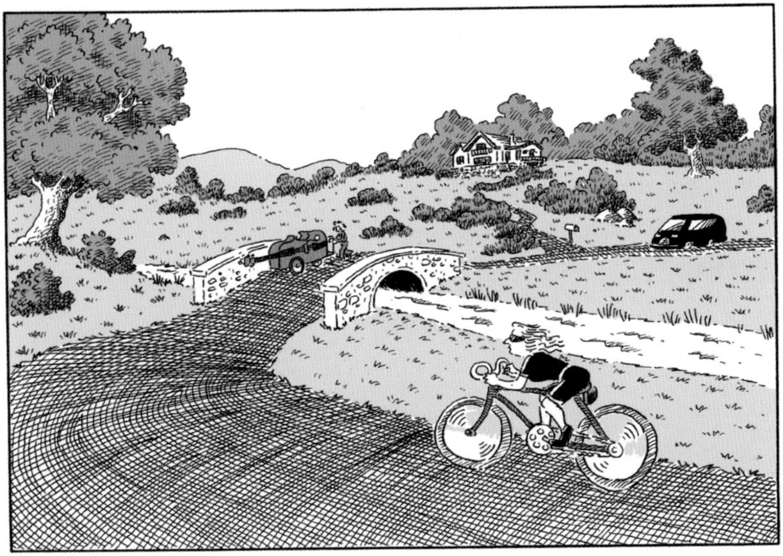

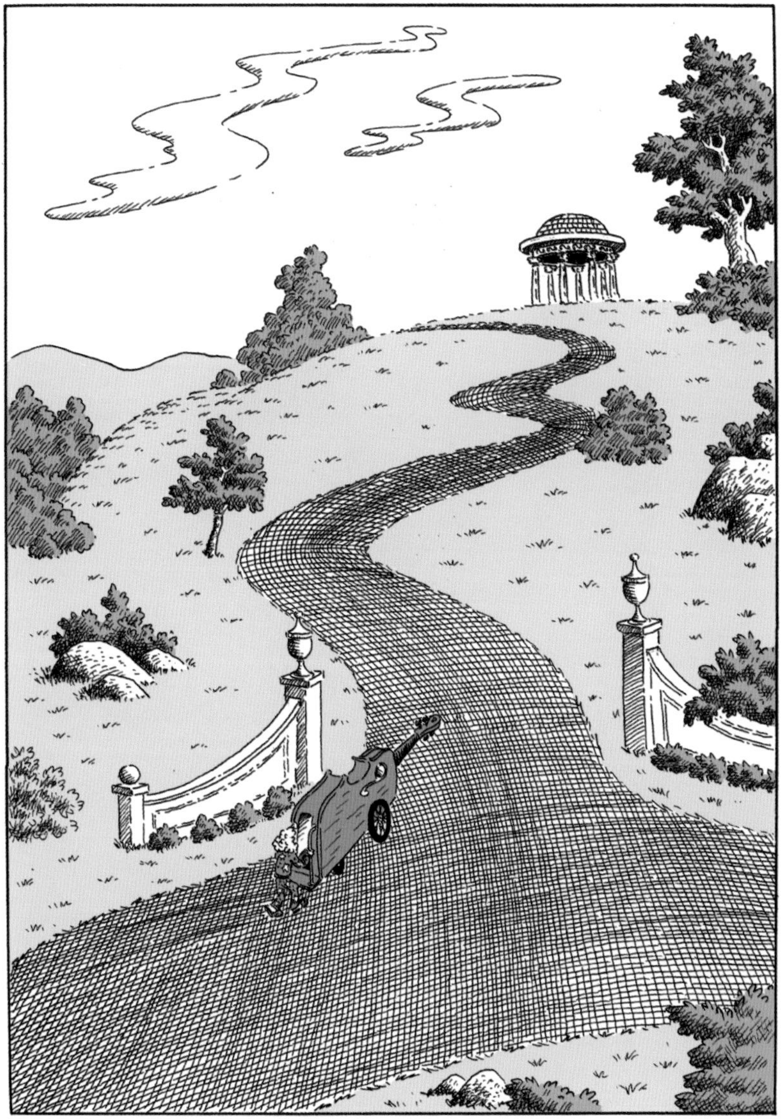

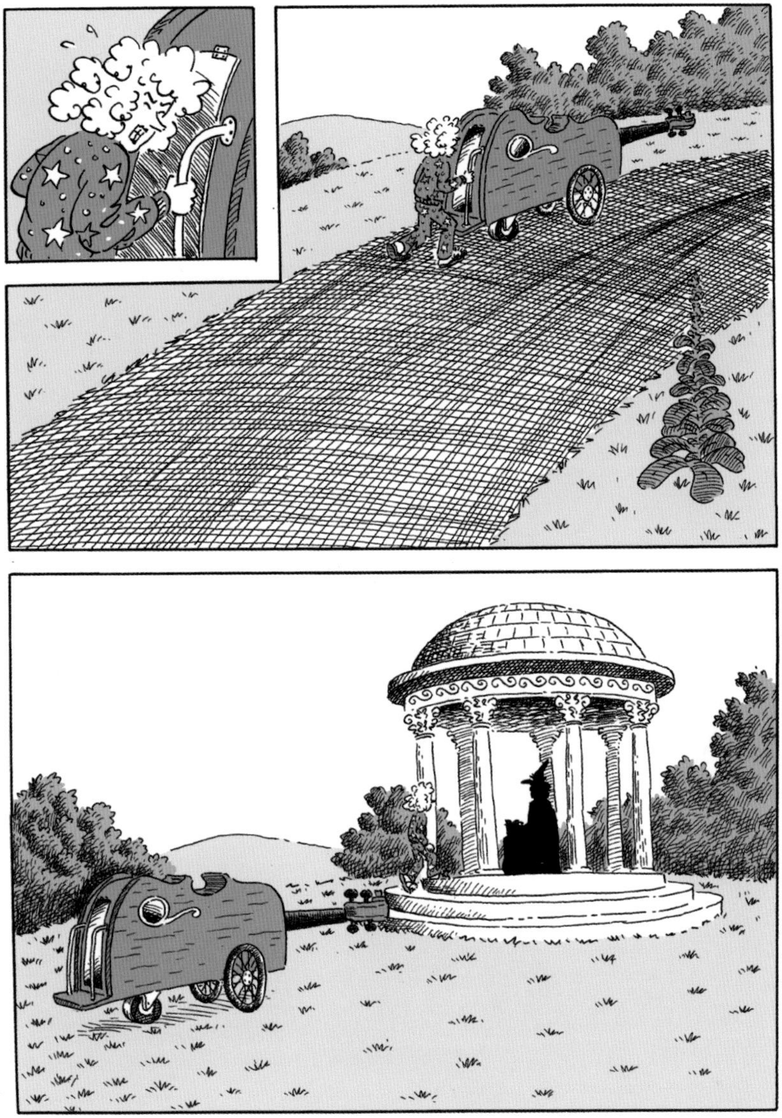

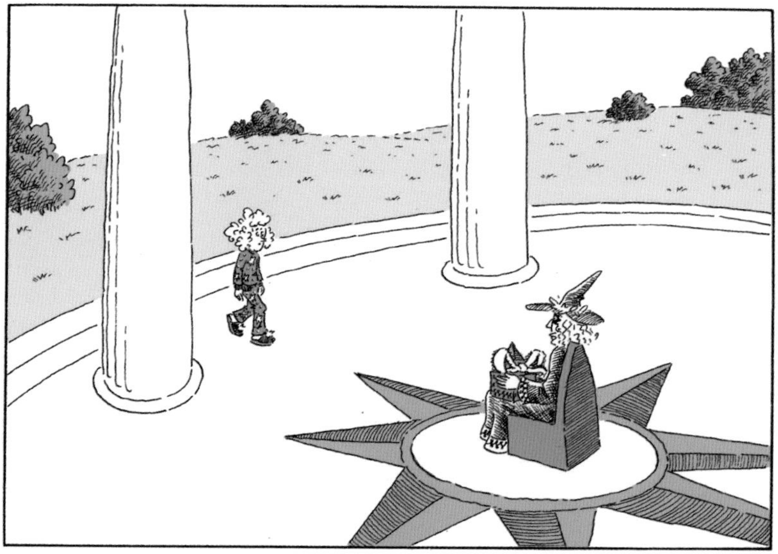

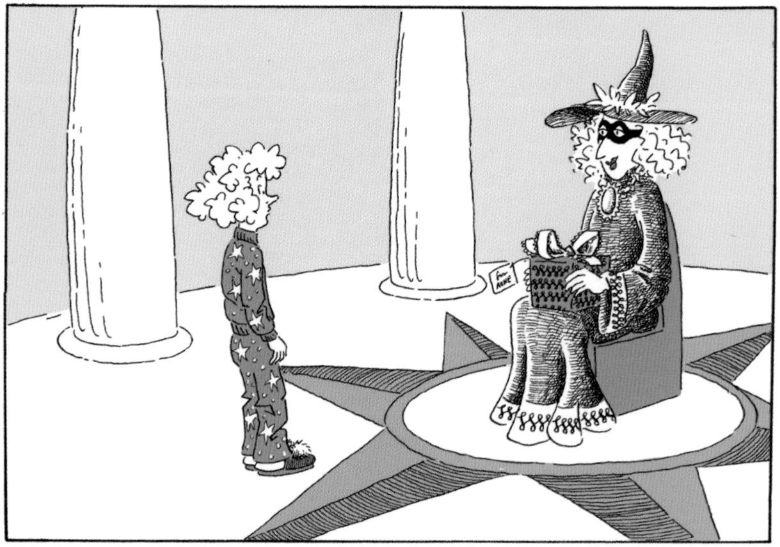
For ANNE

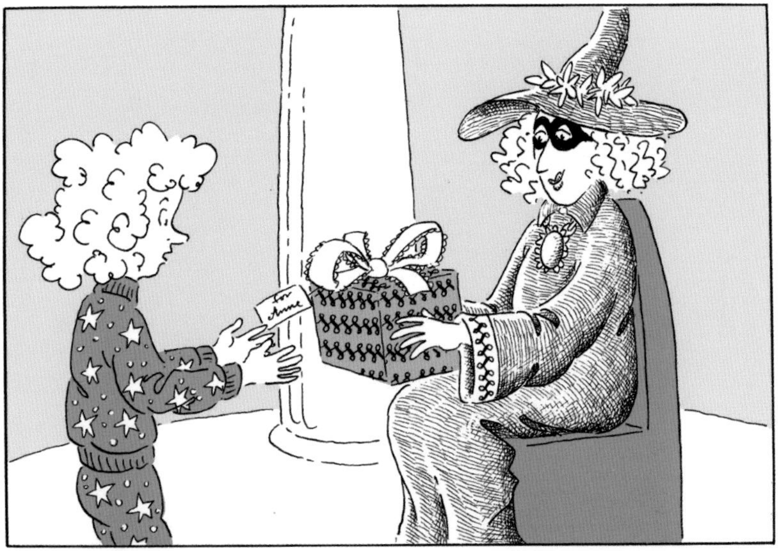
for Anne

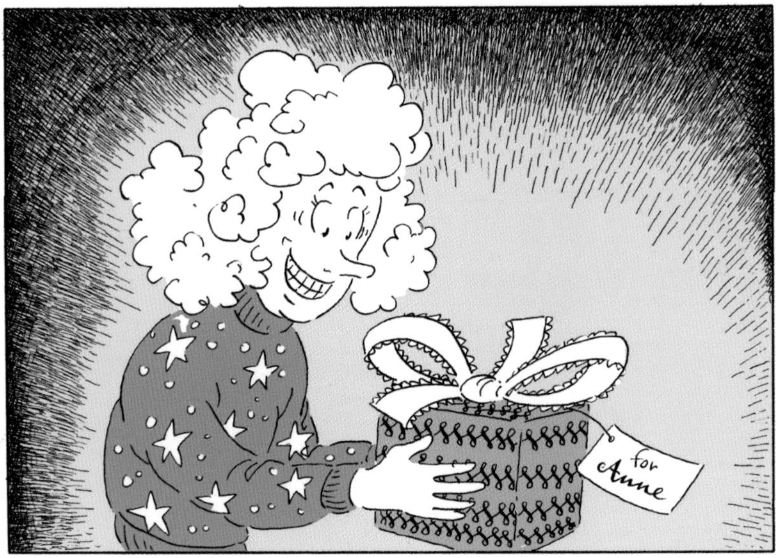
for Anne

8

TRUNK IN
THE ATTIC

Don't you hate it when you wake up from a dream just before you get to the good part?

Otto and I had decided to try out for the talent show. We had practiced a few songs, but I wasn't too happy with any of them. I thought we should write our own. Otto said, "Why not? Let's go for it." So we did. It included my wolf howl, and we worked on it almost every day after school.

It was almost Halloween. We were planning to wear wolf masks, and I wanted to play howling wolf sounds on my violin for trick-or-treating, but Otto pointed out that it's hard to play an instrument while you're carrying a big bag full of candy.

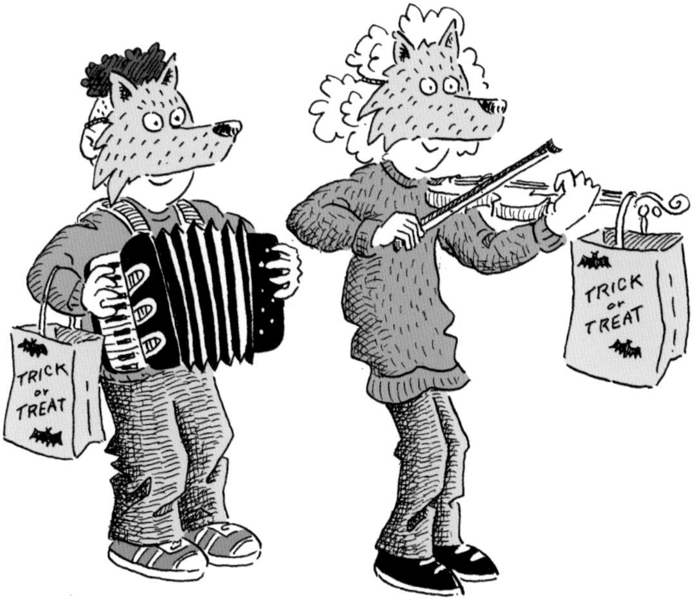
TRICK or TREAT
TRICK or TREAT

We hadn't heard from Dad since we had gotten to Megatown. Sometimes the grown-ups had talks about him after I had gone to bed. Sometimes I listened in. Once I heard Mom say she thought she had been deserted. But Nana said, "I'm sure he'll call any day now."

So then Mom started working again, even though she hates waitressing. I think she wanted to feel independent.

One night I was at home with Nana and Grandpop while Mom was at work. Our TV show ended, and Nana asked me,

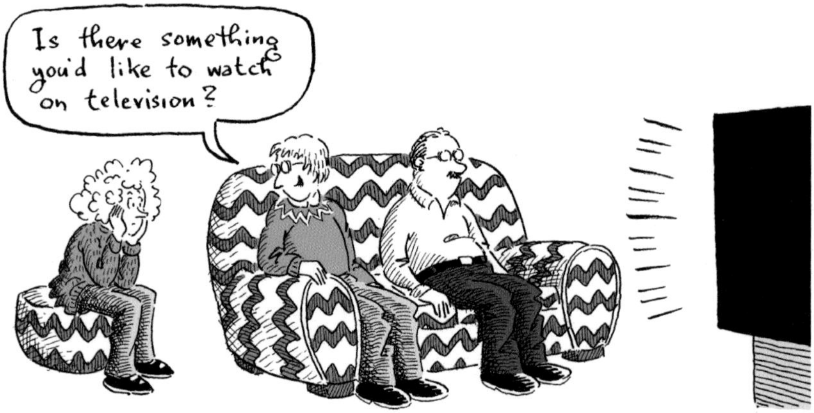
Is there something you'd like to watch on television?

"No, not really," I said. "But . . ."

"Yes, Dear?"

"Well, I wondered if there was a shelf or something I could have. It's for my collection."

Nana turned to Grandpop. "I think there's an old bookshelf in the garage. Do you think you could get it, Reuben?"

He nodded and shuffled off to look for it.

"I didn't know you had a collection," Nana said. "What is it that you collect?"

"Well, it's figurines and things, from a TV show called *The Blimptons*. I used to watch it with Dad, and now I watch with my friend Otto. Dad buys me the figurines. Remember how we said we had had a couple of packages from Dad after he left? They were Blimptons toys for me. But we haven't had one since we've been here."

"I've been keeping them in my suitcase," I added.

Nana said, "How odd."

Odd? "You meant that I keep them in my suitcase?"

"No, Dear," Nana said. "That your father buys them for you. May I see them?"

Nana came with me into my room. I put my suitcase on the bed and took The Blimptons out one by one. Nana was silent, watching me.

Then she picked up a figurine of Franny, and I saw she was smiling.

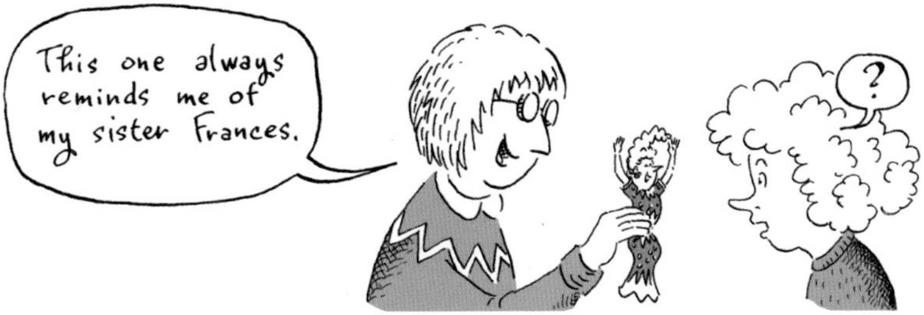
This one always reminds me of my sister Frances.
?

Now I was confused. "That's Franny Blimpton," I said. "I didn't know you watched the show."

"No, I don't watch the show." Then she put her arm around me and said, "Oh, Anne, we've missed him so much!" She held me for a little while and then looked at my face and touched my hair. I didn't mind.

"Let me show you something," she said.

We went up to the attic. It had a lot of boy stuff in it, just like Otto had imagined — comics and games and books. Nana went over to an old trunk and lifted the lid.

It was full of paper. My father's school stuff, mostly, but a lot of drawings too. And there were drawings of *The Blimptons!*

"But the show only started two years ago!" I said. "How did you get these? Who drew them?"

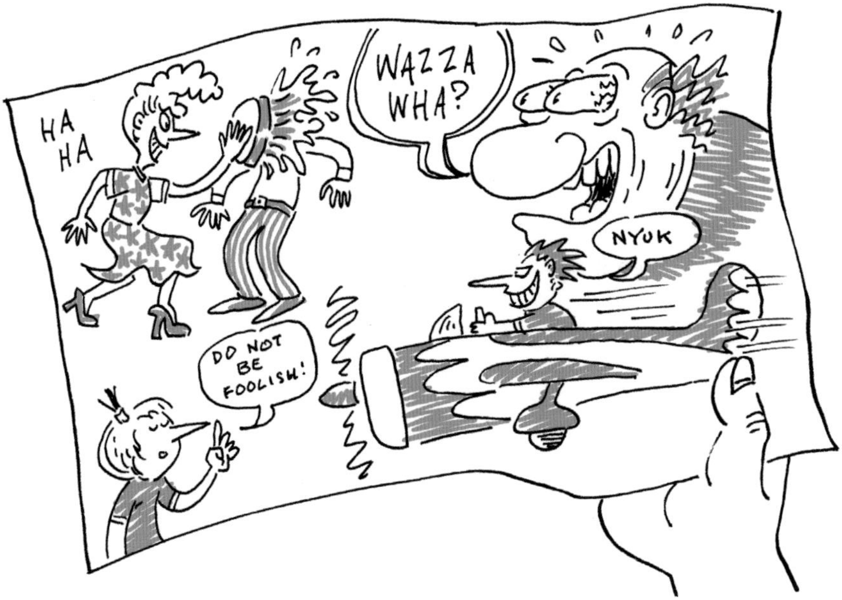
HA HA
WAZZA WHA?
NYUK
DO NOT BE FOOLISH!

"Your father drew them when he was a boy. With his friend, Malcolm Buehl."

"Malcolm Buehl! He's the creator of *The Blimptons*. He's *famous!*"

"I know that, dear," Nana said. "He was a very nice little boy. Very energetic. I was so surprised when he treated your father like that."

"Like what, Nana?"

"Well, after he saw *The Blimptons* on TV, your father wrote Malcolm a letter. He didn't ask for money, or anything like that. He just said that he was glad to see that Malcolm had made something so successful out of the cartoons they had drawn as kids, and he hoped that Malcolm would get in touch with him. He didn't say anything to you and your mother about that?"

I shook my head.

"Oh. He told us right after he got his reply. It must have been well over a year ago. Maybe he had been saving it up for a nice surprise for you and your mom — to introduce you to his famous friend. But then it never came about, because Malcolm's lawyer sent Ross a letter saying that Ross was a swindler and a phony. He said if Ross made any further claims about having invented *The Blimptons*, the 'full legal resources of the Blimpton Corporation would be used against him'!"

Just then Grandpop called up the stairs. "What are you girls up to up there?"

We went downstairs and he showed us the bookcase from the garage.

Grandpop, that is PERFECT!

Just needs a little cleaning!

88

Later, I put my collectibles on the shelf. At first I was going to throw them all out. Then I thought I could sell them to Otto and make a lot of money. But then I said to myself, "These are Dad's characters just as much as yours, Malcolm Buehl! You dirtbag! *You're* the swindler, not Dad!"

And I started thinking about ways to get even with that crook, Malcolm Buehl.

I didn't come up with any good ideas. And then it was Halloween and I ate a lot of candy, and then I had the dream where a witch was giving me a package. I wonder what would have been in it. *Something from Dad? Antique toys from the attic? More Blimptons drawings? A Malcolm Buehl bobblehead?*

9

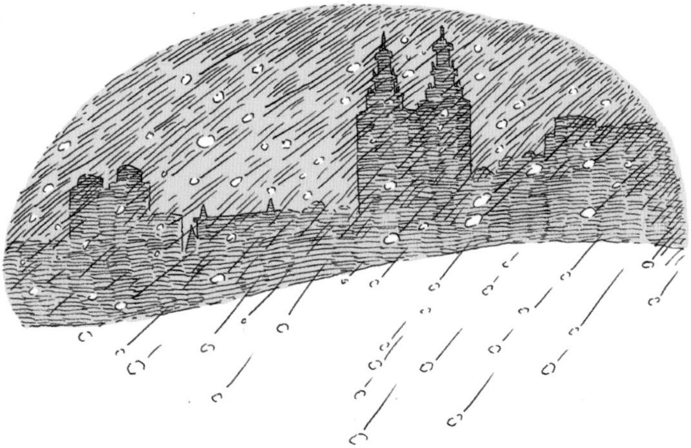

SNOW DAY

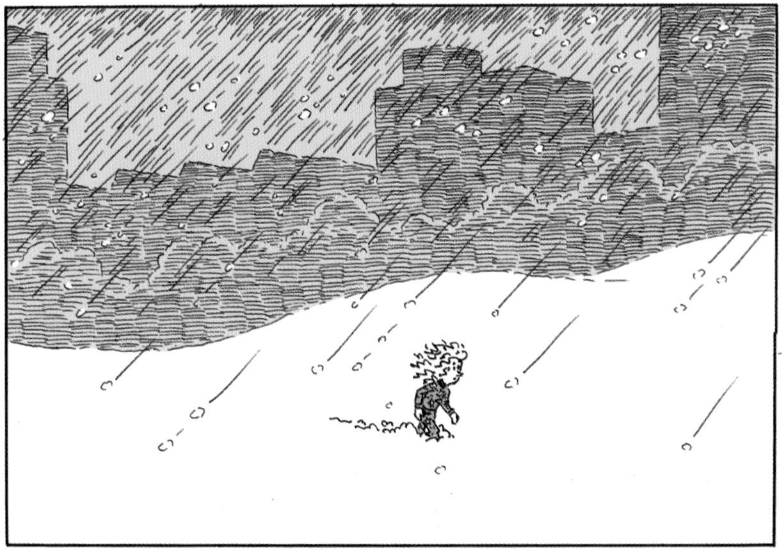

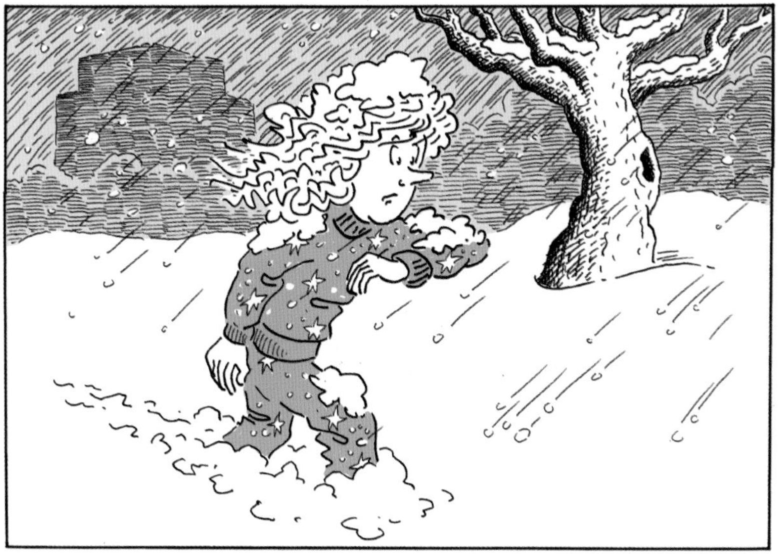

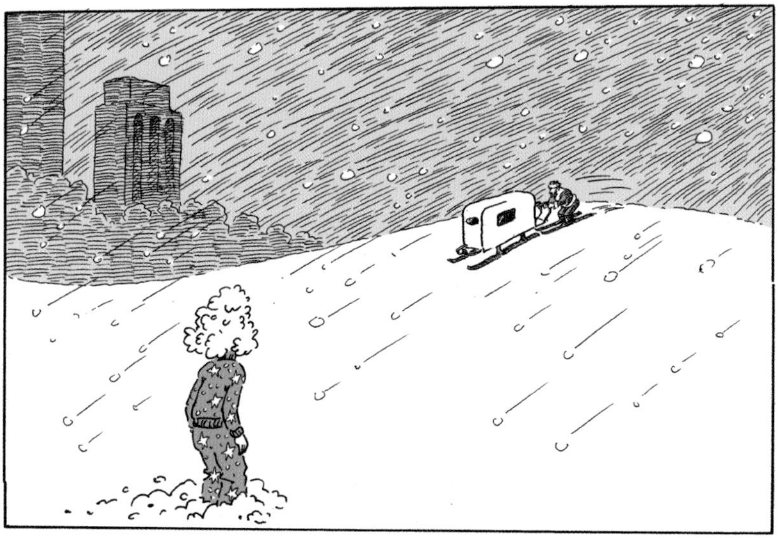

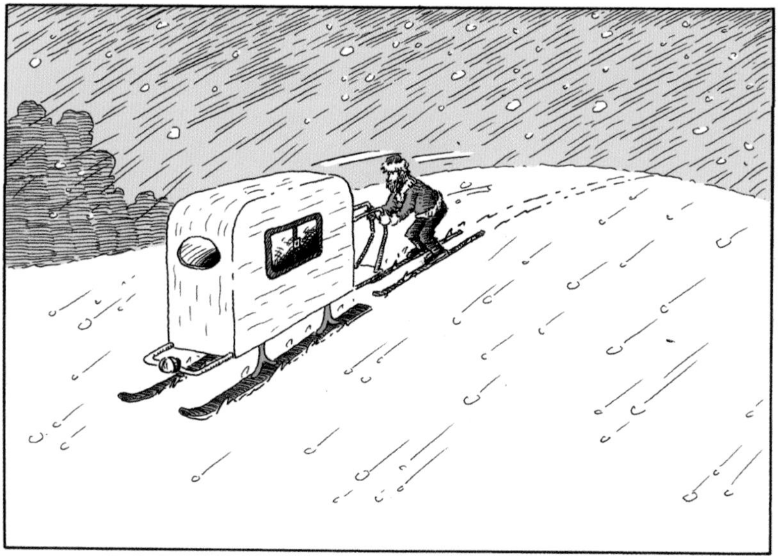

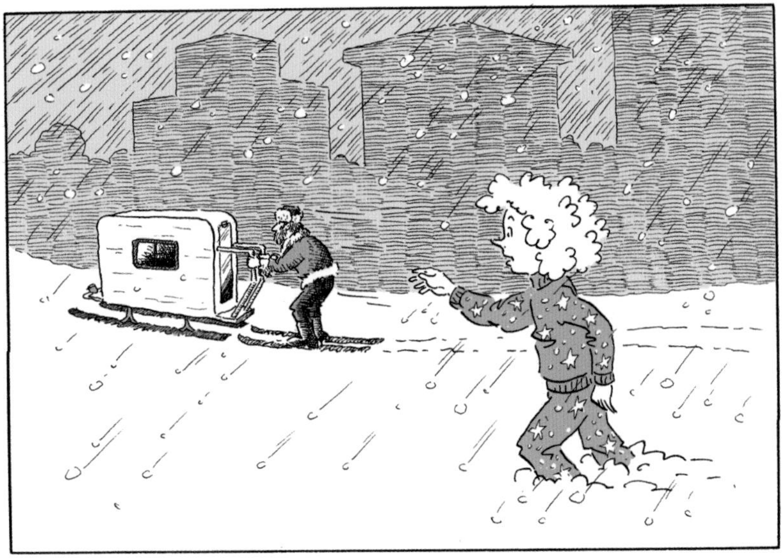

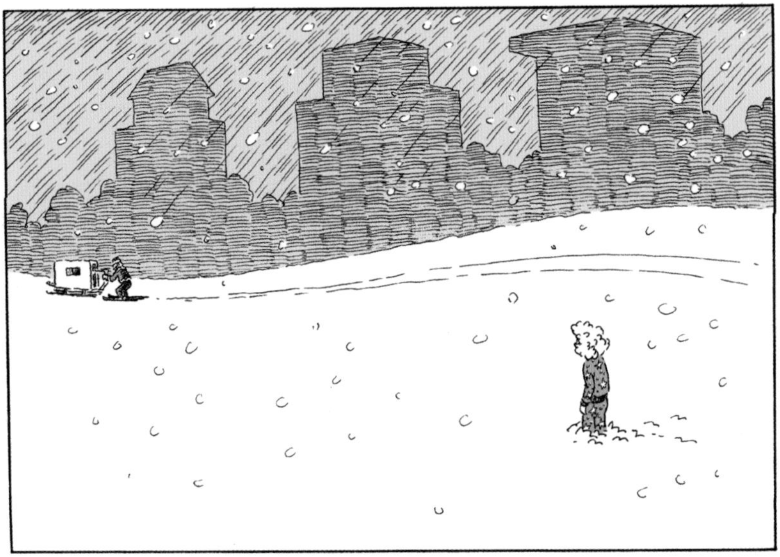

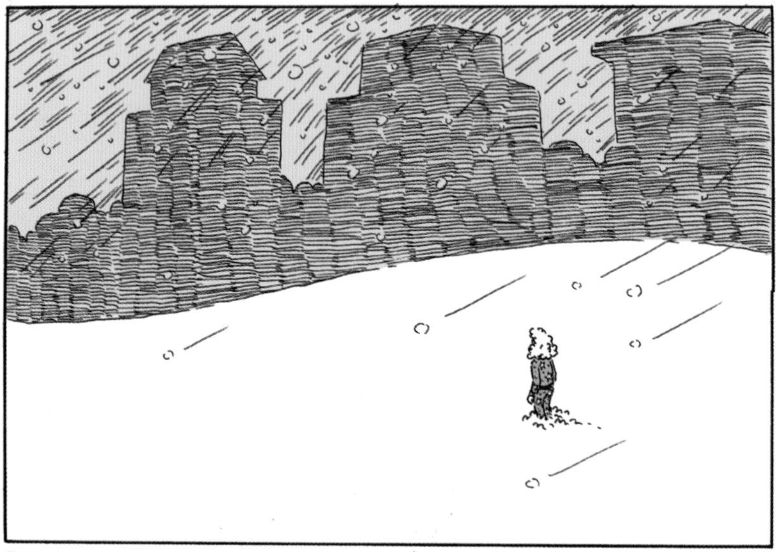

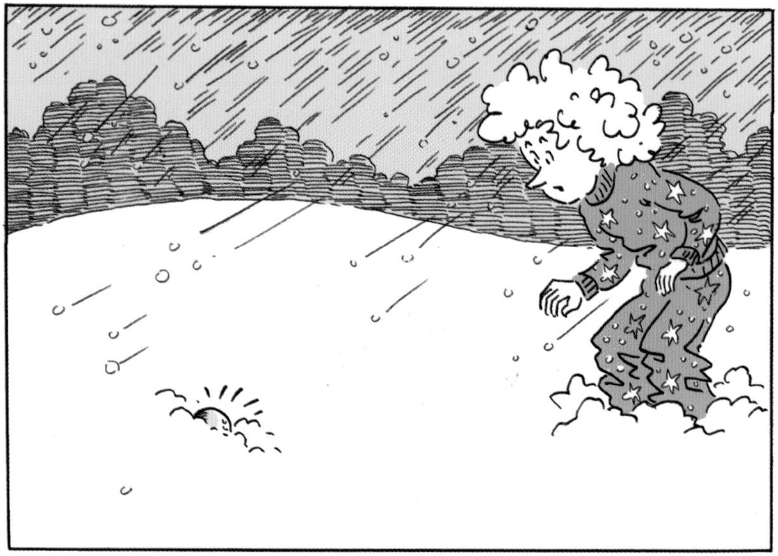

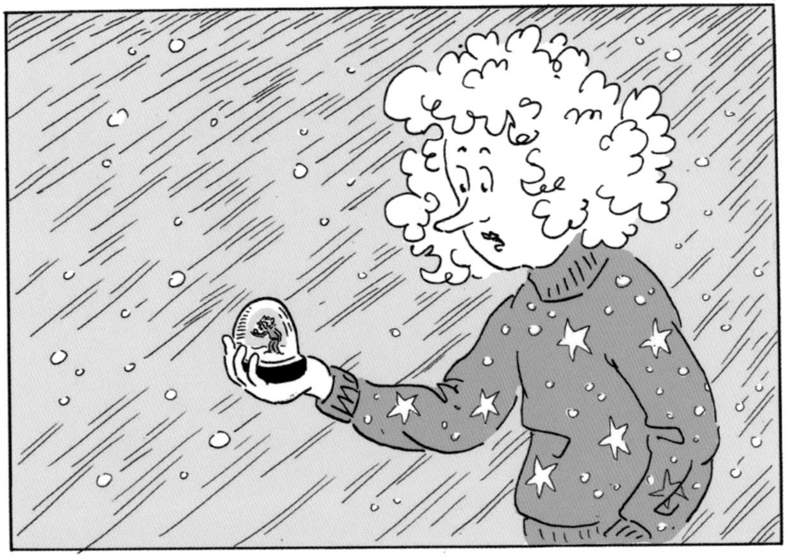

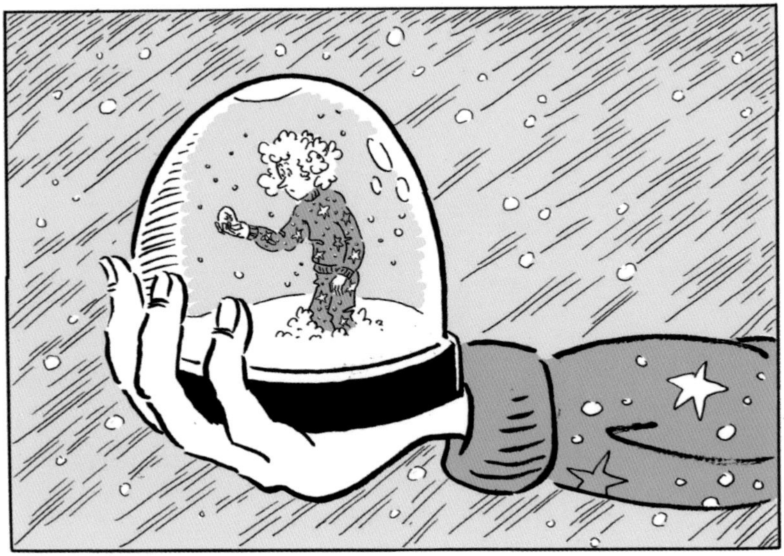

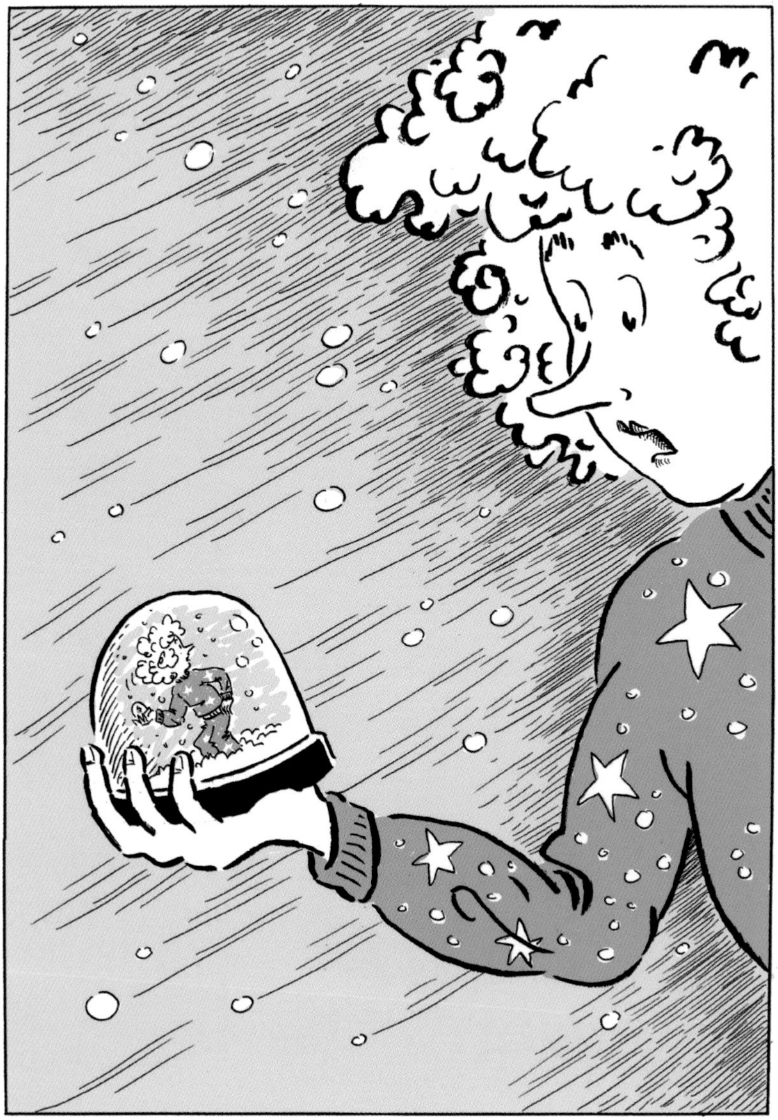

10

THE CITY

Right after Halloween we had a freak early snowstorm. It wasn't like the snow in New Mexico, where every branch hangs down under big, heavy blobs of white snow, and it's all bright and glittery and the sky is deep blue. In Megatown the streets get plowed and salted and everything turns to grey slush.

School was closed so Nana took me and Mom and Otto to the city on the train. We went to a museum and then we walked in the park.

The snow was still clean there. People were sledding down the hill and skating on the pond.

We didn't have any sleds or skates so we walked along a path through some woods and watched the birds at a bird feeder. Nana's cheeks got pink and she said she hadn't been to the park in a good ten years.

We went to a restaurant in the museum for lunch. I asked Nana to tell us about Dad and Malcolm Buehl when they were kids. Nana said that Dad's nickname was Rooster, and Malcolm's nickname was Troll. Mom gave a little snort and said,

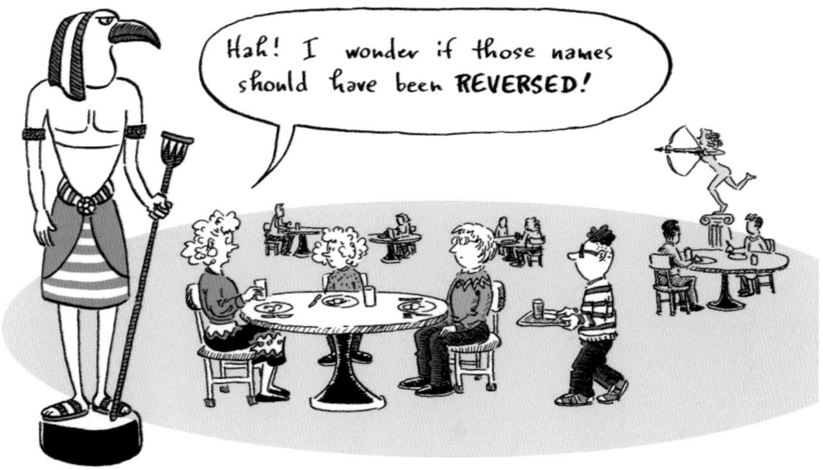
Hah! I wonder if those names should have been **REVERSED!**

Nana looked offended and said that Rooster came from Ross (Dad's name), and Troll was because Buehl means someone who lives on a hill. Ross used to kid Malcolm that it really meant someone who lives *inside* a hill.

Mom blushed and said, "I'm sorry, Anita (Nana's real name). I'm afraid I'm feeling a little resentful."

Then it was Nana's turn to look sorry. She patted Mom's hand and said. "No, you're right to feel that way dear. It's a terrible thing he's doing, not contacting you and Anne like this."

Then they both looked at me and Otto and clammed up.

I'm not sure that I like the city all that much, but I *love, love* the park, and also the train you take to get to the city and back. Coming home after dark, you can see things swooshing by in the background at the same time as you can see your own reflection in the window.

Otto and I had our own seat. Mom and Nana had to sit a few rows behind us on the other side.

I had already told Otto all about Dad's Blimptons drawings and what happened when he wrote to Malcolm Buehl.

Now I said,

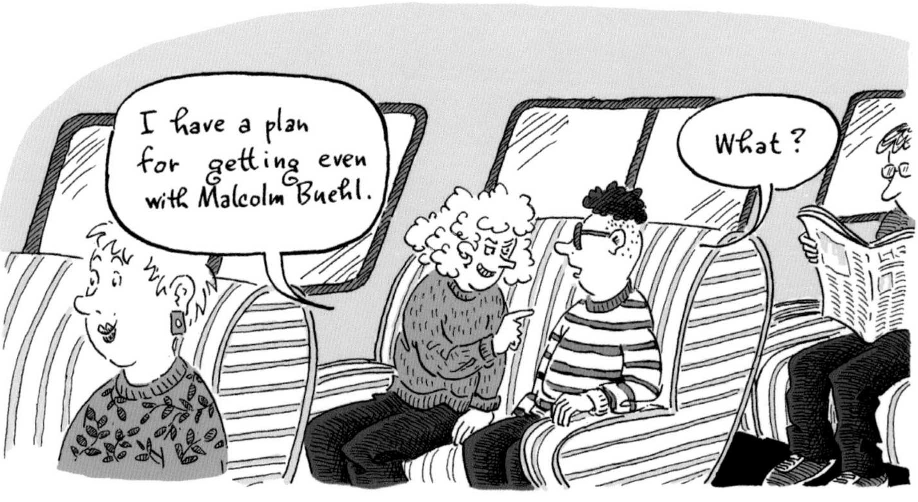
I have a plan for getting even with Malcolm Buehl.
What?

"Well, you know that show on TV called *Hollywood Exposed?*"

"Never heard of it," said Otto.

"It comes on right after the news, and for some reason Nana usually turns it off, but I've seen enough of it to get the general idea. My plan is to go on *Hollywood Exposed* and give them the story of what a rat Malcolm Buehl has been to my dad.

"What d'you think?" I asked Otto. "Can't you picture it? The announcer would be like, *'TONIGHT ON HOLLYWOOD EXPOSED, AN INTERVIEW WITH THE DAUGHTER OF THE MAN WHO REALLY INVENTED THE BLIMPTONS!'* I'm emailing them tomorrow!"

"What if the 'full legal resources of the Blimpton Corporation would get used against' your dad?"

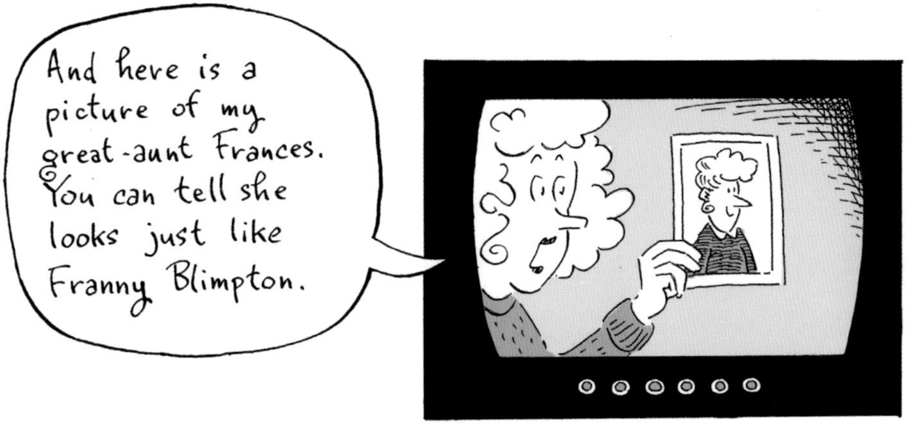
And here is a picture of my great-aunt Frances. You can tell she looks just like Franny Blimpton.

"Oh," I said. "I never thought of that."

"And," Otto continued (Otto is a very sensible kid), "what if Malcolm Buehl's lawyers said that you had drawn your dad's supposed cartoons yourself, and you were a swindler and a phony too?"

I decided my plan needed more work.

But the really big news was that when we got back home, after we had dropped Otto at his house, there was a package for me from Dad!

Everybody was there, but I took the package into my room to open it. It was a Libby Blimpton snow globe. With no note. Just "From your Father" like the last one I got.

I had to look at it by myself for a little while.

It got sent to our old address and forwarded, and it took over a month! So guess what? Dad hadn't let us down as much as Mom thought he had. He was still in touch.

I rushed back into the living room to show Mom and Nana and Grandpop. They were all excited, except Mom looked a little put out. I wished Dad would send her something, too.

I was happy that Dad had sent me the Libby Blimpton snow globe, but later it made me feel all *forlorn*. He didn't even know where I was!

That night I dreamt that I was walking in the snow in that park in the city, and he skied right by me without stopping. But he *did* leave me a snow globe.

11

SHOWDOWN

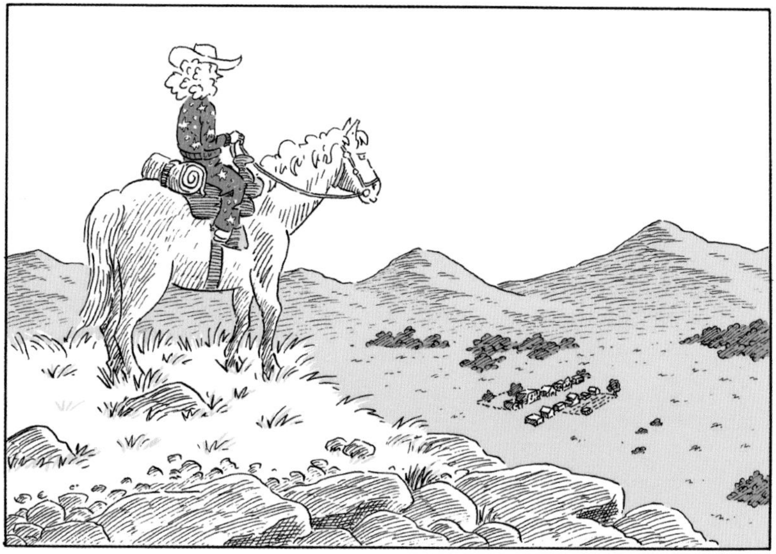

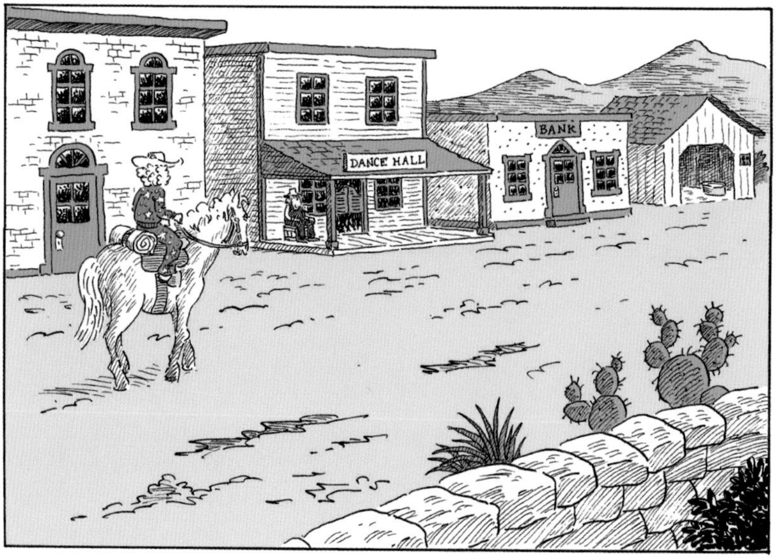
DANCE HALL
BANK

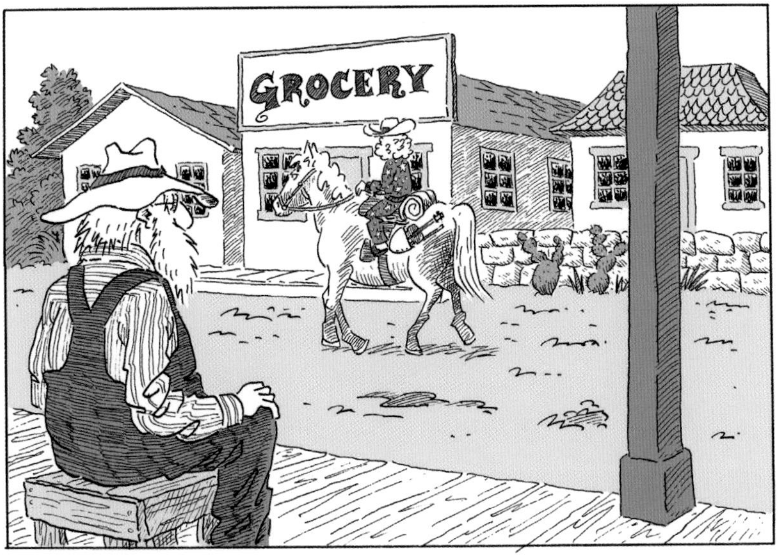
GROCERY

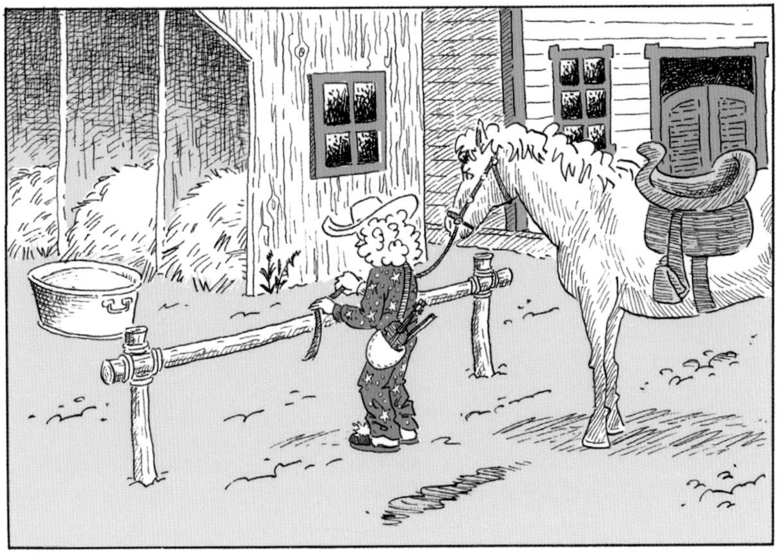

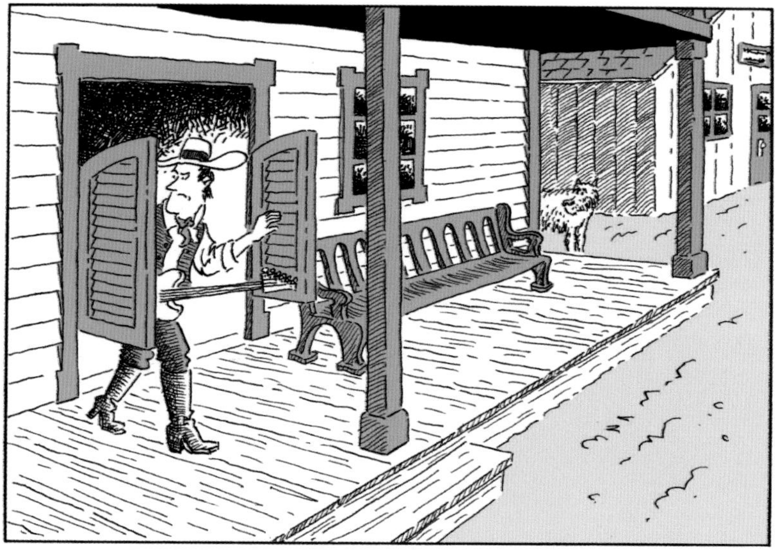

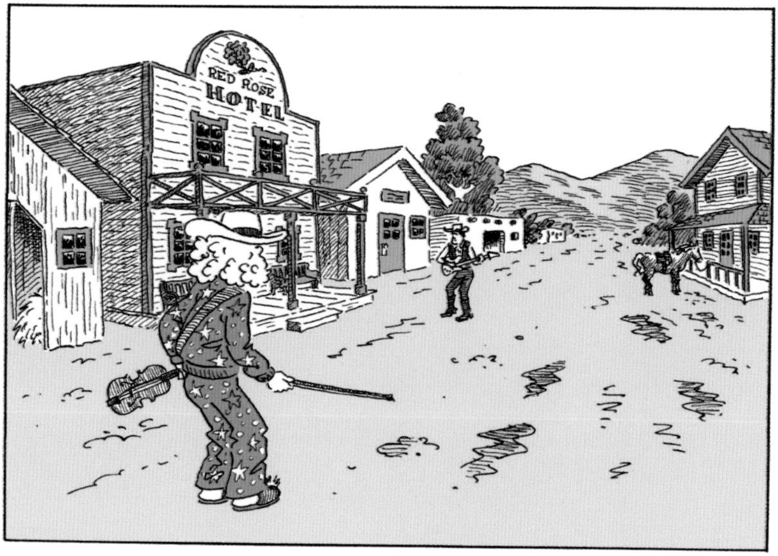
RED ROSE
HOTEL

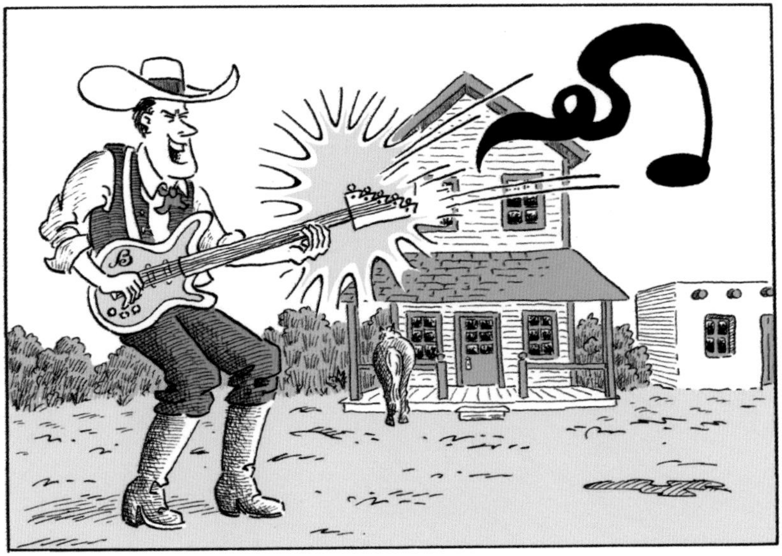

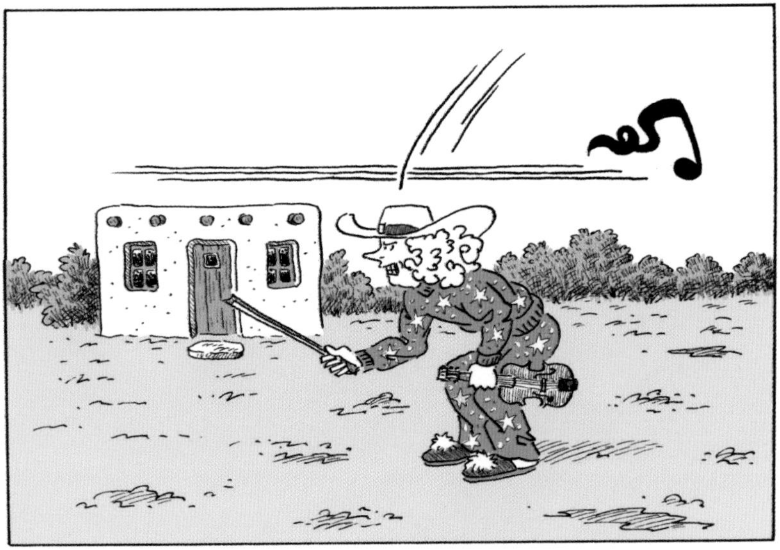

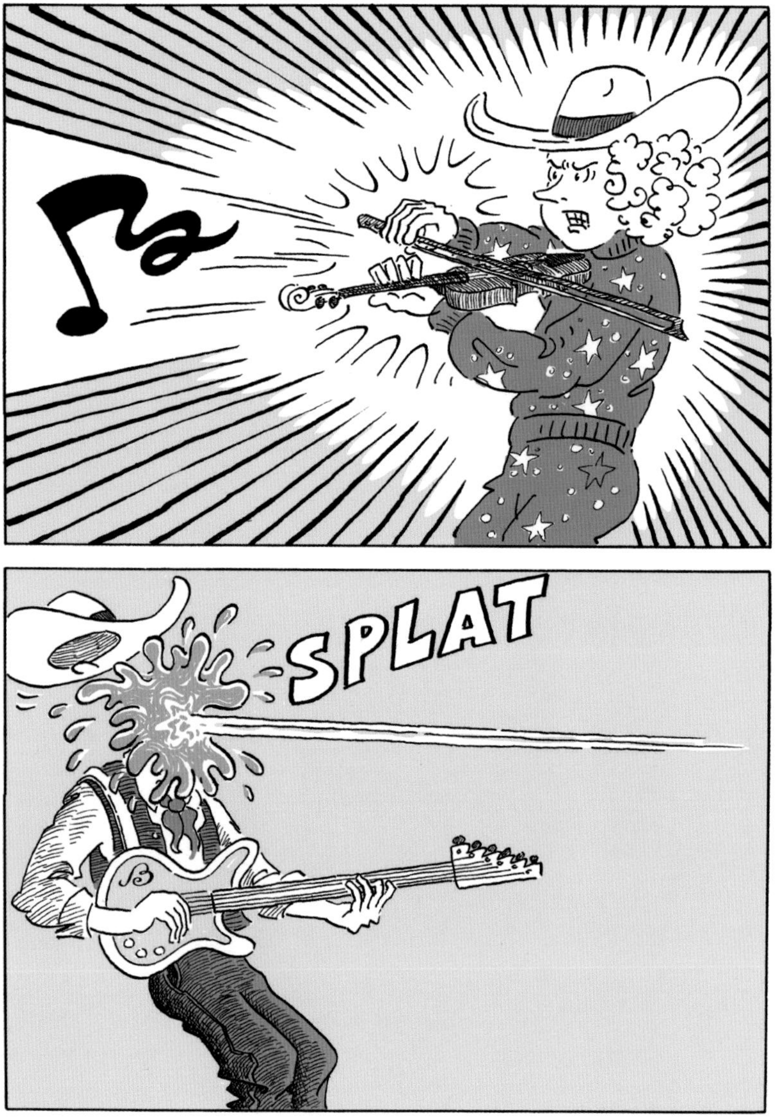
SPLAT

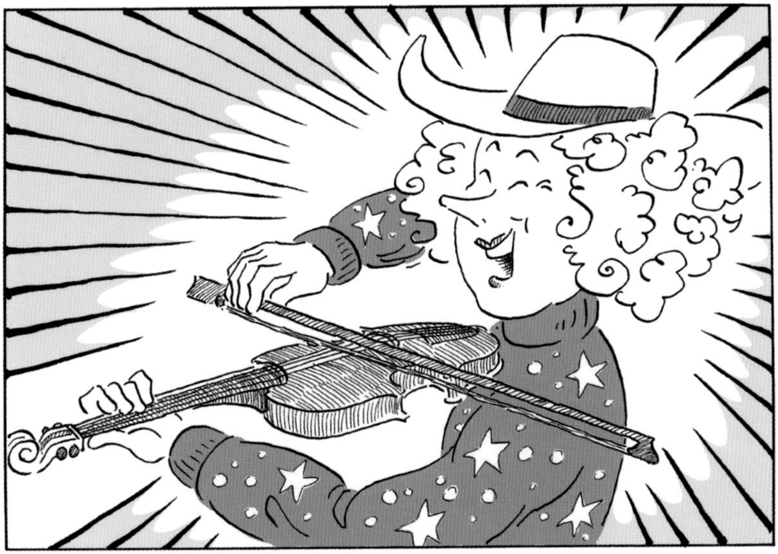

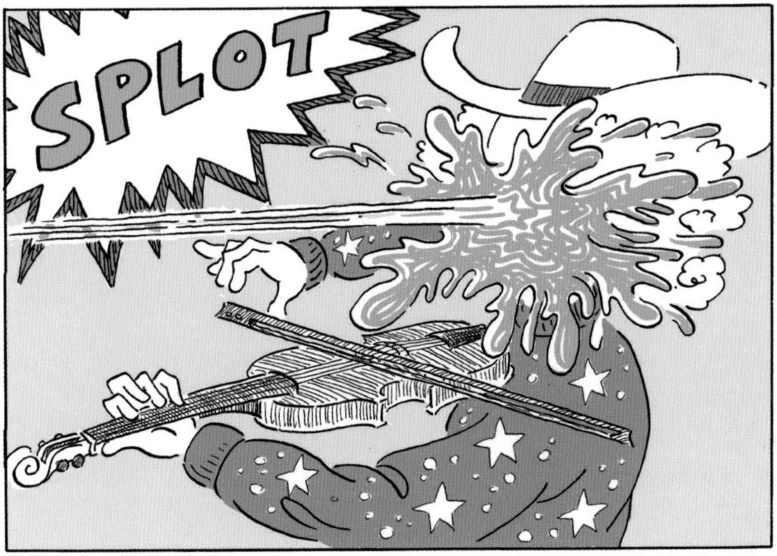
SPLOT

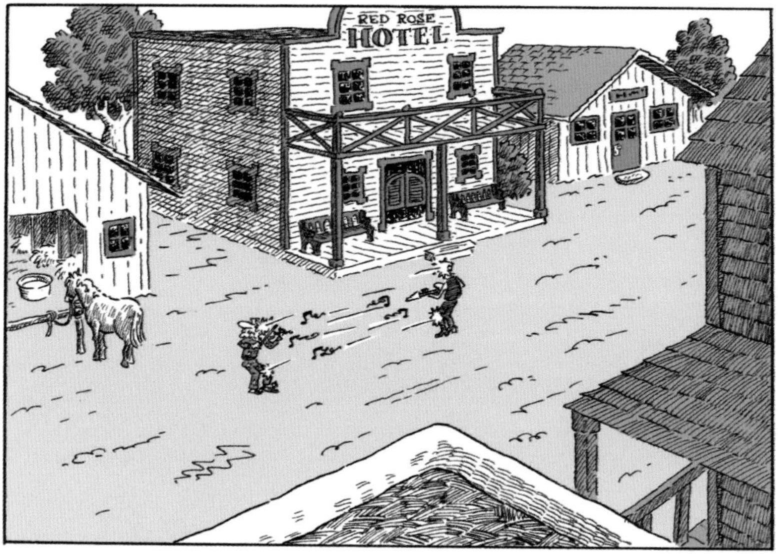
RED ROSE
HOTEL

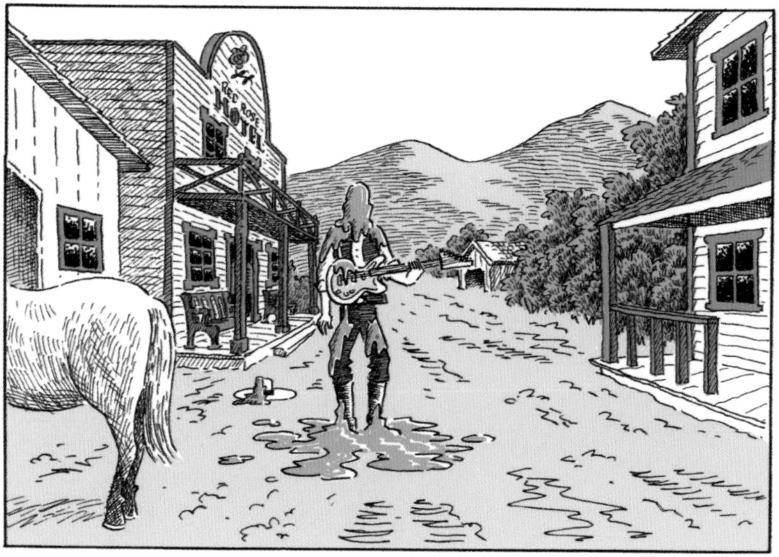
RED ROSE
HOTEL

12

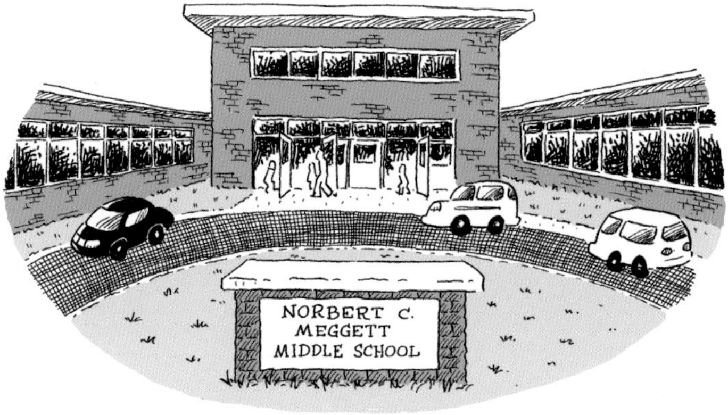
NORBERT C.
MEGGETT
MIDDLE SCHOOL

TRYOUTS

The tryouts for the talent show were stressful for me — and Brendan didn't make it any easier.

Mom was working, so Grandpop and Nana drove Otto and me to the school after dinner. Grandpop brought his phone so he could record us.

I wasn't nervous until we got there and I saw all the other kids. But we weren't up first, and after watching a few acts, I noticed that everybody who tried out was getting in, no matter how bad they were, so I felt pretty good about our chances.

Otto and I thought it was funny that the Kubitsky twins were going to sing a duet of "Sammy the Snowman." What a dorky song!

But I was surprised. They actually sang like angels! It almost sounded like bells when they sang together.

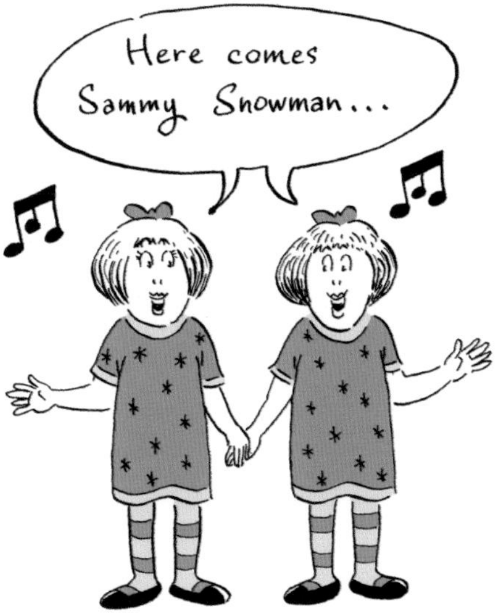
Here comes
Sammy Snowman...

We came after creepy Brendan. I didn't even know why he was in middle school. He looked more like a high school kid. I thought maybe he had stayed back. But he *was* good, I had to admit, if you like loud, seventies, heavy metal music. He even had his own back-up, pre-recorded on his computer, and his voice was husky, almost like a grown-up man.

Then we played our song. It started out slow and sad and then worked itself into a sort of wailing frenzy. When we finished there was complete silence. You could hear the last note echoing and fading away. Mr. Deville looked sort of stunned. Then he said, "Uh, very unique. That should wake the audience up! Congratulations! You're in!"

Afterwards, Brendan came over to me and said,

Nice tune, Anne!
It sounded like
the noise my
cat makes when
someone steps on
her tail!

(And I'll bet he steps on her tail on purpose!)

I wanted to cry and I wanted to kick him in the shins at the same time. Instead I just walked away. I did cry later though, in the car after we dropped Otto off.

Nana said to Grandpop, "She's all het up. It's enough to make anyone nervous, playing on that big stage for the first time."

Grandpop said, "If that tall boy said something to hurt your feelings, Anne, I wouldn't worry about it. He's probably jealous because your music is so original."

I asked if they thought we were any good, and Grandpop said, "Good enough for me to put this video on YouTube!" Then he said we had made a few mistakes, but nothing that a little more practice wouldn't fix. And he suggested that we tone down the frenzy and concentrate more on the melody, "which is very sweet," he said. But he added that that might just be the preference of an old geezer.

Grandpop might be absent-minded and forgetful, but I suspected then that he might know more about music than I had thought.

Later, in my room, I got to thinking that Grandpop hadn't really said we were *good* — just good enough to put the video on Youtube. Oh, crap, I thought. *What if it's like one of those videos that goes viral because it's so bad?*

No, I thought. *Grandpop wouldn't do that to me. Unless he doesn't realize how bad it is! Yikes! I'm about to be the laughing stock of the whole world!*

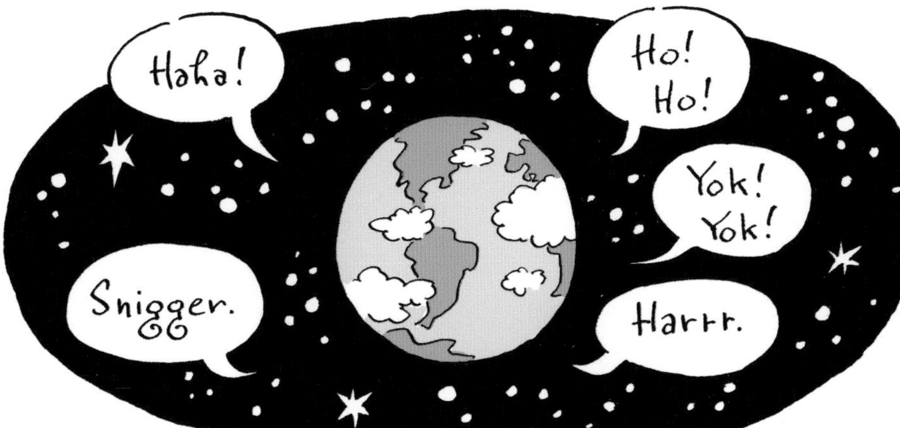
Haha!
Ho! Ho!
Yok! Yok!
Snigger.
Harrr.

I snuck downstairs, and saw that Mom and Grandpop and Nana were all watching us on the computer. I could hear the music. So it was too late anyway. I figured it had probably already gone viral. People were already laughing at me in China! And Brendan Boyle would be laughing at me too!

I wished we had never tried out for the stupid talent show.

The next day I told Otto that he should play a solo in the talent show. I told him I was giving up music.

"Who wants to be a stupid musician, anyhow?" I said. "And besides, Mom says I have to spend more time on my schoolwork." (Which was a total lie.)

Otto said, "Don't worry about what Brendan says. He's just insecure."

"Hah!" I said.

"We're good together," Otto said. "Really good. Okay, maybe we're a little rough in places, but we've still got a few more weeks to practice."

"I've got to go," I said.

I took the long way home.

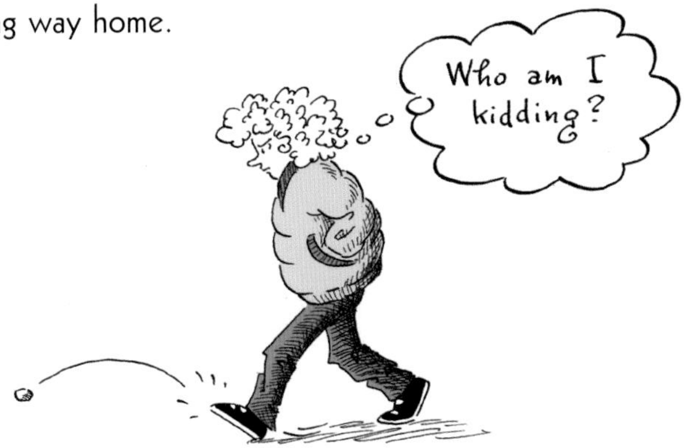
Who am I kidding?

"Let's face it," I said to myself. "I can't compose music. I'm eleven years old. Well, almost twelve."

I wondered what everyone was doing back in New Mexico. It was probably warm and sunny. If we were home, Mom and I could take a drive in the desert. We could catch a horned toad.

That week I glared at Brendan Boyle in class, but I don't think he noticed. Otto ignored me too. And I got a D on my history homework.

After dinner one night Mom asked me, "What's the matter, Honey? Are you feeling okay?"

"Fine, Mom. I feel fine!"

"Well, you don't look fine. Maybe I should take your temperature."

"I don't have a temperature!"

Grandpop watched me with a worried look. We were all sitting around after dinner. I knew I was being mopey and a pain in the neck. I knew it, but I couldn't help it. And it wasn't because I had a temperature.

Grandpop left the room, but he came right back carrying an ancient record player and some old vinyl record albums. He plugged in the record player, lifted the arm and blew the dust off the needle. Then he selected an album, pulled it carefully out of its sleeve, put it on the turntable and placed the needle on the edge of the record.

I had never heard vinyl records before. Of course I knew what they were.

I had never heard music quite like Grandpop's record before either.

It was a little scratchy, but the music was sort of — sort of what? — sort of *uplifting* I guess.

Nana smiled.

Mom tapped her foot.

I almost felt like dancing, myself.

Usually I'm into rap and zee-pop. I've even listened to some atonal electronic music, and some old groups like the Beatles and the Grateful Dead, and of course the classical music that Mom likes. But Grandpop's music was new to me. I guess you could say it was a kind of jazz — fiddle and guitar by two guys named Eddie Lang and Joe Venuti.

I was so grouchy, I didn't feel like liking anything, but I *liked* that music.

Then Grandpop played another record of French songs with accordion, almost hokey, but kind of bluesy. I liked that one too, and I knew Otto would like it, as well.

I was looking through the pile of records when a paper slipped out and fell on the floor.

"Here's an old letter," I said, picking it up. "I guess it got stuck between two of the albums."

I turned it over. "Looks like it never got opened." And I handed it to Grandpop.

"What is it, Reuben?" Nana asked.

"Grandpop put on his reading glasses. "Oh, it's for Ross," he said.

"For Ross? What's it doing with your records?"

"I guess I was going to give it to him the next time he came to visit."

"Let me see that!" Nana snatched the letter and squinted at it.

"Good heavens!" she said. "The postmark looks like. . . yes . . . hmmm, that would make it almost three years old. I hope it wasn't anything important."

"It's just a personal letter," said Grandpop. "Looks like it's from that funny little friend of his, the return name just says, Troll, doesn't it?"

"You're right," said Nana. She put it on the shelf.

"Well, let's not lose it again. We can give it to Ross when he comes."

"But," I piped up, "isn't that Malcolm Buehl? Nana said Dad called him the Troll."

"That's right!" Grandpop snapped his fingers. "Malcolm! That's it. Funny kid. Talked a blue streak."

"Maybe we should open it," I said.

Nana gaped at me. "Open it? Nonsense! I would no sooner open one of Ross's letters than I would rob a bank. The idea, Anne!"

So that was that. The letter sat there on the shelf while we listened to more records, and then everybody went to bed.

I didn't go to sleep right away. I couldn't stop thinking about that letter. How could I keep on planning my Malcolm Buehl revenge without knowing what he had written to Dad three years ago?

It was almost midnight.

I thought about that letter sitting there on the shelf.

I wondered what was in it. I wondered what Mom thought about it. If anything.

If Mom wasn't a grownup, I thought, I bet she would sneak out and look at that letter. She might even open it! And if it was Dad, he would *definitely* sneak out and open it.

So that's what I did. I snuck out and got the letter and brought it to my room. I thought about how you're supposed to be able to steam open letters and reseal them, but I wondered whether that would even work. Besides, I'd have to go into the kitchen and put on the kettle and probably wake everybody up. So I decided I would just make it "disappear" into my secret diary. After I'd opened it and read it, of course.

Here's what it said:

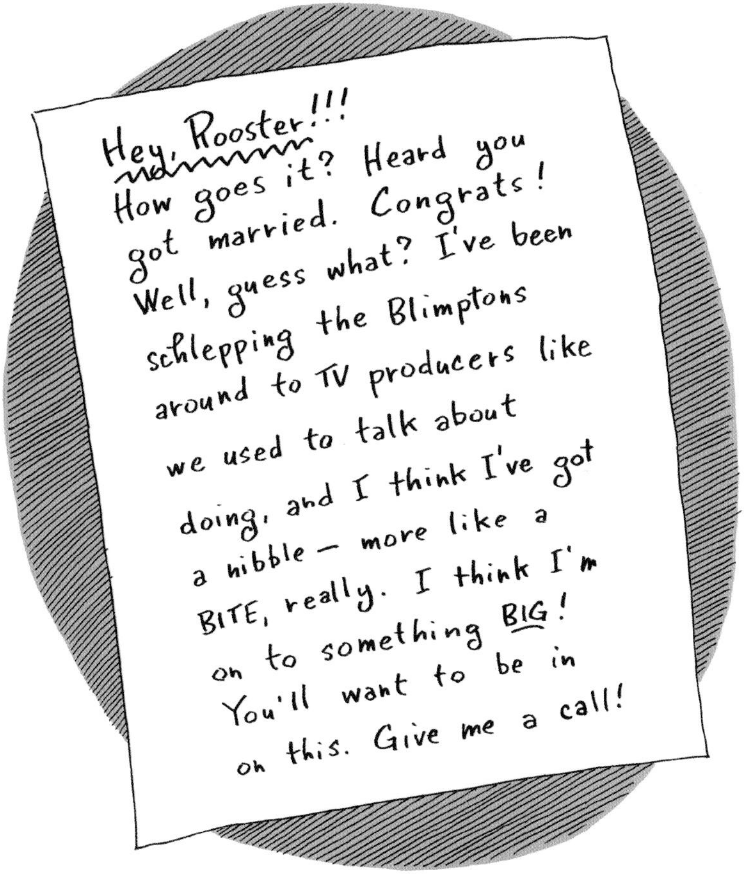

Hey, Rooster!!!
How goes it? Heard you
got married. Congrats!
Well, guess what? I've been
schlepping the Blimptons
around to TV producers like
we used to talk about
doing, and I think I've got
a nibble — more like a
BITE, really. I think I'm
on to something <u>BIG</u>!
You'll want to be in
on this. Give me a call!

And it gave a number. By the time I finished reading it I was hyper-ventilating. If only Dad had known! If only Dad knew now! If only I knew how to reach him.

Then it came to me. It was the middle of the night in Megatown, but it wasn't that late on the west coast, and I had my phone right in my room. So I CALLED THE NUMBER!

I wish I could say that I spoke to Malcolm Buehl, but I just got voicemail, so I left a message.

Hi, Mr. Buehl. You don't know me, but my father is Ross Blossom, and I just read an old letter that you wrote to him, but he never got. I'm sure he would have called you himself, except he's off on a big trip in his pedestrian mobile home, which is something he built himself, and now we're living in Megatown...

I didn't even remember what I said. I babbled. Something about the pedestrian mobile home and Megatown and the talent show and being on YouTube.

I was sure he'd think I was a stupid kid fan. It was a stupid idea to call. He'd *never* call me back, I knew.

Then I fell asleep.

13

BAGEL IN THE SKY

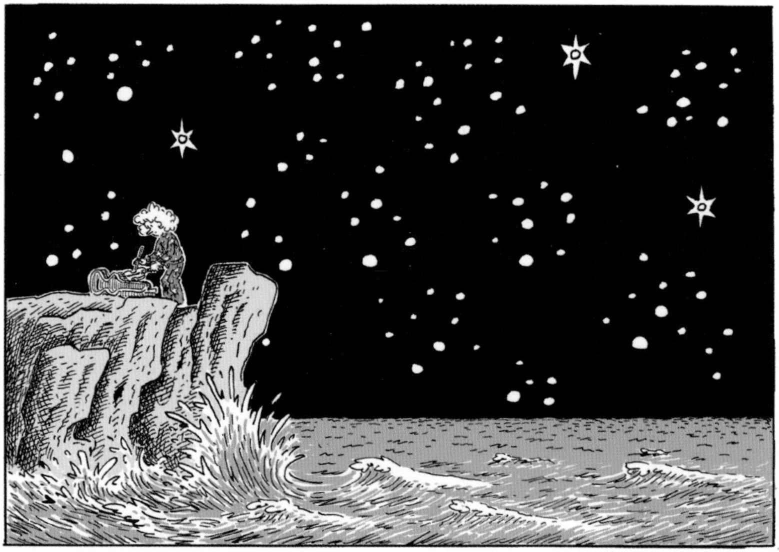

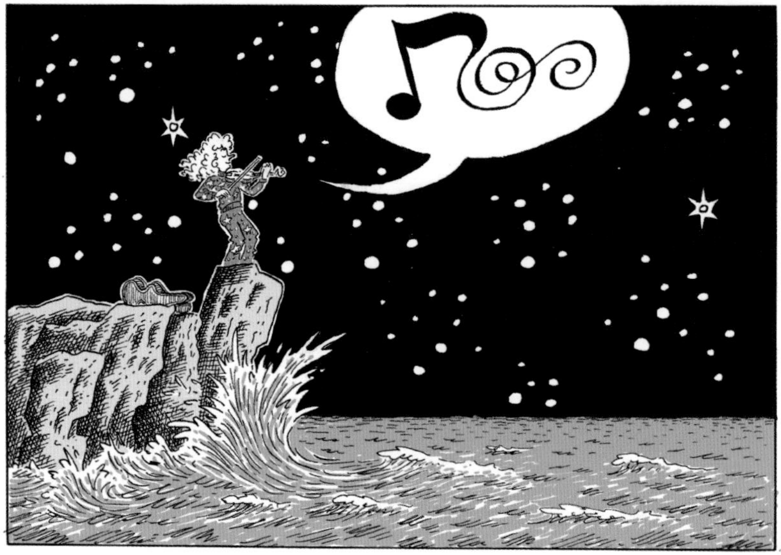

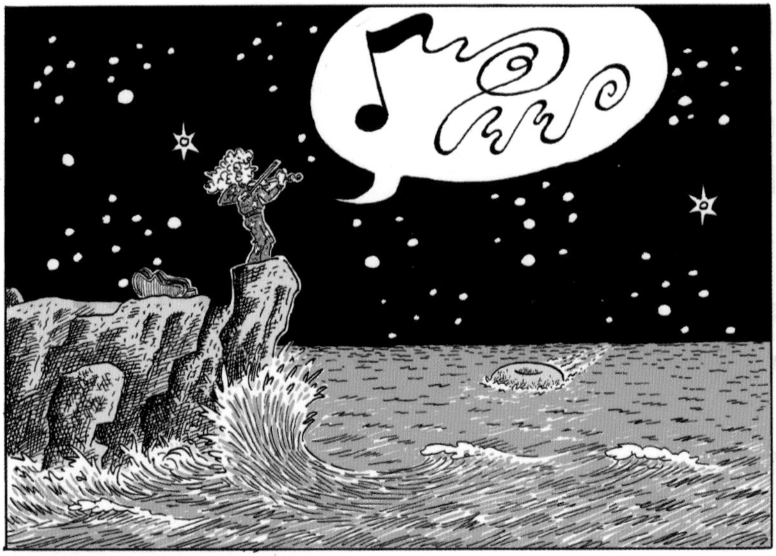

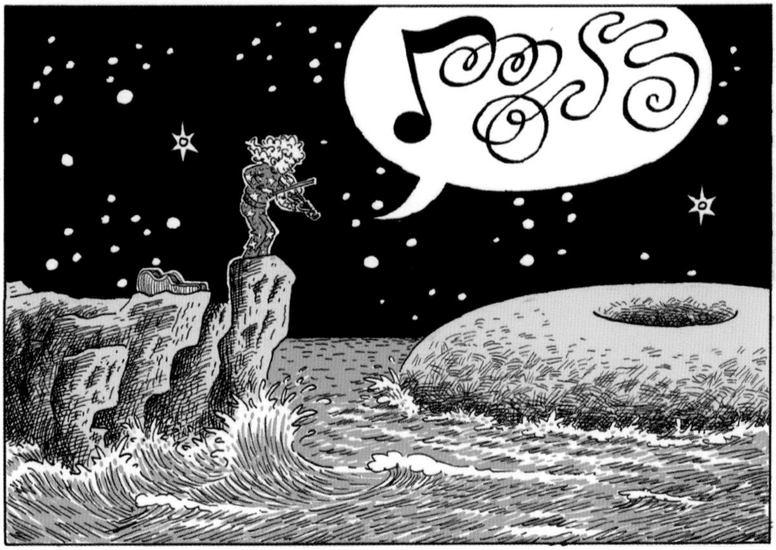

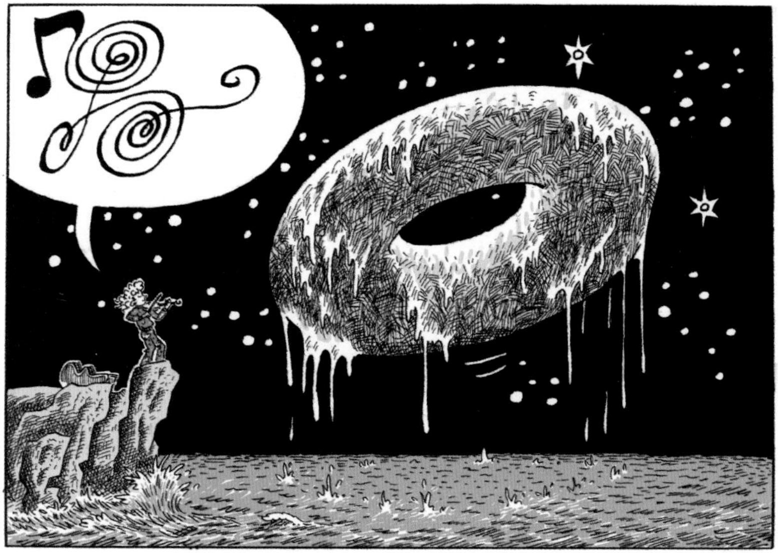

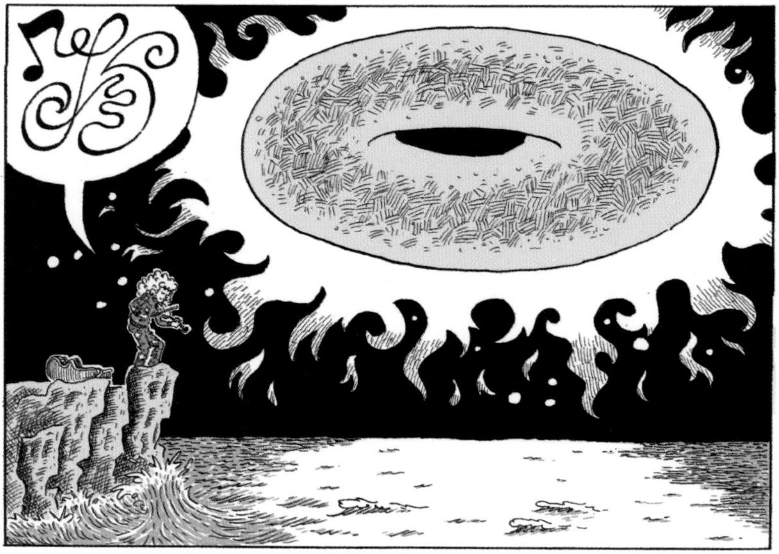

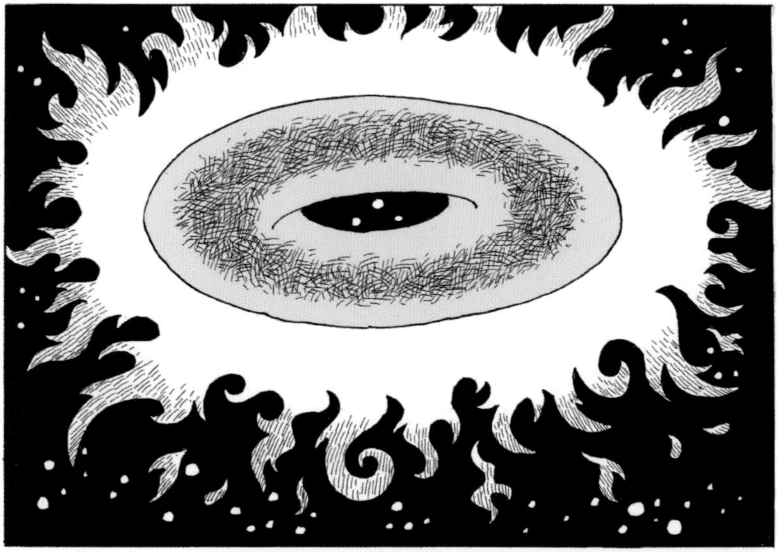

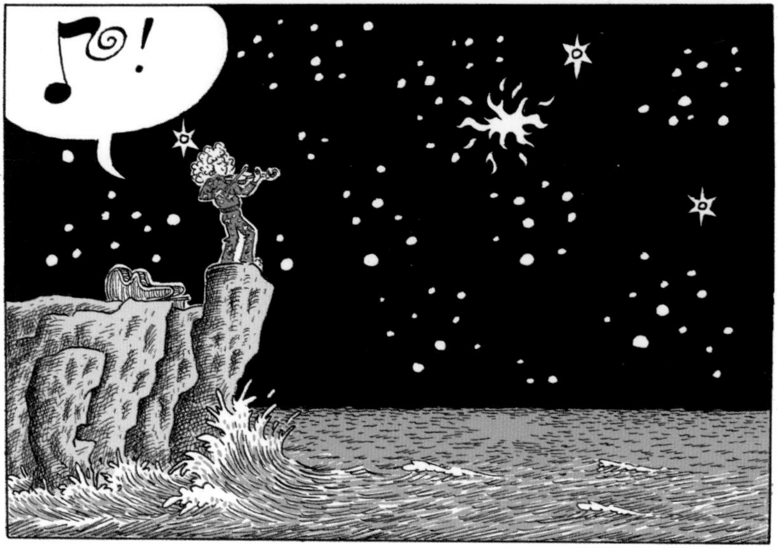

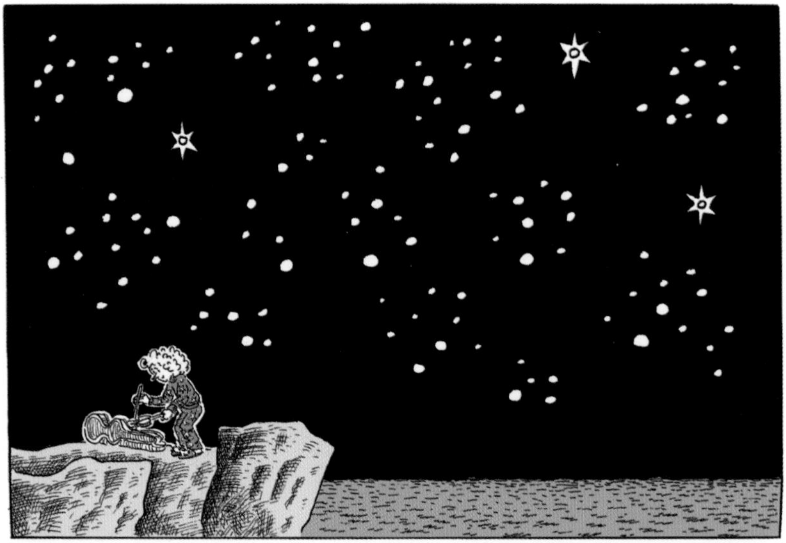

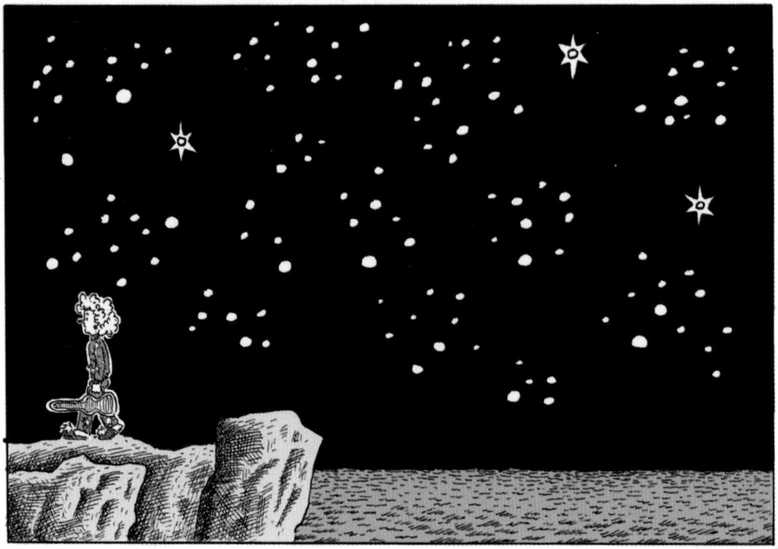

14

THE GREEN BAGELS

That night I dreamt I was playing a lilting melody on my violin, as I stood on a rock overlooking the ocean, under the stars. And a huge bagel rose up to the sky, lifted by the beauty of my music, and burst into flame.

When I woke up I could still hear the notes, but they were fading away, so I jumped out of bed and sounded out the melody on my keyboard app. I couldn't wait to play it for Otto!

My new melody . . . well, it wasn't totally new, but sort of a bigger version of what we had already — with rhythm added. It was sort of a copy, too, of some of Grandpop's records, but I figured everything is inspired by *something*! Right? Besides, what do they expect from an eleven year old?

I decided to wear my stripes and roses leggings.

And after breakfast I texted Otto:

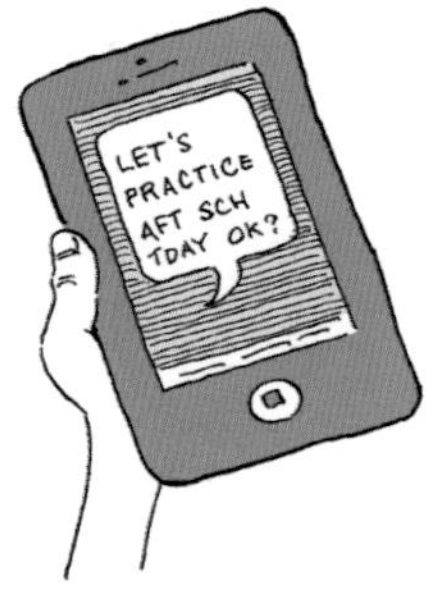
LET'S PRACTICE AFT SCH TDAY OK?

Otto texted back:

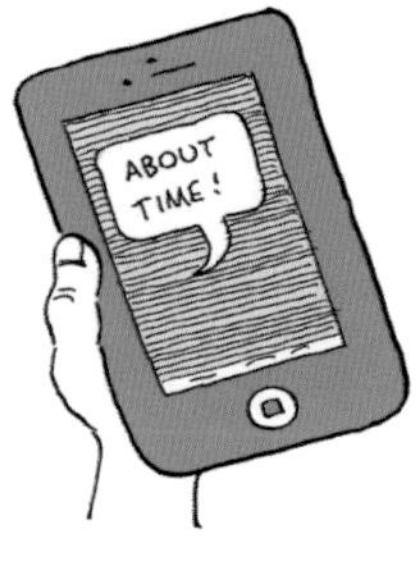
ABOUT TIME!

Otto liked the new melody.

"It's good," he said. "It still has the lonesome wolf sound, but there's more of a melody and more rhythm. I like it."

I was so excited. I said, "It's *great*! We sound so good! I can't wait for the talent show. We're gonna win this thing!"

Otto said, "Well, don't get your hopes up too high. It's a little unusual. I think the judges might go for something more traditional."

"Give me a few more months (well, maybe a few more years), and they'll forget they ever heard of traditional!"

Holding my violin over my head I danced around and jiggled my butt.

Otto frowned at me. "If you do that on stage, I'm quitting!"

I just laughed and danced some more.

Otto said, "It's all up or down with you, isn't it?"

"Up is good," I said.

"I never thought I would be the one telling you to calm down," Otto said.

"Okay, okay. What should we call it?" I asked.

"Call what?"

"Our song, Dope!"

"Oh. Well, lemme think. How about 'Dream of the Blues' after your dream inspiration?"

I said, "You know what's funny, Otto? I've been keeping track of some of my dreams. And you can almost always see where they're coming from. But sometimes they don't make any sense at all. Once I dreamt I was hanging out on a clothesline to dry, flapping in the breeze. Where do you think that came from?"

"I dunno. Somewhere. Everything comes from somewhere. Maybe you saw a picture in a book of clothes on a clothesline. Maybe you were hot and sweaty. Maybe you felt limp and washed out after a hard day. Sometimes when my mom has had a hard day she says she feels like she's been through the wringer. You know, like an old washing machine."

"I know what a wringer is," I said. "But I don't like 'Dream of the Blues.' It sounds too tame. What about 'Howling Wolf'?"

Otto said that was the name of an old blues singer. He said, "How about 'Wolfman Blues'?"

"How about 'Welcome to Weird'?"

"Now you're just being silly."

"No, I'm not. I like it."

"Well, if you're serious, then I have to tell you it sounds sort of show-offy, like you think you're the queen of weird or something."

"Well, aren't I?"

"No, you're just like anybody else."

I used to think I wanted nothing more than to be like everybody else. Now I felt sort of insulted. "Well!" I said. "I thought I was just a little bit weird."

"Everybody is a little bit weird in their own way. I have to admit that your weirdness is a little more interesting than most, though."

"Oh. Well, let's go with 'Wolfman Blues,' then. Or 'Wolfman Stomp'?"

"Okay," he said. "What about us? Shouldn't we have a name?"

I suggested Anne and the Wolfman, but Otto said he didn't think he was the Wolfman type. He said he had an idea, but he didn't think I would like it.

"Why not? What is it?"

"No, never mind," he said. "It's a stupid idea. I'll think of something else. Um . . . how about The Howling Duo?"

I stuck my finger in my mouth and made gagging sounds. "What's your other idea? C'mon, out with it."

"You'll be mad."

"Why should I be mad? I promise I won't be mad. C'mon, it can't be any worse than Howling Duo."

"Okay, okay," said Otto. "I thought we could be The Green Bagels." And he ducked behind the couch in case I was going to throw something at him.

"OTTO!" I screamed. "That *mean*, horrible nickname! How *could* you?"

"Hey, take it easy. I don't think Brendan meant to be *mean*, exactly. Or to hurt your feelings. He was just trying to be funny."

"Well, it did hurt my feelings. I mean my mom's family is Irish, and my dad's family is Jewish. So I am a green bagel."

"So?"

"So people shouldn't make fun of other people's origins."

Otto gave me a funny look. "I'm half white and half black," he said.

"You are?"

"What did you think I was? Swedish?"

"Well, I never met your dad. I guess I thought . . . I mean I never really thought about it, one way or the other."

Otto was just Otto.

"Otto, can I ask you something?"

"Sure."

"Would *you* like to be a Green Bagel?"

"I would be *proud* to be a Green Bagel," Otto said.

That made me laugh. "Okay," I said. "At least it's unique, right?"

"Cool," said Otto. "Show 'em you don't care. Show 'em you like it. And you're proud to be who you are."

15

BEEP BEEP

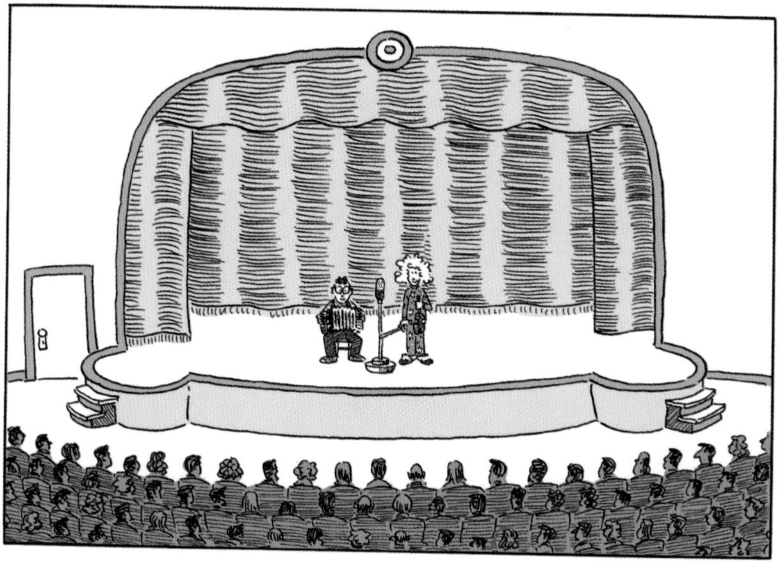

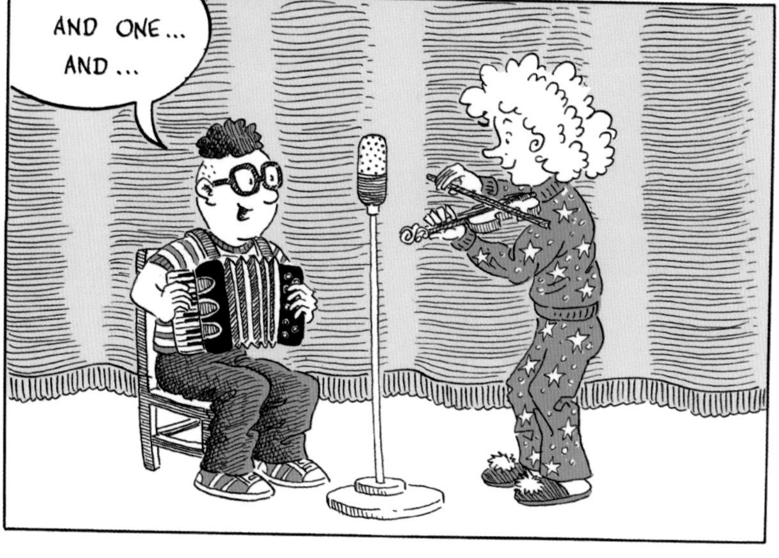
AND ONE... AND...

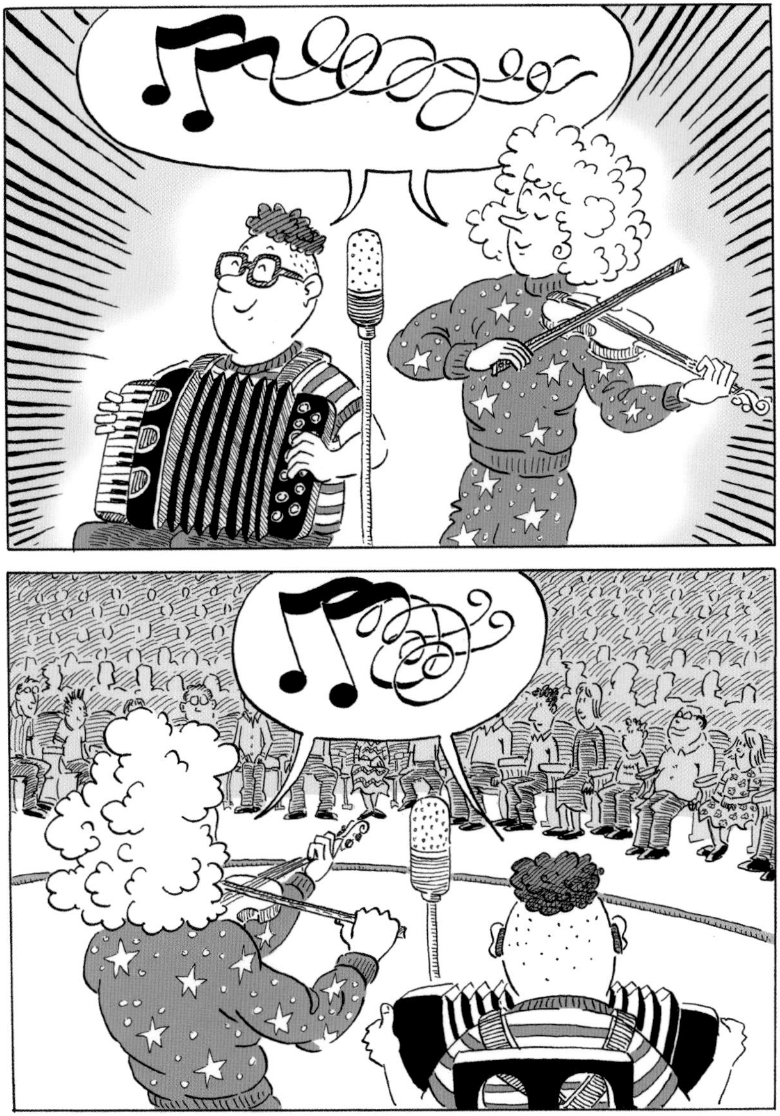

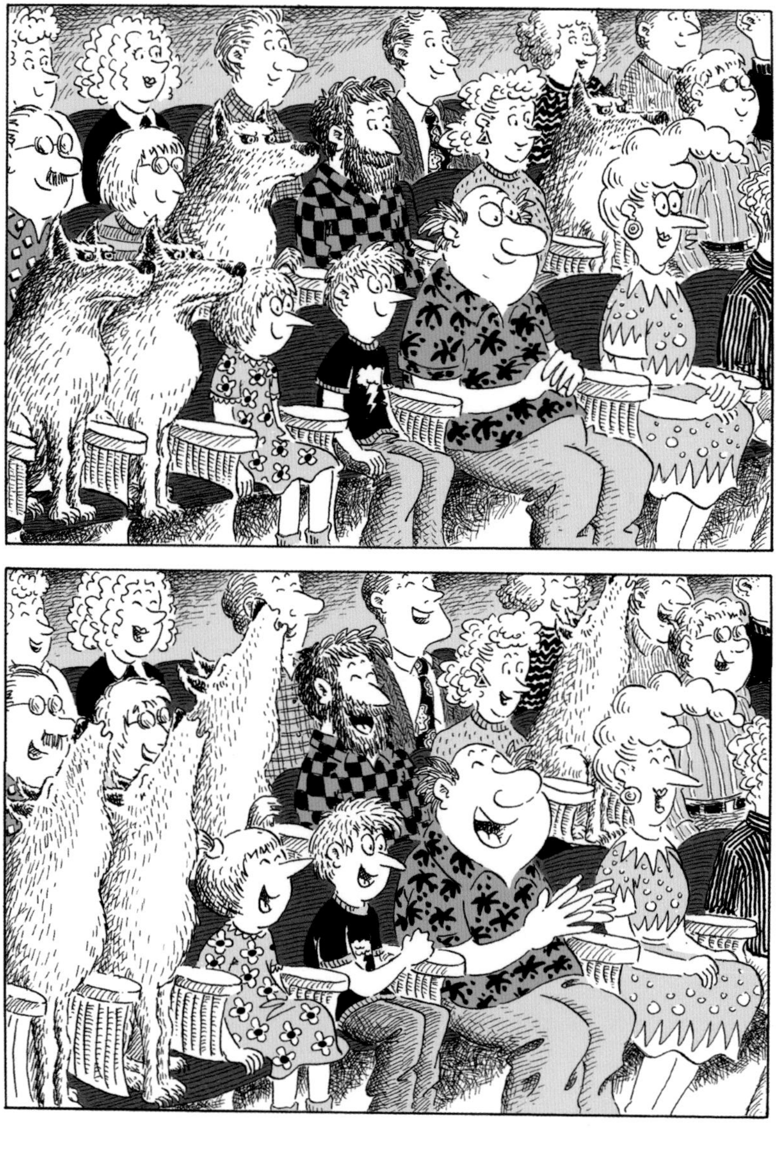

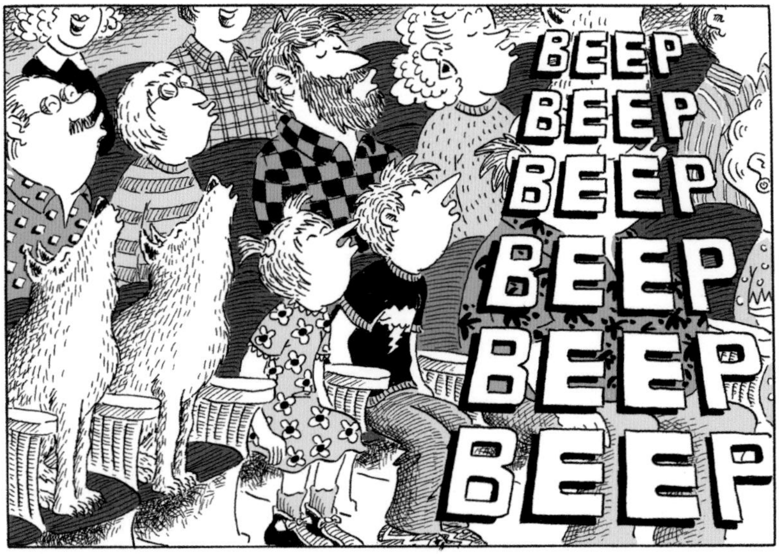
BEEP
BEEP
BEEP
BEEP
BEEP
BEEP

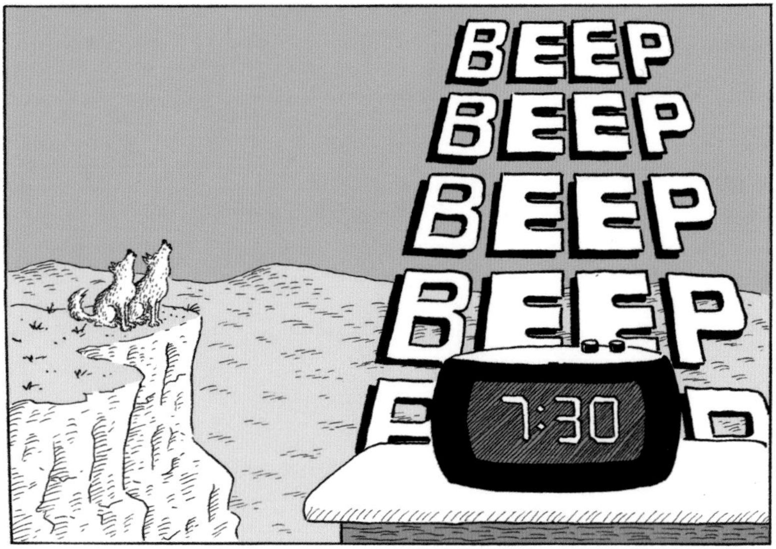
BEEP
BEEP
BEEP
BEEP
7:30

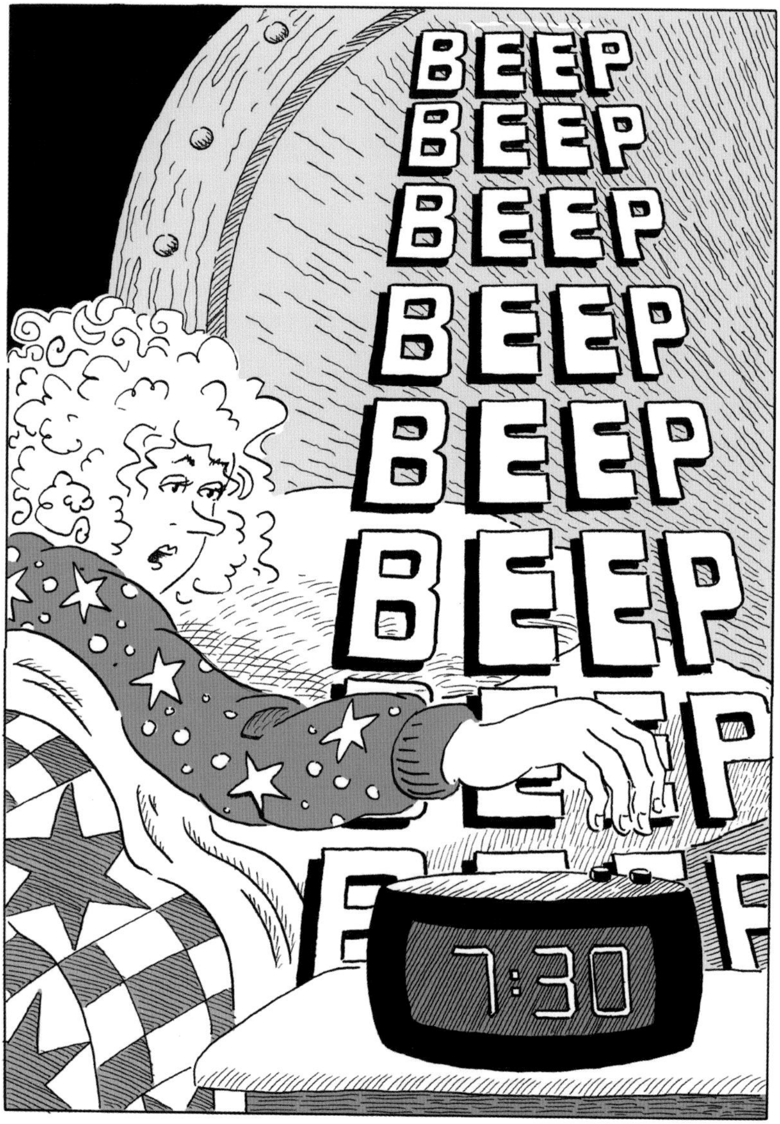
BEEP
BEEP
BEEP
BEEP
BEEP
BEEP
7:30

16

SHOWTIME!

Some dreams seem so real you can't believe you're dreaming. And sometimes, real life feels like a dream.

The morning of the talent show I had cold feet.

"You don't have to come, you know," I said at breakfast. "I can get a ride over with Otto's mom."

"*Not come*?! Of course we're coming!" said Mom.

"Coming where?" asked Grandpop.

"It's Anne's talent show today, Reuben," said Nana. "We're all going."

"I think I might be sick," I said.

"Nerves," said Grandpop.

Nana made me some of her special, stomach-settling tea, and they sent me over to Otto's for a final practice.

"Otto will calm her down," I heard Mom say to Nana as they watched me drag myself along the sidewalk.

In the end I did ride to the school with Otto and his Mom, but when I peeked through the curtains I could see my family seated in the audience.

"And now, let's give a warm Megatown welcome to the KUBITSKY SISTERS!" Mr. Deville announced.

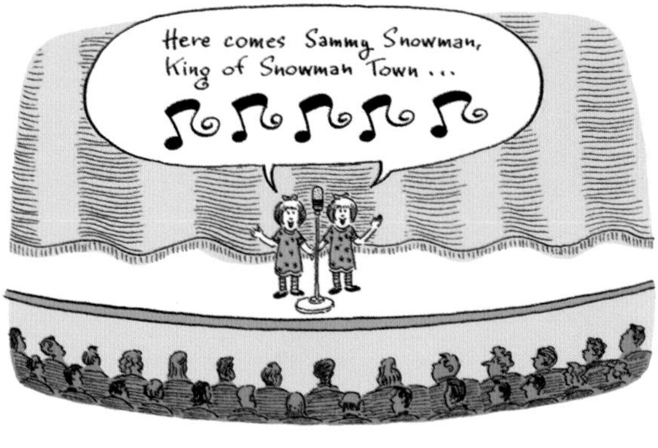
Here comes Sammy Snowman,
King of Snowman Town . . .

"They're good," Otto whispered to me.

"I can hear that for myself," I snapped.

The audience went crazy for the twins, and with good reason.

Next up was Brendan Boyle. He looked very relaxed, whistling while he set up his equipment.

BOYNG, TWANG, BOYNG!

Backstage, I gasped. "Otto! That's our song!"

"Just warming up, folks," Brendan said to the audience with a smile.

BLANG! He began his piece.

"That creep!" I hissed. "He stole our song for his warm-up! Now it will look like we're copying *him*!"

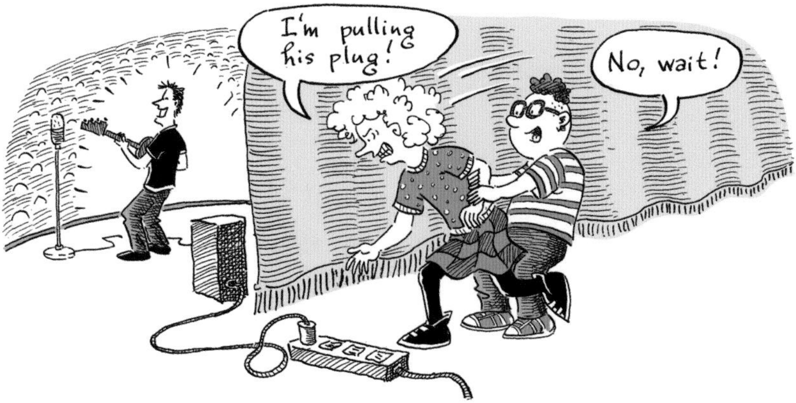
I'm pulling his plug!
No, wait!

Otto pulled me back. "You can't do that! It was just his warm-up. Nobody will remember. It'll be okay."

Too soon Brendan was finishing up and it was our turn.

"I can't do it, Otto," I said. "You'll have to go on alone."

"Relax, you'll be fine."

"But I just forgot everything! What's the first note? What key did we decide on?"

Brendan passed us on his way off the stage.

"Thief!" I growled at him.

"And now," announced Mr. Deville, "the GREEN BAGELS!"

I stood paralyzed, holding my fiddle in one hand and my bow in the other.

I stared at the audience, and there was *Malcolm Buehl*!

I blinked and looked again.

He was gone.

"Oh, I get it!" I whispered to Otto. "This is all a dream, right?"

"No," he whispered back, "but if it helps you to think that, go ahead!"

Then he said out loud, "This is an original song, written by Anne Blossom. We call it WOLFMAN STOMP."

I lifted my bow.

Otto whispered, "And one, and two . . ."

I drew the bow across the strings and it all came back to me. We sailed through the song. The parents in the audience clapped in time and stomped their feet. I got so into it that I even added a few flourishes, and when it was over we floated off the stage to cries of *Bravo!* And *Yee-hah!*

It's over! I thought. *I did it! They liked us!*

Then we had to sit backstage while Peter Platt did card tricks and Giovanna Santos back-flipped all over the stage in a leotard.

Finally Mr. Deville took the microphone. "And this year's winner," he announced, ". . . is,"

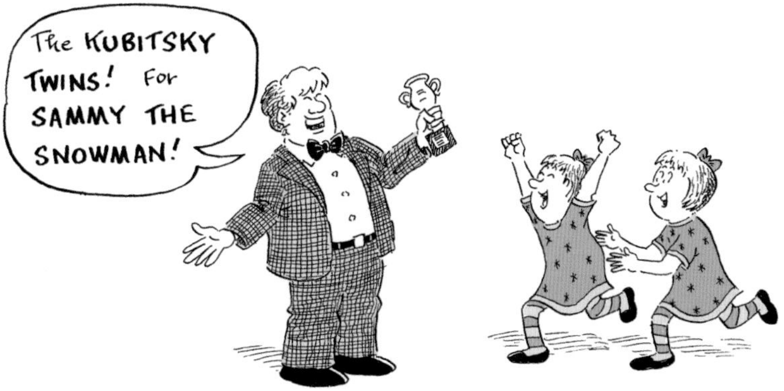
The KUBITSKY TWINS! For SAMMY THE SNOWMAN!

"'Sammy the Snowman'?" I gasped. "We lost to 'Sammy the Snowman'?"

Otto started to laugh. "I told you we were too weird for these judges."

I was so relieved it was all over that I had to laugh, too. "But weird is good," I said. "And the crowd liked us!"

When the twins came over I was able to say to them, "You deserved to win. Your singing is really beautiful."

"We would have given the prize to you," they said.

Isabel Morton, looking cute in a polka-dot dress came up to Otto.

For once Otto couldn't think of anything to say. Brendan Boyle glowered.

Later Otto and I walked outside to find our families.

Instead we found . . .

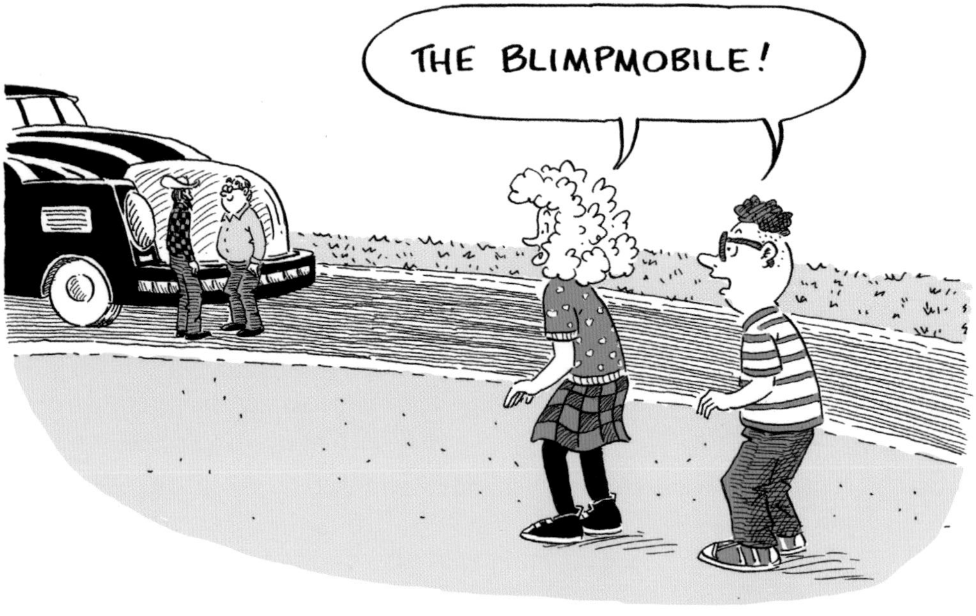
THE BLIMPMOBILE!

It was parked in front of the school, life-sized and in person! Now I *knew* I was dreaming.

Then I saw the two men standing next to it.

IT WAS DAD! And Malcolm Buehl! They had come in the BLIMPMOBILE to see the talent show!

I ran up to them as fast as I could.

But when I was almost there I suddenly felt shy, so I just stood there and said, "Uh . . . Hi."

But my dad knelt down and opened his arms and I ran into them and I was crying. It was just like those kids on TV whose dads come back from the war and show up in the classroom for a surprise. I always thought it would be embarrassing to be one of those kids, but I wasn't even thinking about being embarrassed and I was crying all over my dad's shirt.

"Hey," he said. "Hey, Annie."

After I calmed down, Malcolm Buehl shook my hand and said, "Great show! Great to meet you! You've got real musical talent, doesn't she Rooster? And your partner, too — Otto, isn't it? Great to meet you, Otto! Saw your video on YouTube, but you've made some improvements since then. How do you kids like my bus? Wait'll you see the inside. Looks just like a posh living room, doesn't it?"

"These couches fold out to make beds. And look at all the storage shelves under here. There's a place for everything. Pretty cool, huh?

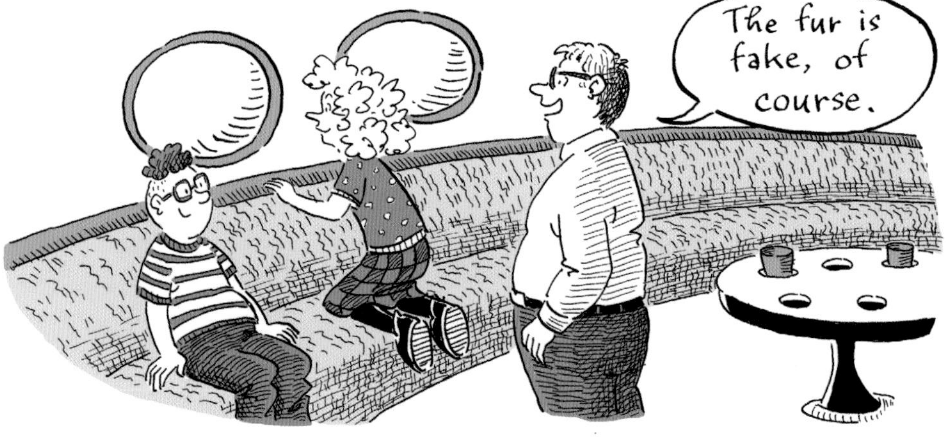
The fur is fake, of course.

"You know your Dad designed it, Anne, back when we were kids, right down to the screw propellers and water jets to make it amphibious. Did you know that your dad was the idea man behind The Blimptons? Smart guy. Musical, too. Like father, like daughter, eh?

"This is the passenger pod. This is where you ride while we're traveling. See, it's got safety belts and an observation window."

My father said, "Uh, I better . . . uh . . ." He gestured towards the window where you could see Nana and Grandpop standing outside, and then he went out to join them. I guessed they already knew he was there. They must have met up when I was backstage. Nana was *beaming*.

Then I saw Mom. She was standing a little way off by herself. "There's my mom," I interrupted Malcolm. "I better go . . ."

He put his hand on my arm. "It's okay," he said. "She'll be meeting us at the deli. She thought you kids would like to ride in the bus."

"How did you get here?" I asked Malcolm. "How did you find Dad? Did you get my message?"

"Can't you guess? It was your phone call. As soon as I heard it, I remembered a news item about a crackpot who was pushing a mobile home around L.A. I never guessed it was the Rooster. But as soon as you mentioned 'pedestrian mobile home' it clicked.

"Just what Ross would come up with. I had some of my guys track him down. Told him what was what back in Megatown, and we watched you on YouTube together. We decided to surprise you. He's quite a character, your father. Nobody quite like him.

"Now if you'll just get buckled in, we'll take off. I understand your grandparents have a little party planned for you two. Green bagels all around!"

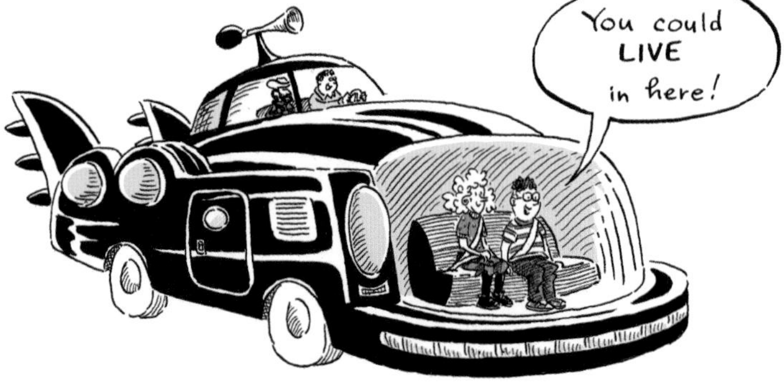
You could LIVE in here!

Everybody was there — Mr. Deville, the other kids from the show, their parents, and of course my family and Otto's mom.

The bagels were green. Bright green, not moldy green.

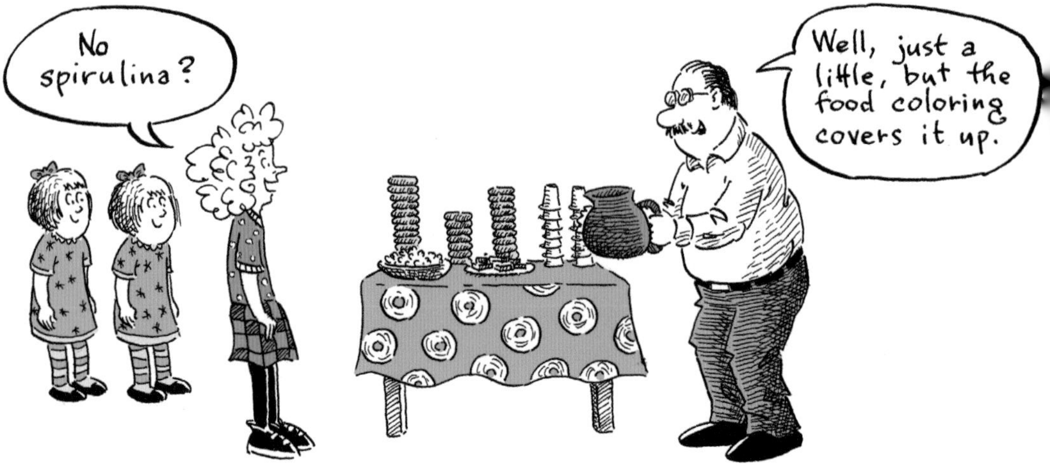
No spirulina?
Well, just a little, but the food coloring covers it up.

17

INVITATION TO
THE DANCE

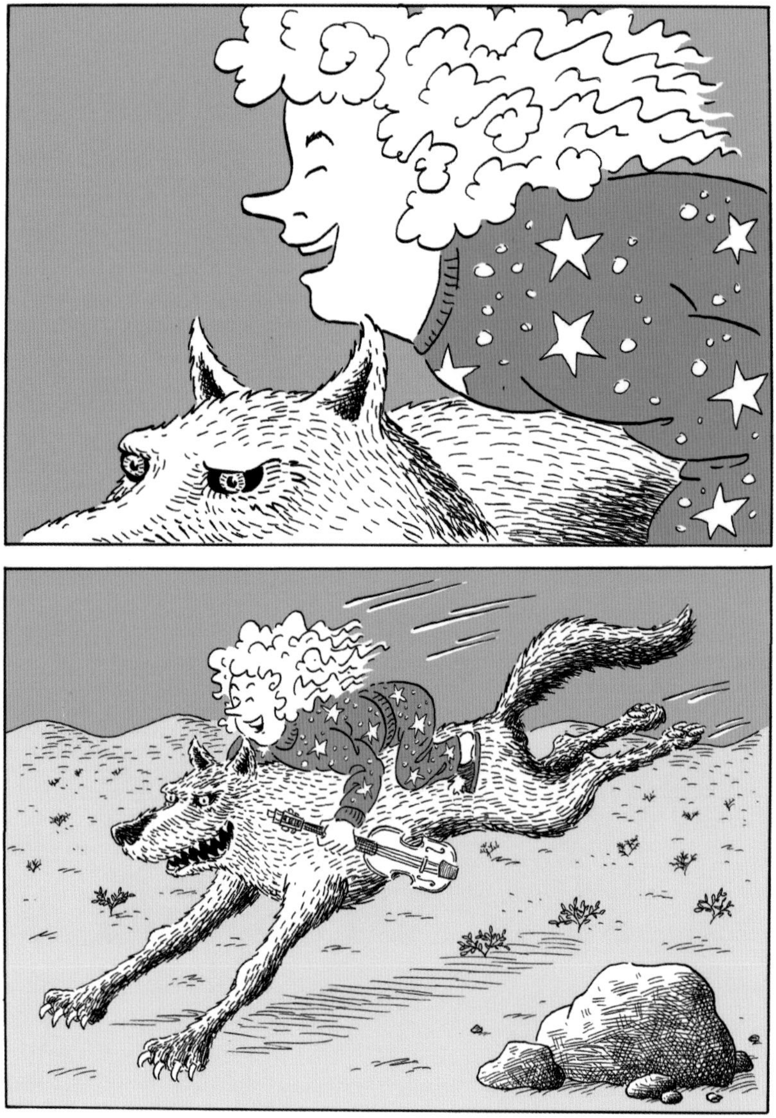

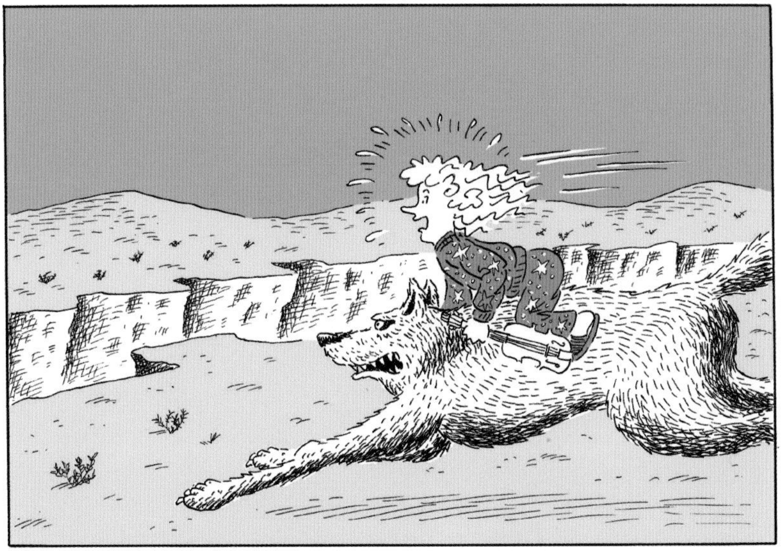

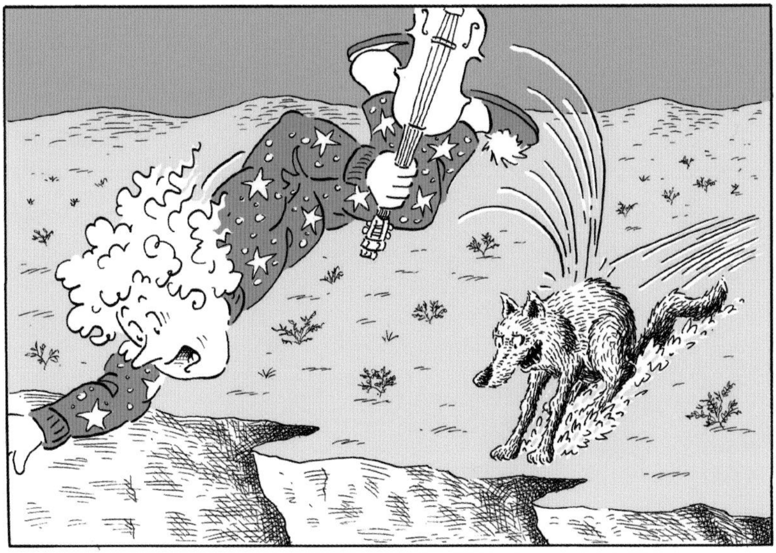

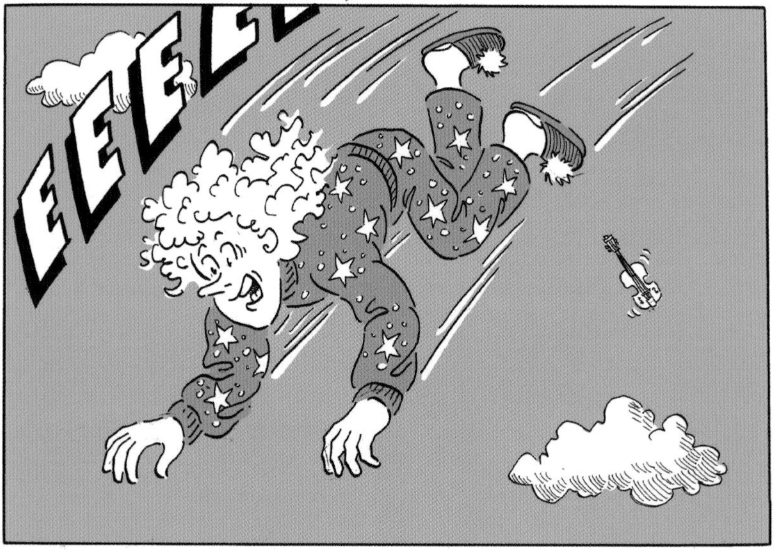
EEEE

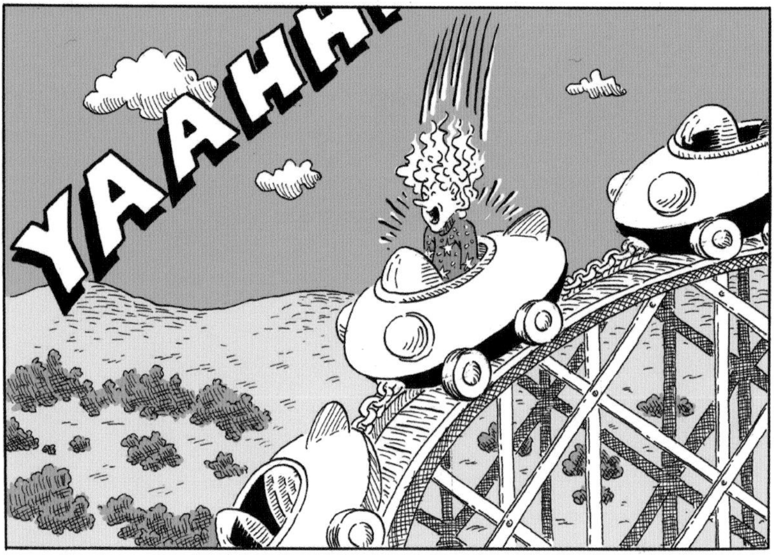
YAAHH

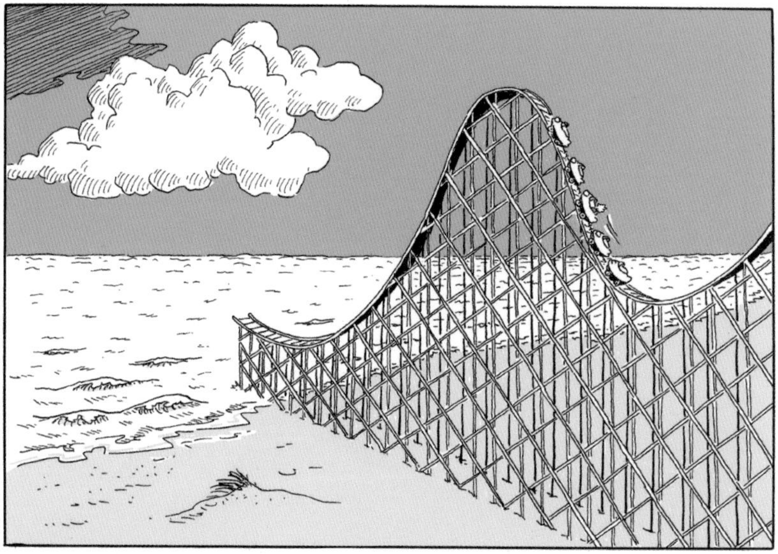

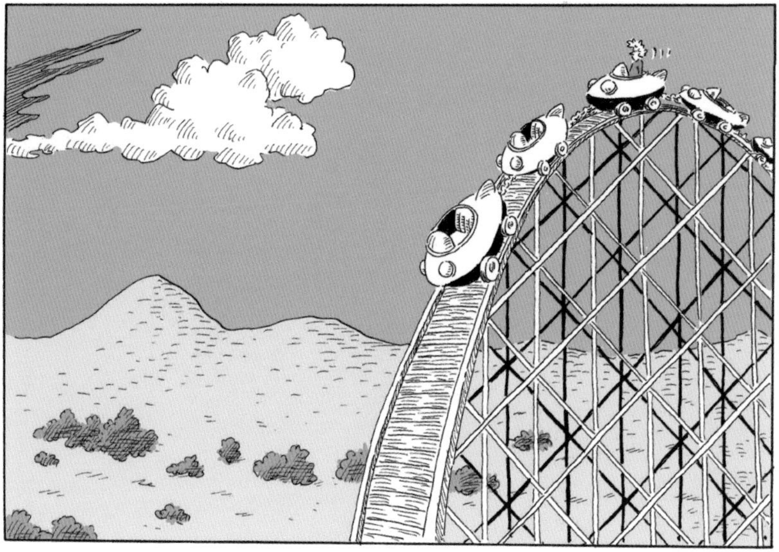

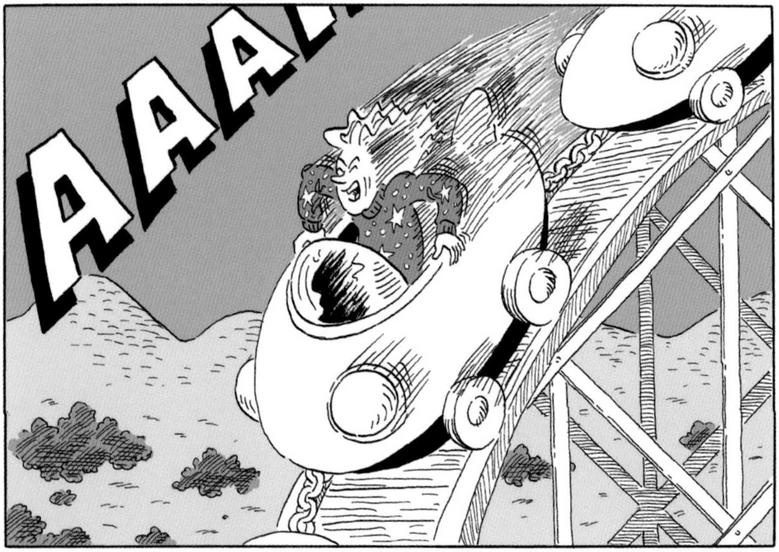
AAAA

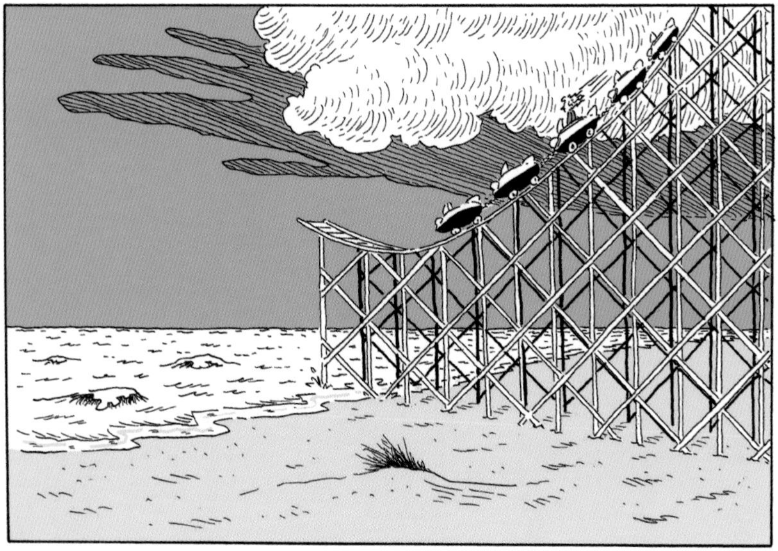

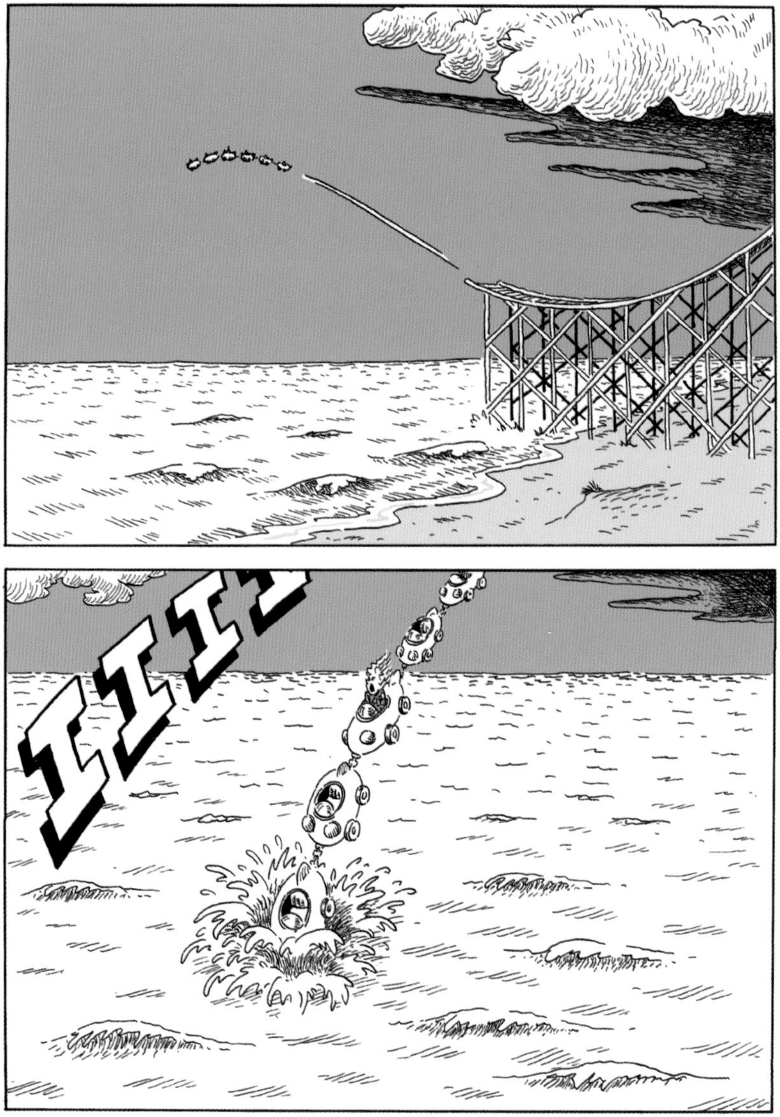
IIII

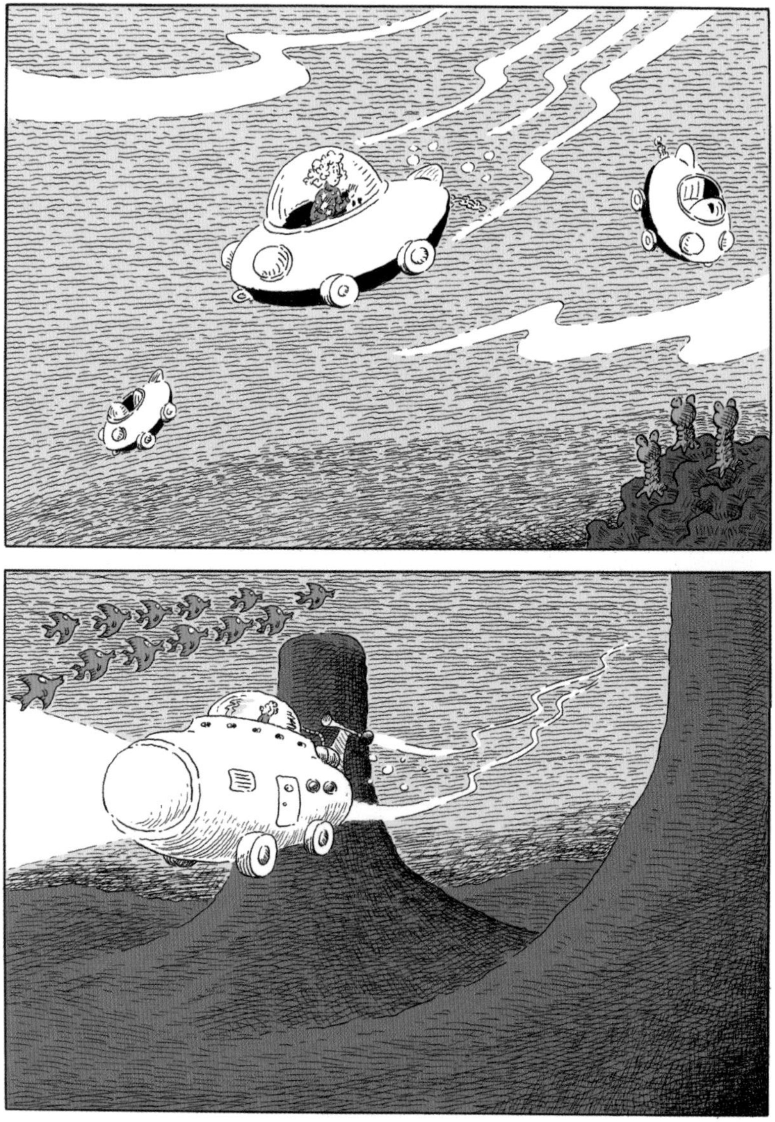

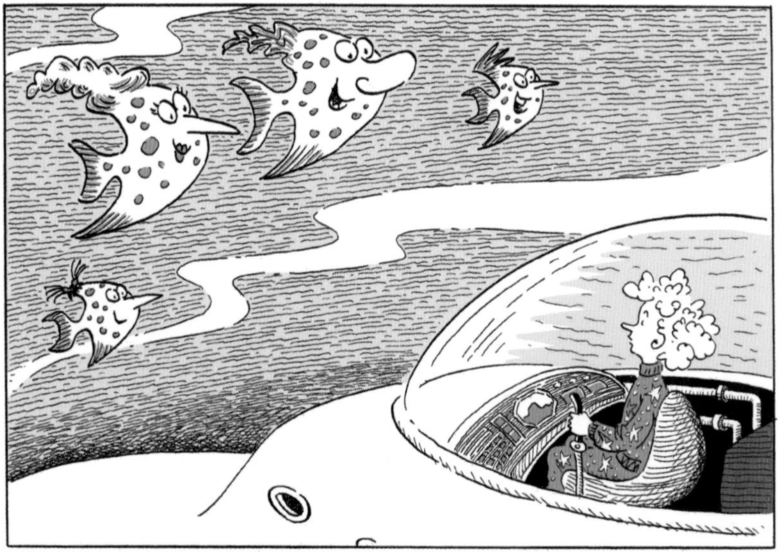

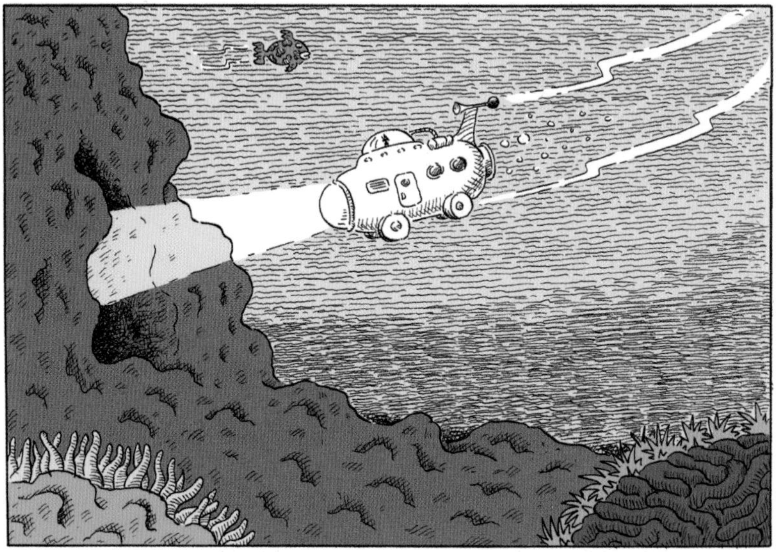

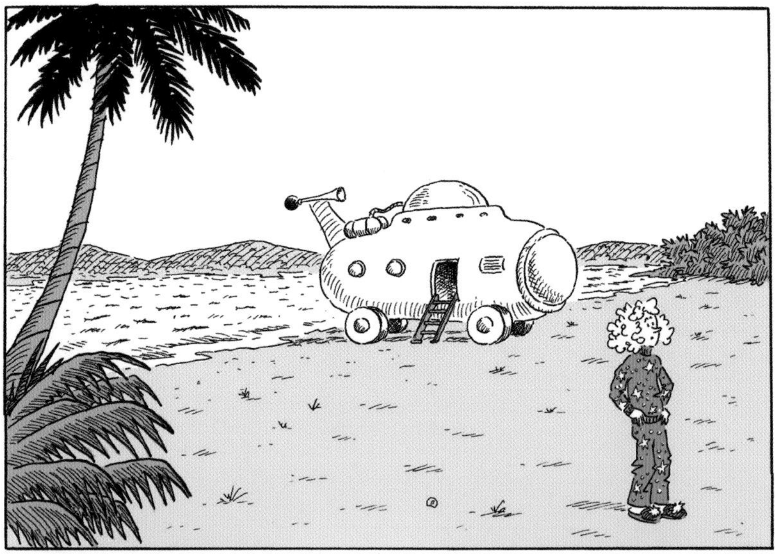

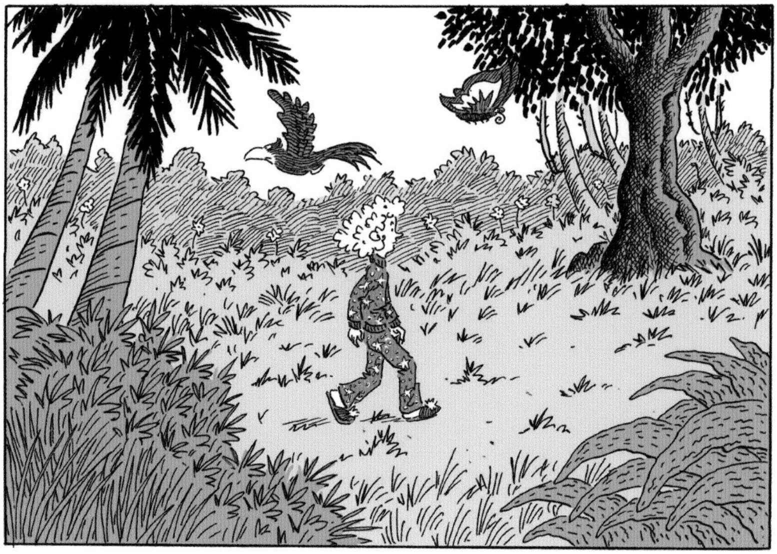

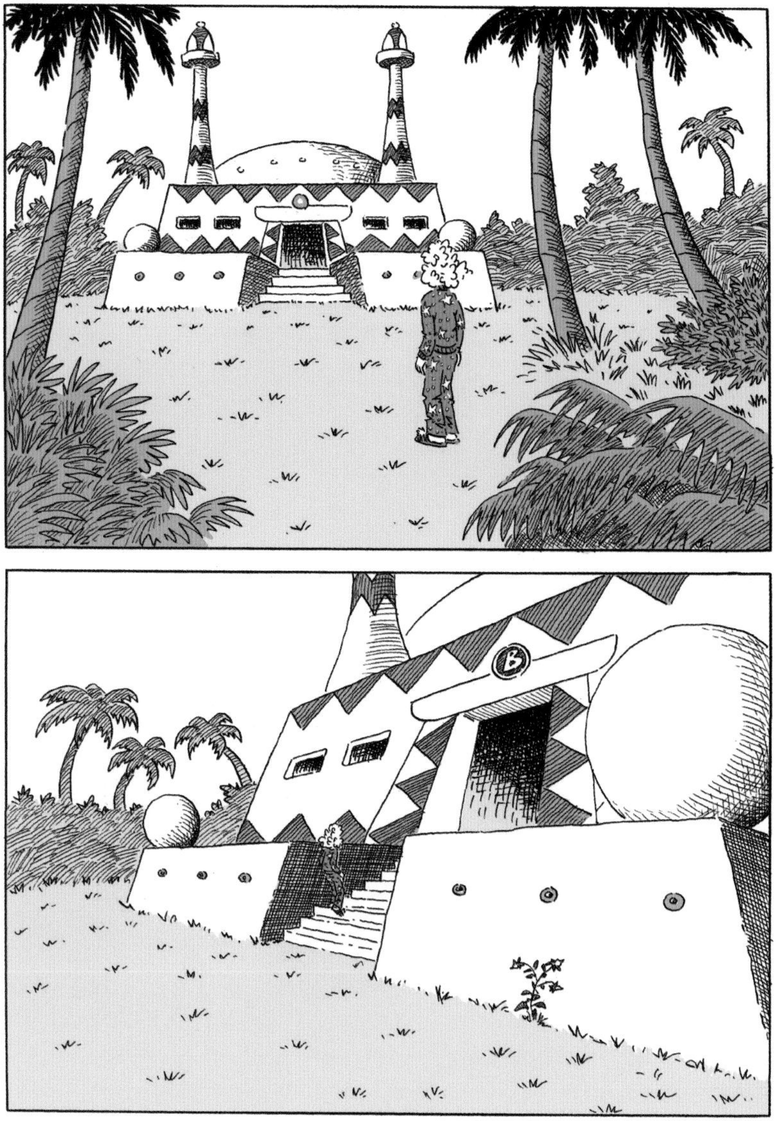

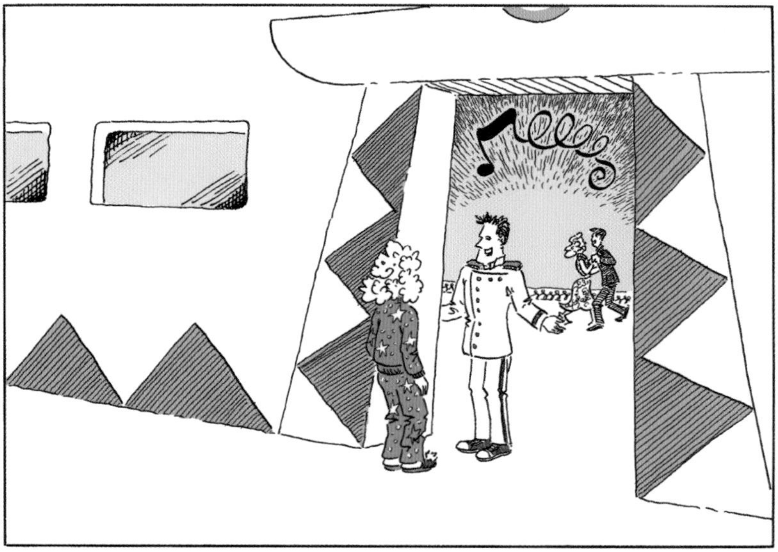

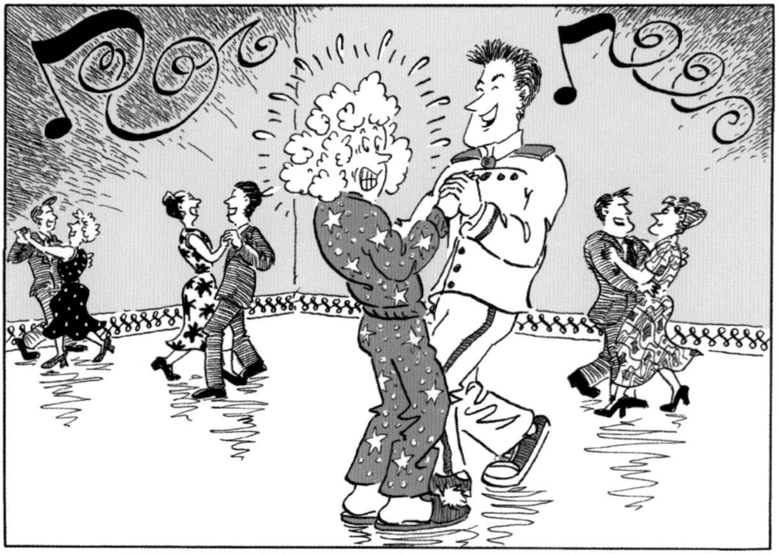

18

FAMILY CONFERENCE

EWW! When I woke up I couldn't believe that I had just had a dream about dancing with Brendan Boyle! But after I thought about it, I decided it wasn't so bad. It was a fun dream. And besides, Brendan Boyle had come over to me at the Green Bagels party, and said he was sorry if he teased me too much. He didn't mean to hurt my feelings, and he thought our song was pretty impressive. So that was nice of him, wasn't it?

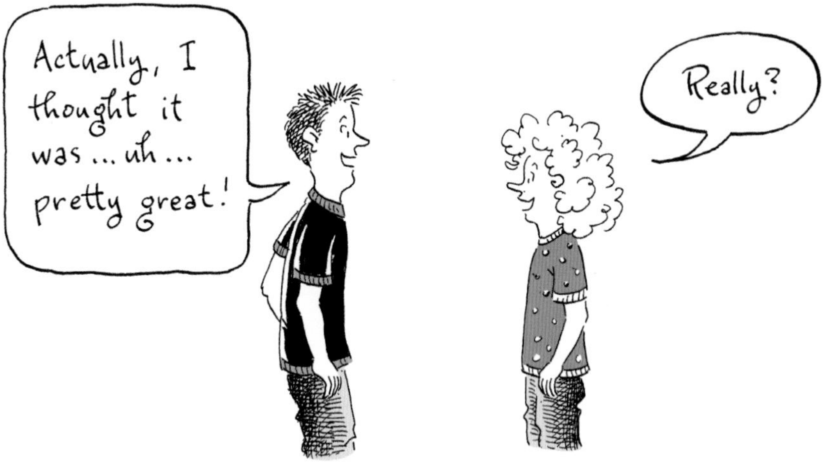
Actually, I thought it was ... uh ... pretty great!
Really?

I thought I might ask him to jam with us. Otto said that Brendan is awesome at beat boxing. Besides, at the party I was so happy to have my dad back that I felt as if I liked everybody. I even felt as if everybody liked me!

But later, after we got home, I started to worry about what would happen to my family next. Would Mom stay mad at Dad? Would Dad go away again? Where would we live? All of these things were going around in my head.

I asked Mom about it. And she said, "I think it would be a good idea if we had a family meeting to talk about just that."

So we all sat around in the living room.

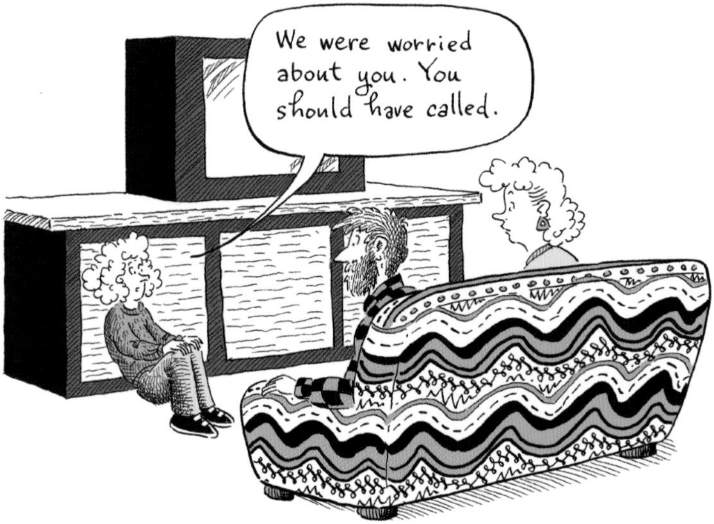
We were worried about you. You should have called.

Dad frowned. "I thought talking to Mom would keep me from feeling homeless. But I sent packages."

"Yeah," I said, "but they were just for me. And the third one came so late we thought something had happened to you!"

"You know I love you," he said.

"And Mom?" I said.

He looked over at Mom.

"More than anything!" he said. "I just get excited about finding my big blockbuster. Not for myself so much. But for Naomi. I know you worry about money, Love. And then I get wrapped up in my project . . ."

His eyes lit up as he began to tell about his trip. "I joined up with a tent city for a while, organized by some incredible homeless people! We built a few pedestrian mobile homes. Of course we had to scrounge up the supplies, and take on a few odd jobs to make some cash." His voice trailed off.

"It all takes time," he mumbled. "And sometimes I forget about the profit motive. You know those nine-to-five jobs are hard on me," he added miserably.

He looked around the room at all of us.

"But isn't Malcolm going to share some of The Blimptons profits with you?" I said. (This was true.)

"Oh, yeah," Dad said. "I was forgetting about that."

I was sure that was true too. Dad just doesn't think that much about money — for himself, anyway.

Mom sat forward.

I'd like to say something.

"I was *very* worried. And I felt abandoned. And angry, too. You were just gone too long, Ross. *Much* longer than the time you went to Lake Taco to try out the underwater tricycle. And the trip to Florida for the Parcheesi convention to show off your 3D game — that was only two weeks *and* you called me — twice! This time I didn't just feel abandoned, I *was* abandoned. We all were!"

"I'm . . ." Dad began, but Mom said, "Let me finish."

She stood up and paced around.

"We know what Ross is like," she said to Nana and Grandpop who were sort of cowering in their chairs. "And we love him in spite of it. Or maybe because of it. Well, things have got to change. The Blimptons money is going to be a godsend. It will mean you don't have to take jobs you hate, Ross, so I hope you will be happier, and maybe not so inclined to go off on your own. In any case, I think you should promise us — and I know you keep your promises — that if you go off from time to time, you'll keep in touch with us."

"I'll call three times a day!" Dad said. "I promise! Cross my heart!"

Dad is such a kid.

"Well, once every few days would probably be sufficient," said Mom. Mom is such a parent.

"But what happens now?" I asked. "Are we all going to live here together?"

"Here? In Megatown?" Dad squirmed a little. "What about New Mexico?"

"We rented the house out," Mom said, "for the whole year, and they can renew for another year."

"Two years! In Megatown?" he repeated. He squirmed again and looked toward the window. Then he burst out, "No offense Mom and Dad, but it's the *sameness* of it all!" He looked at all the furniture crowding Nana's small living room. "And there isn't much space," he added.

"You could have the attic," Grandpop said.

Dad looked upward. You could tell the wheels were turning inside his head. "The ceiling is a little low," he said slowly. "But there's potential." He smiled. "Yes, there's potential here!"

I went to bed feeling good. I was so tired I didn't even hear the hammering and sawing going on. But when I woke up...

Dad had attached the pedestrian mobile home to the house with a tunnel going from the garage!

We all stood outside to look at it.

"I thought you weren't allowed to add anything to a Megatown house," I said.

"We'll see about that!" Dad said. "From here on, I'm fighting those idiotic restrictions! They violate human rights! I'm staying right here in Megatown, where I can be close to you and Mom and Nana and Grandpop, and lead the crusade against Norbert Meggett!"

"But, Dad, are you really going to stay in your pedestrian mobile home and come into the house through that little tunnel?"

"No, of course not. The pedestrian mobile home will be our new guest room! And that's just the beginning!"

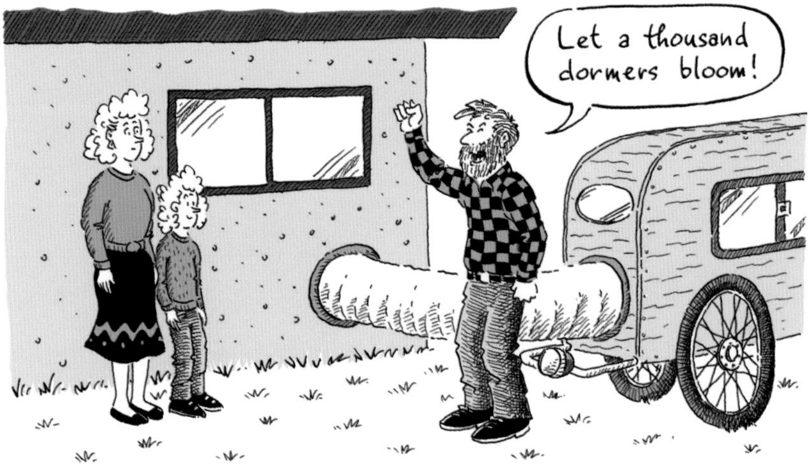
Let a thousand dormers bloom!

"Oh, Dad, you're such a weirdo!"

I was glad we were staying. Dad would have fun fighting Norbert Meggett, and Mom and Dad would both be happy at the same time!

And besides, Otto and I still had a lot of music to make.

WATCH OUT FOR PAPERCUTZ™

Welcome to the awesome ANNE OF GREEN BAGELS graphic novel by Susan Schade and Jon Buller from Papercutz, those healthy bagel-eating souls dedicated to publishing great graphic novels for all ages. I'm Jim Salicrup, the Editor-in-Chief and a big fan of *The Blimptons!*

If you picked up this wonderful hybrid graphic novel because you previously enjoyed SCARLETT "Star on the Run," I hope you also enjoyed ANNE OF GREEN BAGELS.

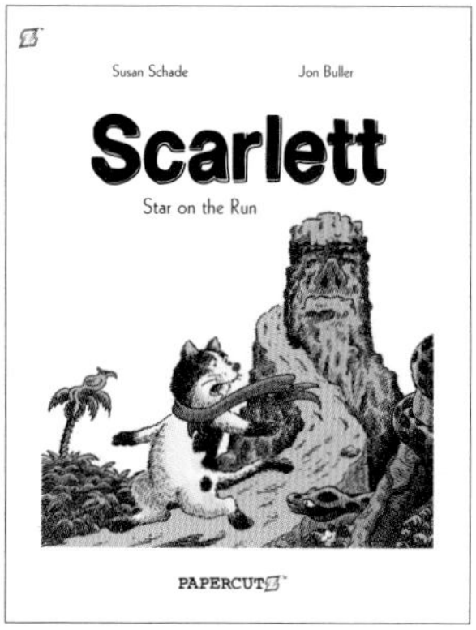
Susan Schade
Jon Buller
Scarlett
Star on the Run
PAPERCUTZ

If you haven't seen SCARLETT, and you enjoyed ANNE OF GREEN BAGELS, then you're in for a treat. SCARLETT is done in the same format of alternating chapters written in prose with chapters done as comics. But just as ANNE OF GREEN BAGELS is filled with great characters and lots of surprising plot twists, so too is SCARLETT. Both graphic novels are difficult to describe, but I'll try to tell you a little bit about SCARLETT. Actually, I'll cheat and just copy what it says on the back cover of the SCARLETT graphic novel:

"Scarlett is a small, spotted cat who is also a huge movie star. And she talks! But she is sick of her caged life in the movie studio and dreams of one thing—escape! So, when she discovers an open window, she runs for her life. Along with Trotter, a dog who escapes at the same time, she finds refuge with a grouchy old man who lives in a secluded cabin. But will they be able to elude the terrible drone spycams that are pursuing them?"

Sounds exciting, right? Well, that's just the tip of the iceberg! It gets even wilder and it's all one big exciting adventure! But to help you get an even better idea what SCARLETT is like, we're presenting the first few pages of SCARLETT on the following pages. We hope you like what you see and pick up a copy of SCARLETT of your very own.

Both SCARLETT and ANNE OF GREEN BAGELS are examples of the kind of great graphic novels Papercutz publishes. To see more, just check out our website at www.papercutz.com. We're certain you'll find something there to enjoy!

STAY IN TOUCH!

EMAIL:	salicrup@papercutz.com
WEB:	papercutz.com
TWITTER:	@papercutzgn
FACEBOOK:	PAPERCUTZGRAPHICNOVELS
FAN MAIL:	Papercutz, 160 Broadway, Suite 700, East Wing, New York, NY 10038

Thanks,
JIM

Check out *SCARLETT,* also by Susan Schade and Jon Buller, in this special preview...

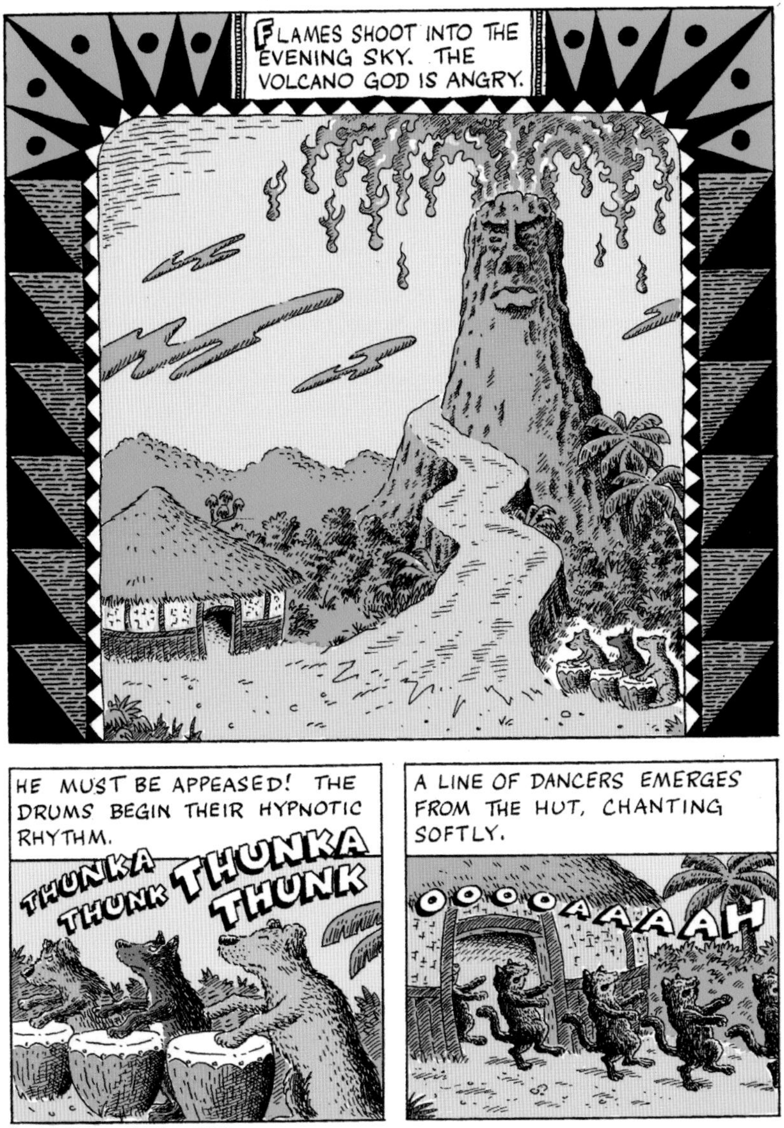
FLAMES SHOOT INTO THE EVENING SKY. THE VOLCANO GOD IS ANGRY.
HE MUST BE APPEASED! THE DRUMS BEGIN THEIR HYPNOTIC RHYTHM.
THUNKA THUNK THUNKA THUNK
A LINE OF DANCERS EMERGES FROM THE HUT, CHANTING SOFTLY.
OOOOOAAAAAH

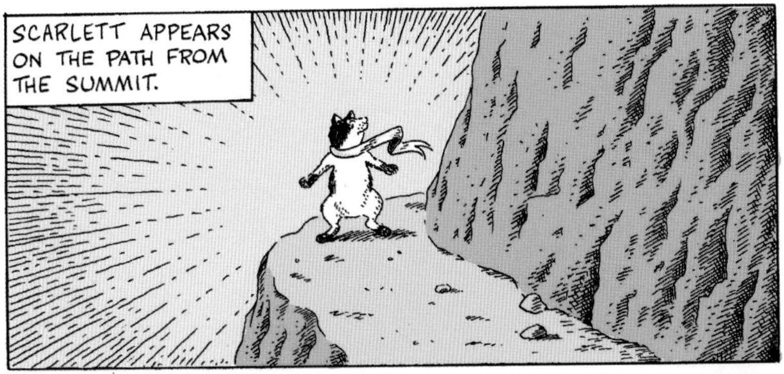
SCARLETT APPEARS ON THE PATH FROM THE SUMMIT.

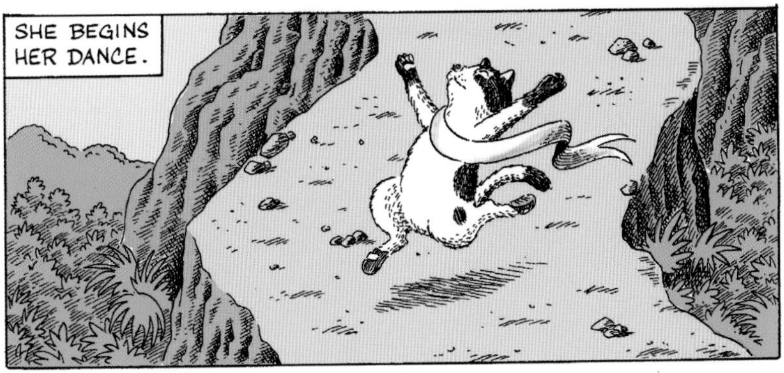
SHE BEGINS HER DANCE.

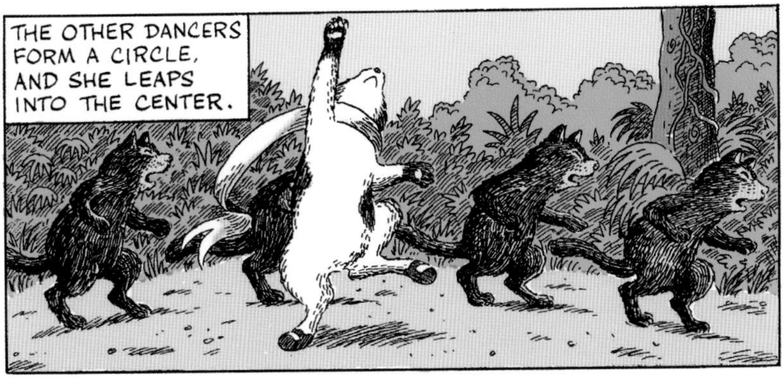
THE OTHER DANCERS FORM A CIRCLE, AND SHE LEAPS INTO THE CENTER.

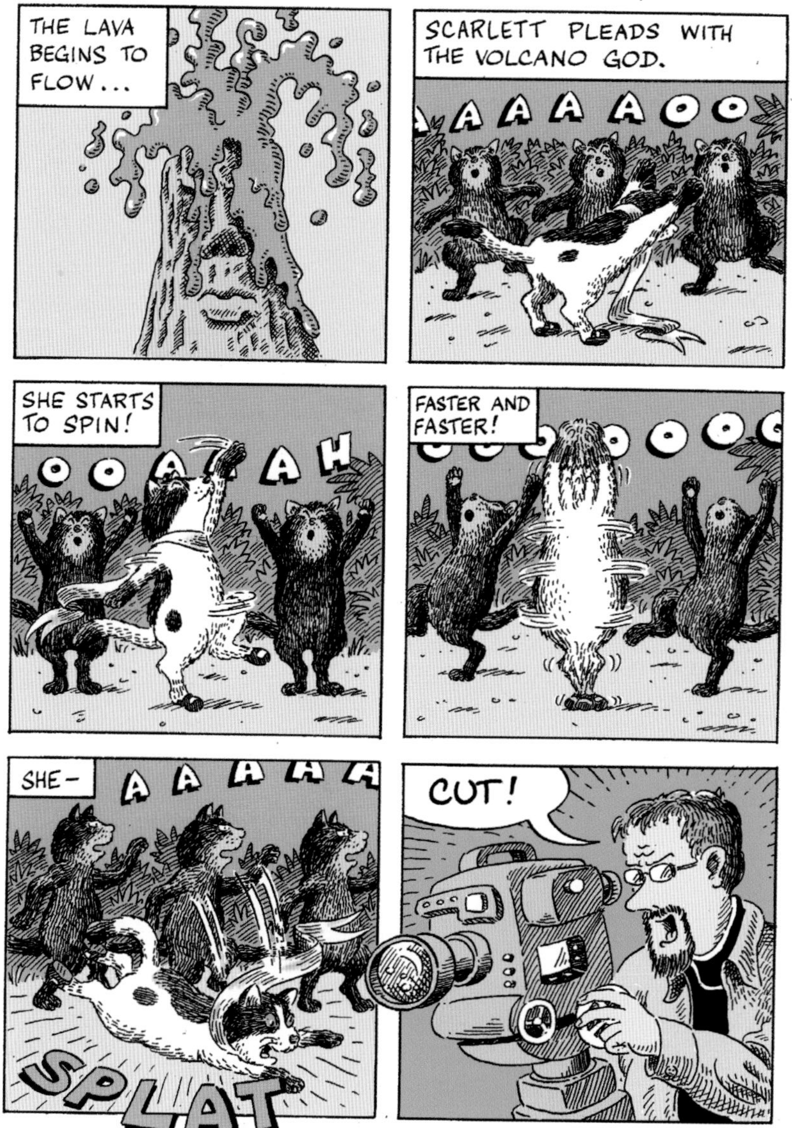
THE LAVA BEGINS TO FLOW...
SCARLETT PLEADS WITH THE VOLCANO GOD.
AAAAAOO
SHE STARTS TO SPIN!
OOAAAH
FASTER AND FASTER!
SHE-
AAAAA
SPLAT
CUT!

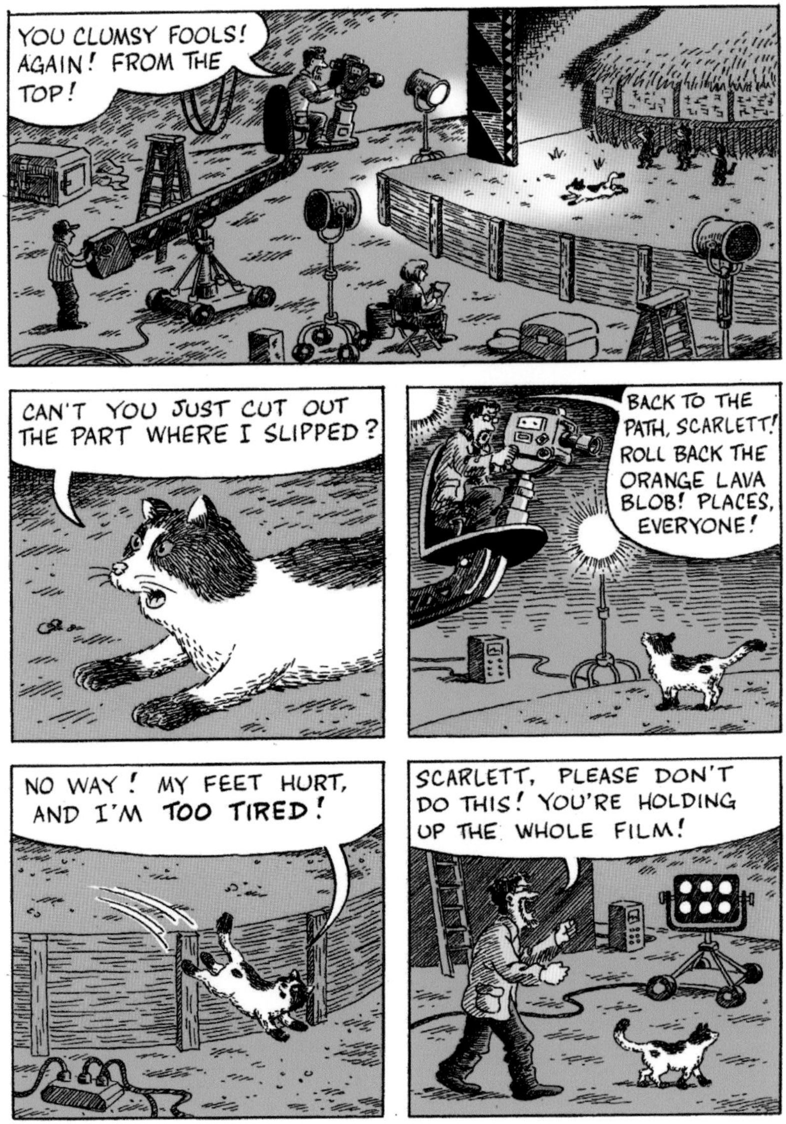
YOU CLUMSY FOOLS! AGAIN! FROM THE TOP!
CAN'T YOU JUST CUT OUT THE PART WHERE I SLIPPED?
BACK TO THE PATH, SCARLETT! ROLL BACK THE ORANGE LAVA BLOB! PLACES, EVERYONE!
NO WAY! MY FEET HURT, AND I'M TOO TIRED!
SCARLETT, PLEASE DON'T DO THIS! YOU'RE HOLDING UP THE WHOLE FILM!

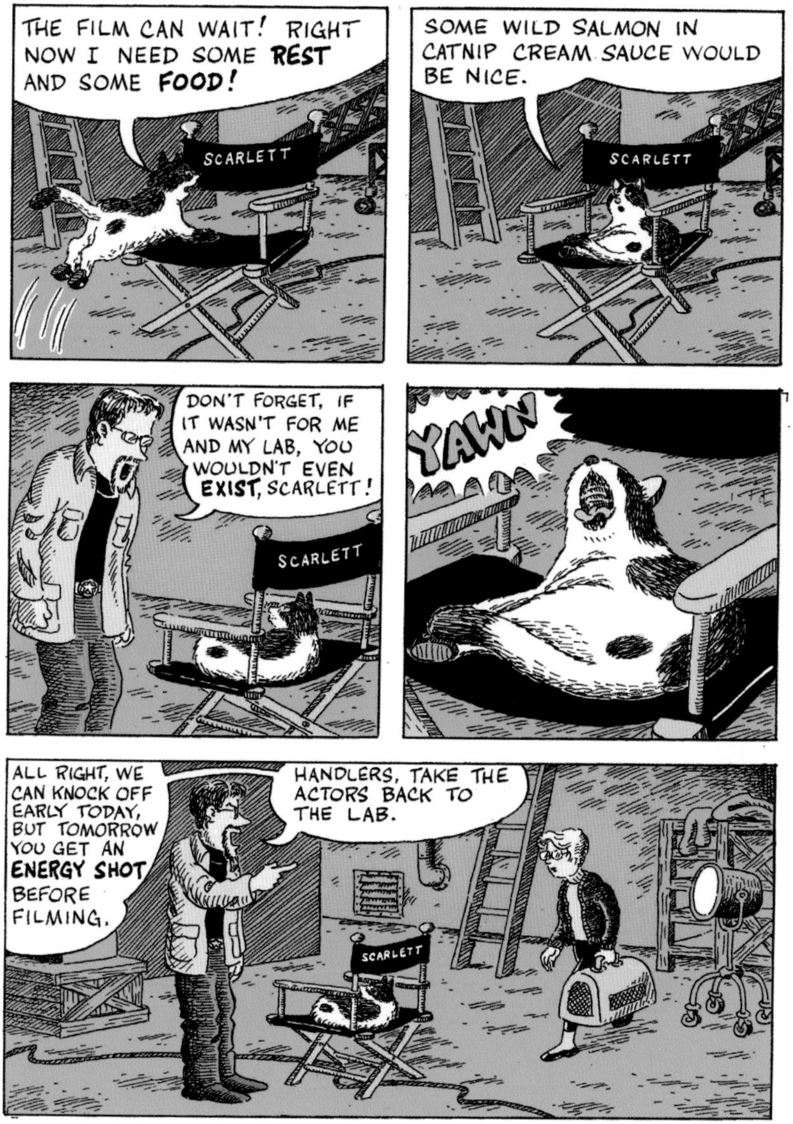
THE FILM CAN WAIT! RIGHT NOW I NEED SOME REST AND SOME FOOD!
SCARLETT
SOME WILD SALMON IN CATNIP CREAM SAUCE WOULD BE NICE.
SCARLETT
DON'T FORGET, IF IT WASN'T FOR ME AND MY LAB, YOU WOULDN'T EVEN EXIST, SCARLETT!
SCARLETT
YAWN
ALL RIGHT, WE CAN KNOCK OFF EARLY TODAY, BUT TOMORROW YOU GET AN ENERGY SHOT BEFORE FILMING.
HANDLERS, TAKE THE ACTORS BACK TO THE LAB.
SCARLETT

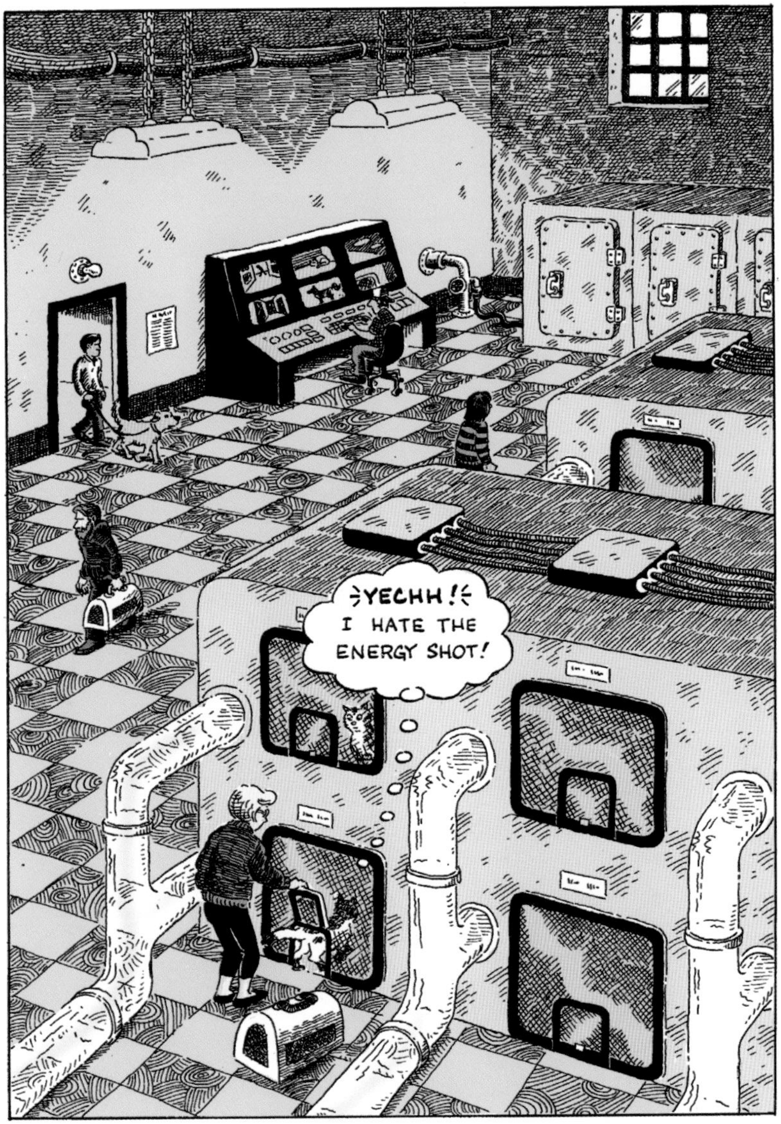
YECHH! I HATE THE ENERGY SHOT!

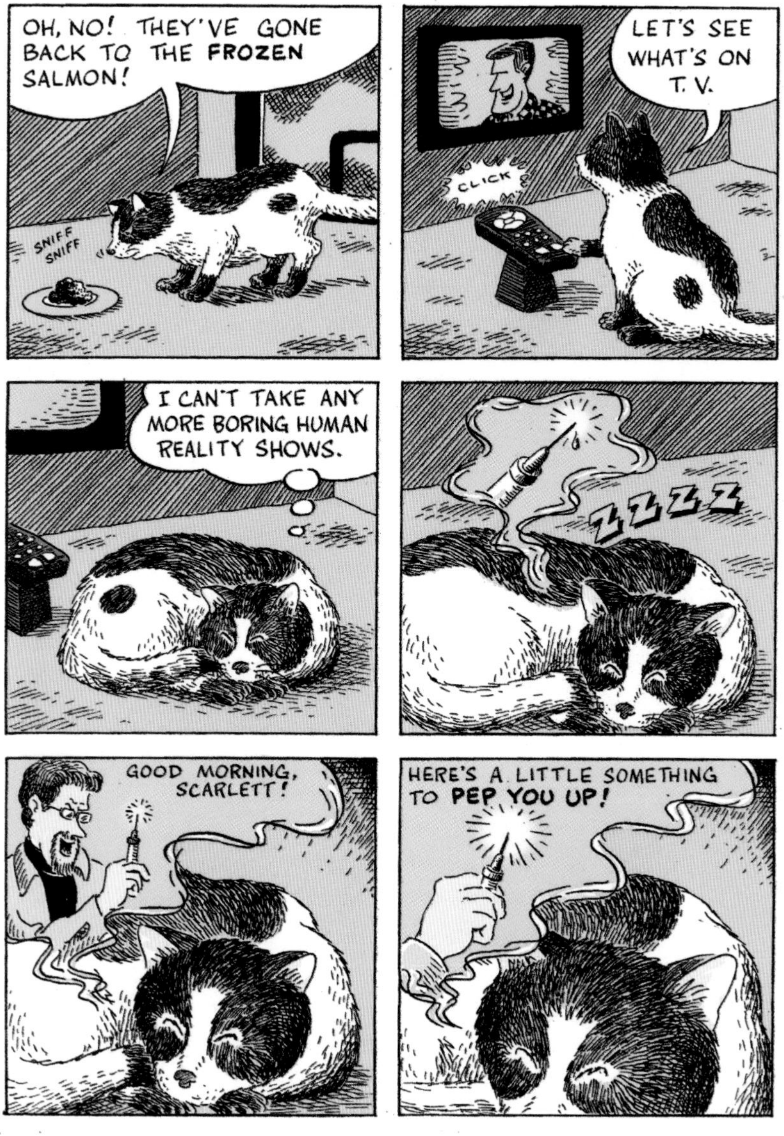
OH, NO! THEY'VE GONE BACK TO THE FROZEN SALMON!
SNIFF SNIFF
LET'S SEE WHAT'S ON T.V.
CLICK
I CAN'T TAKE ANY MORE BORING HUMAN REALITY SHOWS.
ZZZZ
GOOD MORNING, SCARLETT!
HERE'S A LITTLE SOMETHING TO PEP YOU UP!